WillowBrook Series

Book Two

The Magic of WillowBrook

Written by DC Daniel

Published by   ©Bookster Publishing LLC

7601 4th St N Ste. 300

St. Petersburg, Fl 33702

Booksterpublishing@icloud.com

ISBN: 978-1-965808-96-2 (softback)

ISBN: 978-1-965808-90-0 (hardback)

ISBN: 978-1-965808-98-6 (e-book)

Cover design and graphics created

by Bookster Publishing LLC

Printed in the United States of America

First edition, December 2024

Digital Information

Author's Note: Transparency and Creative Process

As the author of the *WillowBrook* series, I want to assure all readers that every aspect and every element of the series—its intricate plots, unique theories, and rich character development—has been meticulously crafted by me without reliance on AI for conceptual creation. After the book was written, *Bookster Publishing* took over the editorial process to refine and polish the final manuscript.
The editing process was carried out by the skilled team at *Bookster Publishing Company*, with all corrections made by human editors to ensure the highest standards of publishing quality.

Visual Elements

The book's cover art and internal illustrations were created through a collaborative process involving both AI tools (specifically AI Genitor with Gencraft training) and Adobe Photoshop, and Canva, under the guidance of *Bookster Publishing* Company's design team.

Audio Transcriptions and Accessibility

All audio transcriptions of the series are narrated by human voice actors to deliver an authentic storytelling experience. For those who prefer to use AI-compatible reading devices or programs, that option is available. However, when you purchase directly through *Bookster Publishing*, human-narrated audio files are included as part of your order.

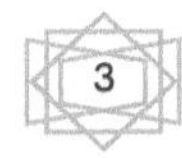

Giving Back

To purchase books directly from us @
https://www.WBSOM.org

For the next year, until December 31st, 2025, we are proud to donate 13% of the direct website purchases. The proceeds from every softcover and e-book PDF purchased through our website (WBSOME.com) will be used to restock Neighborhood Book Boxes and Little Libraries worldwide. Your purchase helps bring magic to readers everywhere. Give the gift! Light up the young readers' minds.

Contact us

If you have any questions or need assistance, feel free to reach out:

Email: BooksterPublishing@gmail.com
Website: www.BooksterPublishing.com

Thank you for joining me on this magical journey through the WillowBrook series! Your support helps keep the magic of reading alive.

Preface

When I set out to write the WillowBrook series, I never anticipated how deeply it would shape my perspective. What began as a simple exploration of personal growth transformed into a journey of discovery—one that revealed hidden truths about my own challenges, victories, and insights.

This book is not a roadmap or a list of answers. Instead, it's a tapestry of experiences—some drawn from my life, others inspired by the remarkable people I've met and the stories they've shared. Within these pages, you'll find reflections and lessons that I've gathered along the way. My hope is that as you read, you'll see glimpses of your own story and perhaps uncover new ways to view your path.

I owe a great deal to the incredible people in my life who stood by me during this creative process. To my family and friends, thank you for your endless encouragement. And to my circle of supporters—your insights, patience, and belief in this project have been invaluable. I am forever grateful.

Finally, to you, the reader: thank you for stepping into this space with me. Wherever you are on your journey, I hope this book offers you something meaningful—whether it's comfort, inspiration, or a reminder that we're all connected by the threads of energy and our vibrations as a shared humanity.

Life isn't about reaching a perfect endpoint; it's about embracing the twists and turns along the way. I'm so grateful to travel this road with you, as we step into the Magic of WillowBrook.

Always stay humble, sending you love, light, and gratitude as we take this step together.~ DC Daniel

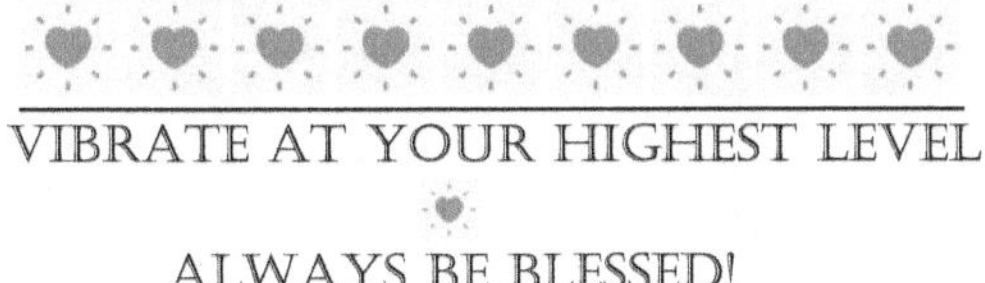

VIBRATE AT YOUR HIGHEST LEVEL

ALWAYS BE BLESSED!

Table of Contents

WillowBrook Motto

I am happy

I am healthy

I am radiant, I am bright

Filled with energy and passion

Shining like the morning light

I am beautiful

I am grateful

I am mindful

I am calm and stress-free

Embracing all the good around me

Living life in balanced harmony.

Become the Light Being

you are supposed to be.

"Let your smile change the world, but don't let the world change your smile." ~DC Daniel

"Keep your head up, and Just keep swimming." ~DC Daniel

"Keep your Mana shining bright, and never stop believing in the power of your dreams." ~DC Daniel

"Be extraordinary in the journey of life, because Extra Ordinary people become extraordinary light beings." ~DC Daniel

"My current situation is not my destination." -DC Daniel

DC Daniel

Chapter One
Three Girls,
One Extraordinary Destiny

Sarah, I understand you say you have these special powers; what do you think the girls' powers will be?

DC Daniel

"It's difficult to predict for either of the girls. So far, they've only revealed a single hieroglyphic sign. If they don't uncover more it before they arrive, they will receive their elemental assignment and learn how to harness their true Universal powers."

"Powers, you mean they get multiple powers?"

"Juno, you know, if they haven't figured it out yet, there are 12 elements. Some get one, other get two, it just depends on What the Order has install for them.

It will be okay because when they arrive at the Manu'ahi Summit, we will stop by Professor SpellBee's Spellbinding Sticks, and she will assist them. Until then, it's anybody's guess."

Miss Juno seems to comprehend and understand what Mrs. Applegate is telling her.

DC Daniel

"Juno, you know, in the world of magic, we call someone like you a glyphless one."

"Why do you keep saying 'Juno, you know?'"

"Well, it rhymes! And since you're a teacher with so much knowledge, it feels fitting to say it that way—with kindness and affection."

"Ha! I suppose that makes sense…"

While Mrs. Applegate is explaining things, the two girls are upstairs, thinking about all the strange stuff happening to them. They remember the glowing symbols that appeared on their skin, meeting HydroKnox, and how Kalei used her waterpowers to save a kid from drowning. They also think about how they floated above their yoga mats during meditation and the mysterious woman, Gabriella, in the forest.

Then there's Trinity, with her crazy powers—she can make things float with zero gravity and even change people's thoughts. Everything is so confusing and puzzling for them.

 "You know Willow, my **kupuna,** or as you all say here in Florida, Grandpa. He would tell me a story called the awakening of the soul.

When a young girl or boy hits a certain age, they may have the ability to tap into their elemental magic.

He would tell me, one day, my **keiki**, you will find your path; I see it in you; your ability to shine and give positive high vibrations.

This is one of the many unique characteristics that make you extraordinary, my dear **keiki**."

Willow and Kalei continue to chat, excited about the supernatural events of the last few weeks.

Willow says to Kalei, "You are my best friend in the whole wide world. No matter what we go through, the up's and the downs, I want us to remain soul sisters."

"Ditto Willow, you are the sister I never had, you know, I heard this once from a famous person. You've heard of Franklin Roosevelt, right? He was one of the presidents.

Anyway, in his big speech in 1933, he said something like, 'We have nothing to fear but fear itself.' So, I'm ready to check out these elemental powers. What about you?"

"So, you're saying we have to face our fears and take action, even if we're unsure about the future?" Kalei asks.

Willow smiles and nods. She reaches out her pinky, and Kalei locks hers in a pinky swear.

"Alright, I'm in! Let's make this future full of awesome adventures!"

The girls chant the best friends forever pack.

"Best friends forever ... We are friends till the end …. Let's share Our hopes, dreams, fears, and happy times …. Friends forever," Kalei repeats.

They reach up in the air , meeting mid-air for a high five. They shout in unison, "BFF's till the END!"

Kalei hears her mother calling from downstairs, and she responds. "Be right there, **makuahine**."

"Kalei, what does makuahine mean?"

"It's my first language; we speak Hawaiian. It is a formal way to respect your mother, in my native language it means, Mother.

My family still speaks in our island language from time to time."

The girls rush downstairs upon arriving in the kitchen.

     DC Daniel

Mrs. Applegate directs the girls to the barstools in the eat-in kitchen. "Girls, we have something to talk to you about, will you take a seat?"

Willow fearfully looks at her mother; she stumbles to get out. "Is everything OK?" Miss Juno seems very pale, confused, and worried.

Mrs. Applegate, with a peaceful look, reaches out her hands to grab a hold of Kalei's hands.

Miss Applegate notices that Miss Juno is not reaching for Willow's hands. She is behaving like a dear staring in the headlights.

As, she turns to Miss Juno, glares at her, and whispers. "You know, being a glyphless one and all may be tough. I get that this may be hard to grasp or believe. But dear, let's shape up. Clara, you have to snap out of it, get with the program."

Mrs. Applegate turns her body back to the girls and grabs both of their hands. She tells them some folklore about the school of divination.

"You know, Kalei, do you remember the story that Kupuna Wahine would tell you about how you'll get your element one day?"

"Yes, ma'am. However, I don't remember much."

"Willow, Kalei has told me everything that happened at camp, from your levitation experience to riding with HydroKnox…. You're one of the chosen ones, Willow."

"Both of you girls need to understand you're coming of age; your 13th birthday will be over in the summer.

Your powers may come into full light a week before your birthday. Now listen closely; I will tell you a little about safety and the practice of magic."

Willow looks at Kalei, surprised. "Magic! Are you serious? The lady in the woods said this. Is this really true?"

"Yes Willow, this is for real, you both must understand it is a special gift to have magic; if you don't respect it (the almighty one can take it away), there are a few rules that I want you guys to memorize. Promise me never to use your skills to harm others."

"Yes, ma'am, we promise," said Willow.

"Yes Mom, I promise," said Kalei.

"Ok, these are the six golden rules every Wixan must follow. "The girls nod their heads to acknowledge what she says.

Sarah continues, " #1. Use your powers to help others, and never use them against free will.

#2. Honor the emerald tablets of knowledge; it is the holy grail of MANA Magic.

#3. Act as if you are a child of the Universe. Use the Laws of Attraction and meditate daily.

#4. Treat your own body as if it is a temple.

#5. Be kind and thoughtful and live with gratitude.

#6. Always… Always, believe in yourself, every day is a choice, to choose good over evil."

Both girls eagerly agree. "Yes, we understand, and we promise."

Mrs. Applegate comes from around the table; Miss Juno, no longer confused, follows suit with Mrs. Applegate. Both mothers embrace in a hug with their daughters.

Mrs. Applegate yells out. "GROUP HUG!" They all smile and give one big loving hug.

Later that night, at home, Willow goes to her mother. "Mum, I am having a hard time believing I am special….

How can I be a chosen one? I'm just an ordinary girl born into an unloving world. Well Mom that was till I met you."

"Well, dear, extraordinary things happen to ordinary people. I may be a **glyphless** mom because I lack magical understanding and powers. But I believe in you." Clara embraces Willow in a loving hug.

As she caresses her hair with a gentleness. "Willow, you are the best kid; you are honest, smart, caring.

I also think you are the most outgoing daughter a mother could have ever wanted. I am beyond blessed to have you in my life, Willow.

So don't ever think you are unloved or unwanted. You are going to do great things with your life."

Willow feels the love in her mother's words and hugs her back, softly saying, "Mom, thank you for giving me this wonderful life with you and Aurora. You are an amazing mom."

Miss Juno sniffles, overwhelmed with emotion, as she senses the profound connection between her and the child, a gift from the divine. She recognizes Willow as a wondrous being entrusted to her care.

Understanding this, she resolves to allow Willow to flourish, embrace her innate magical potential, and share it with the world.

The next day, the girls make their way to the fridge for a drink. It's a cozy house on a Saturday afternoon.

Keanu and Chase are hiding in the kitchen with plastic jelly spiders, ready to prank Willow, Kalei, and Trinity, who are chatting in the living room.

Keanu whispers, "Chase these spiders look so real! Are you ready?"

Chase grinning ear to ear, "Totally! The girls are gonna freak out."

Keanu says, "Okay, let's go."

Keanu and Chase sneak into the living room, each holding a couple of plastic jelly spiders. They creep up behind the girls and suddenly throw the spiders on them.

Keanu shouts "Spiders!"

Willow screams, "Ahhh!... Get it off me!"

Kalei laughing nervously "Oh my, you two are total freakazoid's, I can't believe we are even related Keanu."

Trinity jumps up, "No way! Keep it away from me, its gross!"

Keanu and Chase start laughing and continue to chase the girls around the living room, holding the spiders out in front of them.

Chase teasing the girls. "Watch out, they're coming for you!"

Willow runs away yelling. "You guys are the worst!"

Kalei giggles, "Stop it, seriously"

Chase throws a few at her, Trinity dodges two spiders as she yells, "This isn't funny"

The girls run towards the kitchen, trying to escape the boys. As they dash through the doorway, they hit the saran wrap that Keanu and Chase had set up earlier.

Willow slams into the saran wrap, "What the—?"

The girls simultaneously fall into one another.

DE Daniel

Keanu grabs the roll of packing scran wrap, then Chase grabs the other end of the wrap. Chase stands still holding it, as Keanu runs around the girls entrapping them.

"Keanu laughs and yells out, "Looks like you've got yourself wrapped up in a tight situation!"

Kalei laughs, "Oh no, we have been plasta~fied!"

Trinity pulls at the saran wrap" Help! We're stuck

Keanu is doubling over with laughter, he yells, "Gotcha! The spiders were just the beginning!"

Chase high-fives, Keanu, "Best prank ever!"

Willow laughs despite herself, "Okay… okay… you got us. Now help us get out of it."

Kalei still giggling, "Yeah, this was pretty clever."

Trinity looks at them smiling, "Just wait until we get you back!"

Keanu and Chase help the girls peel the saran wrap away, all of them laughing and chatting about the prank.

Keanu grins, "Don't get your big girl pants in a wad, it's all in good fun."

Chase smirks, "Yeah, but I think we're safe from revenge for a while, right?"

Willow playfully says, "Oh, we'll see about that."

Kalei with a mischievous look, "You'd better sleep with one eye open tonight. Revenge will be sweet."

Willow is laughing, "Yeah, you never know when we might strike back."

 The break continues, and the next few days are filled with banter and camaraderie.

 A few days before they leave for Hawaii. The girls are getting their foot lockers packed and their stuff ready for the exciting trip to the island.

The night before the trip to fly to the Island. Everyone gathers at Mr. and Mrs. Applegate's home for a bonfire and cookout. Everyone is there, Miss Juno, Willow, Mr. and Mrs. Applegate, Kalei, Keanu and his best friend Chase.

They all have a great time; Willow stays the night at Kalei's. Kalei sets Whizzy the Wizard's alarm to wake at 6 am. They all fall fast asleep, in anticipation of the exciting day tomorrow.

Whizzy the Alarm Wizard, rings loudly

"RING

RING

RING!

My extraordinary magical ones! The sun is up, so it's time for you to rise and shine. It's a magical morning, and soon the adventures of the island await you!"

Kalei looks groggy, and responds, "Ugh… Whizzy, do you have to be so loud every morning?"

Whizzy the Alarm Wizard, with his hands on his hips, glares at her, "Of course, Kalei! How else would I ensure you make it to WillowBrook on time? The early magical ones catch the spell, after all!"

Willow stretches and yawns "He's got a point. We can't be late for our plane to the island. Thanks, Whizzy."

DC Daniel

Trinity yawns and rubs her face to wake up, "Yeah! Yeah! But you don't have to be so cheerful about it? Morning are Hard! Whizzy!"

Whizzy the Alarm Wizard is always full of glee; a smile can be seen under his mustache that is moving rapidly as he talks. "Cheerful? Why not? ladies, a positive attitude is the best way to start a magical day! Besides, we've got quite the adventure ahead.

The adventures of the island, and a magnificent place called Manu`ahi summit. The summit isn't going to climb itself!"

Kalei says, "I suppose you're right. But what do you mean the Manu`ahi Summit, what is that?"

Whizzy says, "Not to worry when the time is right, you will know.... So, girls, let's get ready.

After your vacation on the island, you two have many adventures ahead. You'll have a Magic Banyan Tree to meet, the Manu`ahi Bird tonquer, and spells to learn."

DE Daniel

Willow radiates a natural glow looking at her BFF, "Trinity, This is going to be phenomenal."

Whizzy with his caterpillar mustache moving rapidly, he says, "I heard that Professor Nightingale has some amazing new potions to teach you."

Willow with her eye raised, "Whizzy you know professors at the school? Who is Professor Nightingale?"

"Of course, Willow, I know more than it seems, you know I will leave you with a tidbit of information. Professor Nightengale is half Owl and half human, with a keen sense of sight."

Trinity "Plus, we can't forget about the other classes we'll have. What kind of magic will we get to learn? Soon, we'll be at a real magic school! I'm so excited to meet the professors and all the new friends we'll make!"

Whizzy replies, "That's the spirit! But just remember it's not official until you receive a delivery of your commencement letter. Remember, magic is in the air, and every step you take brings you closer to your dreams. Now, let's get moving! Time waits for no witch!"

Kalei snarkily says, "Alright, alright Whizzy, lead the way with that boundless energy of yours."

Whizzy smiles and points to the door, "Onward, to Oahu, Hawaii. Where your Extraordinary Destiny begins!

The path is paved with wonders, and WillowBrook School of Magic awaits its brightest witches!"

Willow smiles, "Thanks, Whizzy. We're lucky to have you waking us up every morning."

Trinity grabs Whizzy and places him in his travel carrier. She looks more positive, "Yeah, you may be loud, but you make it hard not to smile. Let's marvel at this day!"

Now fully awake and excited, the girls take their footlockers and belongings to the car. Mrs. and Mr. Applegate, Keanu, Willow, and Trinity get loaded into the vehicle.

They set off toward Orlando International Airport, their spirits are high and ready for the self-discovering, spirit-enriching, and magical days ahead.

Chapter Two
Mahalo My Queens

As soon as they land, they walk through the outside terminals in the airport, the warmth of the sun and the warm salty ocean breeze invigorate their spirits. When Willow and Kalei exit the airport

Mr. Applegate says, "Willow, here it is customary to receive a Hawaiian Lei. As an ancient tradition, we welcome you with a great big **Mahalo**."

"And let me not forget my two queens."

"A beautiful Triple Strand Pikake Lei for my dear Kalei, and for you my love, here you go, a Pink Plumeria Flower Lei."

The smell engulfs everyone's senses. They get in an Uber and head directly to **tūtū's** house. **Tūtū** greets everyone with a big aloha, "A big *aloha* to everyone! You have arrived home, and my heart is at peace in your presence.

It has been almost a year, but you have returned with joy and full of love. May we always be united in love!"

The girls head upstairs to Kalei and Keanu's old bedroom. The teen girls stand on the bay balcony, the evening breeze casting ocean mist over their faces. Kalei grabs Willow's hand. "Take a deep breath, close your eyes, and let the feeling of the Tradewinds bring the beautiful smell of the beach, waves and the island's nature."

"Ahhh! It feels so refreshing."

Mrs. Applegate comes to the balcony.

"Girls, you know your birthdays are coming up during our summer trip. And by now, I understand that you both know that you have some special talent bestowed upon you from the **Ancient Elemental Ones (AEO)**."

Both the girls nod their heads in agreement.

"Mrs. Applegate, I know you say we have this special talent, but what does this really mean?"

"You know, Willow, for now, you can call me Sarah until we get to school, at which point you will just refer to me as Professor or Professor Applegate."

"Ok, Sarah."

"**Makuahine**, is this what my **tūtū wahine** has been telling me all these years? Last year, **tūtū wahine** told me that her element was time, and Mum, your element is fire. What do you think my element will be?

"Kalei? What do you mean by Elements? asks Willow.

"Well, girls. Not to worry. The great ones have already determined your element. Upon reaching WillowBrook School of Magic, if your elemental sign hasn't yet been revealed, you'll be given one, just like the Nuffer'do's.

Willow looked confused and asked, "Nuffer'do's? What's that?"

"It means you have only half the magic of a Wixan," Applegate explains further. "You only inherited half of your parents' magical traits. So, you're not a full-blooded Wixan."

Willow's face blurts out with a gleaming smile. "Wait a minute Sarah, hold on, back it up a minute. Did you say magic school…. like a real magic school…… like ones that use incantations and enchantment spells?" She looks at Kalei with an astonished look on her face. "You know, Kalei, I

DC Daniel

really thought you were kidding, when you told me we would go to a magic school, but you are serious."

Willow looks back at Kalei's Mom. "Sarah, is this for real?"

"Yes, my dear child, don't be afraid. You know the lady in the forest, the magical trip with HydroKnox, and all the other incidents. These que`winky dinks were shown to you, enlightening you that you have a magical path ahead of you."

"Yes… bestie, I think this is what the old lady was talking about."

"You mean the one that came out of the woods at the Cove?"

Kalei nods her head and smiles. "If I recall correctly Mum, she said I was a water sign, and Willow was a moon sign."

"You know, girls, we will be going on a trip to WillowBrook School of Magic in a couple of weeks."

Kalei softly whispered to Willow.

"My tūtū always said to be Extraordinary light beings…and always vibrate to your highest potential."

Kalei giggled with Willow as if they could read each other's minds. They glance at each other, snap their fingers, point at each other, and loudly say.

"Then let's be *Extra~Ordinary* people that do **extraordinary** things."

Chapter Three
Enchanted Expeditions

"Hey, mum, you're a fire element. Can you show us a few things that you can do"?

Her mother looked at them with a smirk, using a fire enchantment.

"Firemortus"

She unfolds her hand, using her index finger and thumb to rub them together over the flat palm.

"Voila!"

A flame appears. The girls express their amazement with a loud sound.

"Squeal Veeck"

Mrs. Applegate blows on her hand as the flames get more extensive.

Then she says.

"Flama Fussa Genie"

DC Daniel

The flame quickly rises to one and a half feet tall, forming a fire Genie with a golden turban-wrapped head and a fire-changing body. His arms crossed; the Genie bellows out.

"Your wish is my command."

Then, just like that, she swiftly closes her hand. The Genie disappears. Her hand has no burn marks, and no smoke emerges from this magical illusion. Both Kalei and Willow once again yell out.

"WHOA"

They look at each other and stand in astonishment at what Sarah has just shown them.

"Here is something, girls: after you graduate from your 5th year, you will get a magic elemental ring like this. If of course, you can pass the Grand Masters exam."

"**Makuahine**, your ring is glowing…Why?"

"It's transmitting a message dear."

She twists her ring, and a beam flows from it as it activates

a talking hologram.

"Good day, Professor Applegate…… Beep…… Beep…….

Beep…….

"Important news from the Order of the 12 Elements: You are here sequestered to rejoin WillowBrook in Wixan teachings for 2nd and 3rd year students."

"We have changed our mind about placing Neophyte studies with 1st-year studies. Instead, you would better serve in the Practice of Dimensional Wixan studies."

"We also see you will be escorting two 1st-year students. Please Make your way to Manu`ahi Summit for supplies before the start of new student orientation."

"Beep," "Beep," "Beep"

"Transmission ending"

She taps the side of her ring and the 3D talking Hologram disappears.

Later, during the trip, the girls sit in the living room with tūtū enjoying a few Hawaiian-style snacks on this summer day. The Tradewinds gently blow through the open windows, and the air is cooler than usual for this summer day.

Willow sits there and thinks to herself.

"How am I special; how do I have the ability to cast enchantment spells and possibly change a candlestick into a rabbit or turn a frog into a prince?"

While pondering these exciting thoughts, this Yammering sound comes from this clumsy PuddleHopper named Jasper. Without hesitation, the creature swooshes through the window. His flying squirrel wings help him clear everything off the table in his path. He nearly misses Tutu's Hibiscus Tea, with a special delivery.

Chapter Four
PuddleHoppers & ChatterStones

Squeak! Jasper says. "Miss Willow, I have a special delivery

for you. Squeek! "

He bows down to get a pet on his head, for his delivery.

"Mrs. Applegate, what do I do?"

"Here, Willow, give him this ChitBit. This sunflower jewel powers their forest community. They collect these jewels for deliveries and use them to make the tesla coil light up the entire village."

"Here, Jasper."

"Squeak! Thank you, Willow. Every ChitBit helps, they all go into the hopper. All our lighting is from special lamps with a mix of liquid mercury and sodium.

But we still need electricity from the ChitBit's to power everything else with the Telsa coil."

It wiggles its left hip, creating a pocket for the jewel. Bowing down, it eagerly seeks a rub down. From his head to his tail, afterwords he gives a wiggle and a shake with a smile. Willow pets his back and fur a few more times and it dances around for a minute with excitement.

"Check him out, Sarah. His camouflage gray fur looks kinda rough when I pet him. It's amazingly soft, I'm just loving the vibe he's rocking," she says, caressing her hand over the green and blue feathers covering his neck.

"**Tūtū,** it's so cute! Look at its little whiskers twitching like a mouse sniffing around. Its bat wings are all folded up on its back." Kalei says, "I know I'm only 12 years old, but seriously, I've never seen anything this adorable."

Then, Jasper stands up on his hind legs, shaking his hips as if using an imaginary hula-hoop. The girls burst into laughter

DE Daniel

at the comical sight. When Jasper stops, he bends down, lifts his right arm, and opens his bag, revealing the ChatterStone.

"Go on, Willow, take it. It's yours; it has a special message for you," Jasper says.

Willow pulls the glowing ChatterStone, from the PuddleHopper's pocket. It twitches its bat-like ears, wiggles its squirrel-like nose, and thumps its tail up and down a few times on the ground. It opens its wings, flaps a few times to get going, and pushes off into the air with its powerful legs as it darts back out the window and is gone in a flash.

Willow squeals with excitement.

"Kalei, OMG... Look at this, beautiful stone?"

Sarah explains. "It's a ChatterStone, a Luminary Language Orb."

"What do I do with it, Sarah?"

"Yes, Willow, hold your right thumbprint on top of the center of the blue and white glowing circle."

Kalei does a double cartwheel across the living room and lands it, in joy for Willow, gleaming with an open smile.

"What are you waiting for, girl? Put your thumb on the middle of it," said Sarah. Willow looks at Kalei and puts her thumb on it.

A flash of light, lights up the room, startling Willow, who drops the ChatterStone.

Then, a holographic Telegram protrudes into the desk next to them, producing a lady wearing a golden, teal robe with a deep purple waistline and a ruby red stone in the middle.

Her gray hair was wrapped in a fully braided large bun atop her head. She peers out of her half-lined reader glasses, making eye contact with Willow.

The air fills with a magical drum roll, then Trumpets toot….

Dun, Dun, Dun, Dum….

"Miss Willow, I come from the Order of the 12 Elements. My name is Grace Kittles; I want to give you a big warm WillowBrook welcome."

She continues; "I here have a telegraph for you. To the left of them, magically, a scroll starts to fill with words of everything Mrs. Kittles is saying.

"Grace Kittles ~

School Madam ~

Neophyte Students ~

Welcome new students!

YOUR MAGICAL JOURNEY BEGINS HERE!!!!!!!

That will be all~ Transmission Complete."

A Starlight Mumsnet appears at the end, which is a mini supernova exploding in on itself to a small black hole in the air, disappearing into nothingness. It happens, and, in a flash, the Transmission is complete; the image disappears, and the ChatterStone ceases to glow.

As Willow stood there in amazement, she grabbed her best friend to hug her tight. Kalei looks down to the ground and expresses herself in a lower-than-normal tone.

"I wonder when I'll get my letter, Willow."

Just then, with a loud bang…

"Thug…plunk... Doink…"

Both girls run to the window and glare down. Kalei screams.

"What the grasshoppers." She looks down on the grass.

"You're a silly PuddleHopper …. you missed the window…you guys don't seem to have the landing down."

The PuddleJumper shakes its head in a daze, looks up at the girls, and with a quick hop, they dodge; it swoops in and gracefully glides into the window.

Alice says when she lands. "Squeak, Kalei, you're right. With the recent polar axis shift, our echo-receiving locator in our ears is off by a few degrees. But we do our best, squeak!"

Alice winks at her and folds her wing back on top of her back.

"Well, your silly girl, what are you waiting for? Payment please," says Alice.

"**Makuahine**, do you have another Hopper ChitBit?"

"Here you go, Kalei." Kalei places it in Alice's pouch.

Alice shakes her left hip out without hesitation and displays Kalei's ChatterStone. In her Chirpy and squeaky voice, Kalei pulls out the stone, and Alice leaps off the table and speaks.

"Squeak! Have a magical time, you two stardust Wixans! May your journey be filled with enchantment and wonder as you embark on adventures beyond the ordinary realms."

Alice pulls out some glitter from her pouch, blows it on the girls, and says.

"Let the sparkles of this stardust guide you, and may your hearts be open to the mysteries of the universe."

The girls can feel the air rush past their bodies as the PuddleHopper swoops past them, flapping its bat wings. Alice gracefully flies to the other side of the room and out the other window.

"Willow let's see what my ChatterStone has to say. She puts her thumb on it and activates it."

After Mrs. Kittles announces her bequeathment to Kalei, the announcement ends. A scroll falls out of the sky from the telegraph image. It is a supply list needed for the first day of class.

DE Daniel

WBSOM
WillowBrook School of Magic
Headmaster Maximus Vanderbilt
Grand Wizard master's degree
Ancient Order of the 12 Elements
Grand Sorcerer of the high order of THAUMATURY

We hereby bequest; your presence at
WBSOM
on Solaris Island.
on the 29th of July 2020.

Enclosed you'll find your entry ticket do
that ALA MANU.
The Firebird Transport.

We invite you and your Familiar to
come to orientation on the date stated
above. Kindly proceed to Manu`ahi
Summit (Firebird Alley) which is a
haven for young aspiring Wixan's
seeking to secure supplies.
Your Neophyte 1st yr. studeies
are listed below.

DC Daniel

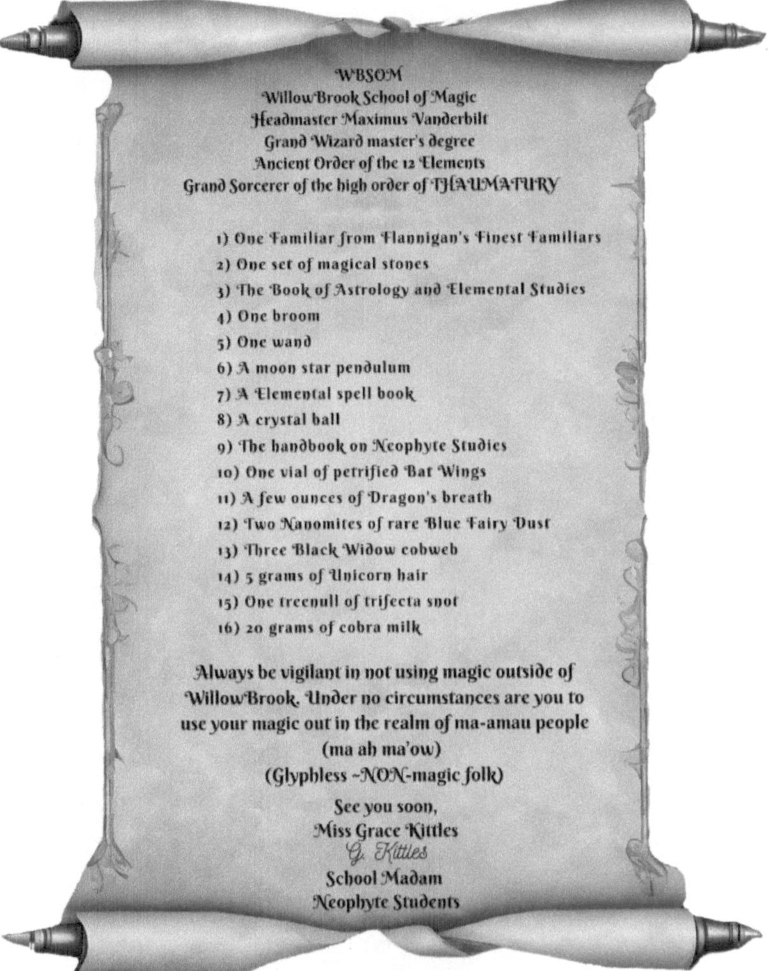

WBSOM
WillowBrook School of Magic
Headmaster Maximus Vanderbilt
Grand Wizard master's degree
Ancient Order of the 12 Elements
Grand Sorcerer of the high order of THAUMATURY

1) One Familiar from Flannigan's Finest Familiars
2) One set of magical stones
3) The Book of Astrology and Elemental Studies
4) One broom
5) One wand
6) A moon star pendulum
7) A Elemental spell book
8) A crystal ball
9) The handbook on Neophyte Studies
10) One vial of petrified Bat Wings
11) A few ounces of Dragon's breath
12) Two Nanomites of rare Blue Fairy Dust
13) Three Black Widow cobweb
14) 5 grams of Unicorn hair
15) One treenull of trifecta snot
16) 20 grams of cobra milk

Always be vigilant in not using magic outside of
WillowBrook. Under no circumstances are you to
use your magic out in the realm of ma-amau people
(ma ah ma'ow)
(Glyphless ~NON-magic folk)

See you soon,
Miss Grace Kittles
G. Kittles
School Madam
Neophyte Students

They both stand there screaming, holding hands, jumping up and down, expressing the excitement of singing.

"We are going to WillowBrook … Yah yah… Yah yah"

"We are going to WillowBrook …Uh hah…"

"We are going to WillowBrook … Yah yah… Yah yah"

"We are going to WillowBrook …Yah yah…"

Chapter Five
Oahu Hawaii the Gathering Place

Over the next few weeks, Mr. and Mrs. Applegate drive the girls along the coast; they stop at various beaches to swim, surf, and sunbathe. They discover hidden waterfalls and breathtaking vistas while exploring the lush green tropical forests.

The days fly by as they immerse themselves in the natural beauty of Hawaii, checking off one adventure after another.

As the sun sets on their last day before the Big Island adventure to swim with the Mana Rays and the trek up to the Manu'ahi Summit of Mauna Loa, they sit on the beach. Willow is reflecting on her experiences of this year, feeling grateful for the memories.

The next morning as the sun rises, it reflects beautiful orange and yellow hues illuminating their bedroom. The island Tradewinds blows a genital breeze through the room.

Willow and Kalei awake to the fresh-smelling breakfast.

Tūtū expresses great energy. "Rise and shine ladies, our island favorite of spam and hotcakes with **haupia**. Everything is at the breakfast nook, the last one in the kitchen is a rotten pineapple,"

"Tūtū, thank you, you know I just love haupia." "Willow, you have to try my Tūtū's Coconut Pudding, it is so delightful and creamy, it's just to die for."

"Sounds lovely Kalei," Willow says as she leaps off the bed and flings her housecoat on, and says, "Remember last one to the kitchen is a rotten pineapple." She takes a big leap out of the room and shouts, "I am outta here."

"Hey Willow, not if I beat you to the nook first," as she tries to leap past her.

Willow arrives first almost knocking Sarah over, as she slides into her.

After Mrs. Applegate collects herself, from the near mishap. She greets the girls at the nook with an embracive ho'opā, after her warm embracive hug and a morning kiss on the forehead, she announces.

"Girls, are you ready for our big trip today? We will stay at Mauna Kea Resort for the night and watch an ʻauana hula. We will swim with more Manta Rays just off Kauna ʻoa Bay at the resort. After arriving back to the resort, we will have a fresh fish fair of Mahi-mahi."

But the best news is tomorrow when wake, we will go to the old wise Banyan Tree in the special lush green meadow. From there, more adventure awaits. We will go to the Summit and get supplies, before heading to WillowBrook tomorrow evening.

"Mrs. Sarah, where are we going to get our wands? Every Enchantress needs a wand, right?" Willow expresses with great enthusiasm. Grinning ear to ear.

"There is this special place called Mana'ahi Summit. Here, we will find all our supplies we need for school."

That evening, after settling into their room at the resort, after a long day of adventure on the Big Island.

"Kalei, I can't believe it, we were so close to the Manta rays yesterday. Remember last week with the manta rays, we could only view them in the distance. But this time was so amazing, It was so cool to touch thier underbelly. It was surreal, as the magnificent sea angels glided over and around us, I can still see the vivid details. It makes me feel more connected to nature, the island, and the sea."

"I understand, Willow; this brings back some of my best childhood memories. My favorite pastime is swimming with dolphins, wild and captive.

There is this place called Sea Life Park in **Waimānalo,** on **Oahu**. They have injuried ones you can swim with.”

As she makes air quotation marks with her fingers, she says, “Maybe I can ask my dad to take us the next time we come to the islands, and we are not officially on magic business.”

“That sounds like a fun time. So, we are heading to Volcano National Park today, where we can see the beautiful vistas and natural views of the Kilauea Volcano.”

“Willow, at least that’s what my dad says. However, be prepared for a story, my dad loves telling stories about the ancestors.

As they arrive, Mr. Applegate informs the kids. “Kids, you know, this volcano is the most active in the world. With the inspiring fury of a volcanic eruption, one cannot help but feel a profound respect for the power of nature.

My **kupuna kāne** *(grandfather)* told me once a long time ago, that his ancestors would give offerings to the volcano gods to help protect the people on the island from an eruption. They believe that these offerings keep the volcano gods happy."

Willow replies surprisedly, "I am lost for words, Mr. Applegate. If this is what the ancient ancestors of the island believed, offerings to the volcano to appease the Gods. I can only imagine what it would have been like here 175 years ago, when King Kamehameha III, rules for the people on the island."

The following day, the girls wake up to Kalei's wizard alarm, which she received from her Tūtū when she was 10. "Wake up, Kalei. It's 7:40. Time to rise and shine… Wake Up Kalei…"

Kalei responds in a half-awake voice, "uhgg… Good Morning, Wizzy."

Then she pulls the pillow over her eyes, hoping to rest a little longer. "Girls…. spells, broomsticks, and black cats wait for no one. You know a new adventure awaits you at WillowBrook. Today is your day… zip and s'kat doodle… let's get 'em bones, ahh` moving…. So… Get up… rise…. and shine…No time to waste on eyelids and blankets…."

"Alright, Wizzy, that's enough bum rushing of cheer and motivation, we are getting up, don't get your wand in a tizzy."

She crawls out of bed, and Willow beats her to the floor, as she yammers about everything for the day, making no sense, just rambling on.

"Alright, alright, Willow, I can feel your excitement, but can you take it down a notch…. just a little bit? This is too much excitement for me this early in the morning."

"Okay, Kalei, I will try to contain myself till you are fully awake. But remember, Wizzy got me piped up and ready for adventure."

"Okay, tūtū is making my favorite for breakfast. You gotta try it; it's called **Spam Musubi**."

"I don't know what that is, but I am dying of starvation; let's get downstairs." Willow walks to the end of the bed and acts like a T Rex, with little hands and a big body, and speaks. "My belly is like a creature, roaring, 'I'm going to eat everything in sight. Get in my belly, I want to eat you… rah!'"

"You crack me up, girl. Your facial expressions are just too much…. Ha ha ha", Kalei says as she rolls and laughs on the bed. They sit for breakfast; tūtū brings their plates and refreshing coconut water. Kalei serves Willow a few Musubi rolls.

DC Daniel

"These are delicious, for many years, my family has made these. It starts with a ball of sticky rice and pan-seared Spam slices. Then my tūtū always puts a dollop of her special sauce before we wrap it in the savory Nori."

"Yumm! Delish…. What are these sauces, Lei lei?"

"Try them, but beware—the green stuff is spicy. It's called wasabi. I like the soy sauce, that's the liquidity brown one; my mom's favorite is the teriyaki sauce, that's the one in the middle."

"Oh, I really like this one; I guess I am like your mom…lol.

Chapter Six
The Magic Bayan Tree

As the sun peeked over the horizon, Steven stood by the breakfast nook, a cheerful smile on his face. "Kids, are you ready for an adventure? Let's hurry to the meadow! Grab your stuff and let's hit the road. Tūtū, can you help Aurora to the cart?"

"Sure thing, Steven!" Tūtū replies, ready to assist.

Excitement buzzes in the air as the group prepares for a day full of possibilities. The vibrant colors of the wild sunflowers sway gently outside, inviting them into a world of magic and wonder.

"Hey, Kalei, do you know the scoop about this school?" Willow asked, her curiosity piqued.

"Well, my dad says it's amazing! His cousin spent four unforgettable years there and became a great wizard," Kalei responds, his eyes sparkling with enthusiasm.

Kalei's brother, Keanu, jumps in with a teasing grin. "But watch out! If you mess up more than twice, you might end up dungeon-bound with the headmaster's three-headed dog! Better practice your disappearing act!"

Kalei shoved Keanu playfully. "Knock it off, you weirdo! Willow, don't listen to him; he's just trying to scare us!"

DE Daniel

Feeling bold, Willow snapped her fingers. "Phew! Get el-weirdo under control! I'm about to unleash my bag of tricks, and I don't even know magic yet!"

"Go ahead! I know whatever you do will be epic!" Keanu replied, clearly enjoying the playful banter.

As the family gazed out at the lush, knee-high field of wild sunflowers, they could feel the excitement building. "Alright, kids, let's unpack the car and get our AirCharm Cart ready for our journey!"

With that, they sprang into action, their hearts filled with the thrill of adventure that awaited them.

Tūtū and Mrs. Applegate perform an incantation.

"By the power of two.... Aeris Lepus."

Willow looks down at the cart as it begins to hover, bags in stow and Aroura securely attached. A cloudy mist flows out from the bottom of the cart.

As the AirCharm Cart starts to Hum, four round metal platforms come out of each corner, ready to have a traveler.

They give each other a group hug and take their places. Mr. Applegate wishes them well. "Bye, ladies, we will miss you; have a magical time."

"Yeah, sis, make sure you brats go to the deadly forbidden forest and reveal yourself to the Deathweavers. Then I will have Mom and Dad all to myself." He sticks his tongue out at her.

Mrs. Applegate commands and points her wand at him. **"bocca con cerniera"**

The Zipper Mouth spell made Keanu furious. He grabs his father's shirt with muffled screams. "Well, son, you can wear that all the way home. Maybe it will teach you a lesson. Don't be so mean to your sister and her friends."

"Ladies, step up on the plate, hold on to the pole, and wave bye to the family. Our journey begins NOW!" she speaks an ebb and flow command to the AirCharm Cart,

"Glidara Levandus!"

The Aira Cart starts to hover and move towards the colorful flowered path. Mr. Applegate waves at the girls walking away, and they wave back.

They travel through the meadow and flowers for a few minutes. Then they arrive at a clearing greeted by a lush, green meadow. Far in the distance, in the center, is a large circular formation of banyan trees, with a glowing middle.

As the group approaches the banyan tree, they notice that this tree is moving; as is the ground around the tree. It seems to be alive, breathing, moving up and down, in and out.

"Kalei, do you hear that strange melody? Look, my hand is lighting up again."

"Mine too; I think it's a water sign." The girls pause and look over at Mrs. Applegate.

"What is that sign, Mrs. Applegate?"

She doesn't respond. When they arrive, they step off the trolley, which continues to float alongside them. Sarah puts her hands on the girls' shoulders and reassures them.

"You two have nothing to worry about. I have been through these magical Banyan tree many times before. It will be okay; this is the magical portal to travel to the other 7 Magic Schools or Manu'ahi Summit and the Ancestral Hypogeum, where the elders live."

"Wow, mom, have you been to WillowBrook?"

"No, my **keiki** *(child),* I taught at Greenland School of Thaumaturgy before I had you and your little brother, and now that you have been accepted, I was offered to come to WBSOM and teach Neophyte studies."

DC Daniel

"So, both of you girls always have me. If you need anything, I will be on the campus. Your dad will take care of Keanu until we return from this summer trip."

"Mrs. Applegate, does that mean you are an enchantress like us?"

"Yes Willow, I too, was bestowed the special gift of our Elemental ancestors on my 13th birthday. As all enchanters and **nā kāhuna kilokilo** *(magic witches)* do on their birthdays."

"MOM… LOOK!!! See those other kids over there. Are they going to WillowBrook too?"

"Dear, I don't know where they are going, this is a passageway, as I said before…. the gateway to the other schools and the Manu'ahi Summit. Who knows where they are headed."

As Willow approaches the group, a whirlwind of emotions sweeps through their thoughts.

Questions linger in her mind:

"How did I, the abandoned child left at the hospital, become a part of this group? Is there a place for me here?"

A gentle smile adorns Willow's face despite a life of demise and trouble. At that moment, a flicker of hope ignites, whispering that, perhaps, her life is on the brink of a profound change.

Willow looks back to the banyan tree. Its branches begin to glow as pixie sparkles fall from the curves of the tree.

The intertwined root system growing from the ground to the sky, twisting and turning making a breath-taking display.

Willow stands as she watches it breathe. The ground seems to move up and down, with soil rolls rippling outward in pluses from the tree.

"Look, Willow, look at the treetop. The tree is expelling pixie dust in the air, making each step towards the tree feel more magical. Willow looks at Kalei.

"Do you hear that crackling?"

"Yeah, it's the tree, I think."

"Ma'am, why's the tree doing that?"

"Ladies, allow me to introduce you to the enchanting Banyan Tree. It draws energy from Mother Earth and the mycelium, it is interconnected through the nuro networks of the surrounding 'Mother Trees.' This magical synergy grants it a power that transcends the ordinary, making it extraordinary."

"Mom, how are we going to pass through a tree?"

"Watch the kids as they go through the tree; it's easy."

Willow walks closer and approaches the tree. Everyone watches in amazement. The tree begins to change as they get closer.

It's roots reconstruct and form an old wise man's face that starts to talk. As each word flows, the tree top expresses more pixie dust.

Willow listens as the Wise Banyan tree's deep voice echoes through the space around them with a rumble from up through the ground it speaks.

"Hello! New and old ones, friends of the past and future, welcome to the mighty Hawaiian Banyan Tree…. Please come forth and say the magic words. Step into my blue waters, and you complete these two things. Then I will grant you access to my **Kupua puka** *(magic portal)*.

The rules are simple, you may only enter if you are in your proper ancestry culture wares and give me your passage access words spoken from your culture in your dialect.

Once these two things are completed, I will give you access to your desired world."

"Now, girls, our time is coming soon; let's all hold hands."

"Okay, now repeat after me."

(e ʻoluʻolu, lāʻau kupuna) take us to *(Manau ʻahi Summit)*."
(Please ancestor Tree of Magic) take us to *(Firebird Summit)*. The girls repeat it back to Mrs. Applegate in sync.

"*e ʻoluʻolu, lāʻau kupuna*" (*please take us to Manauʻahi Summit.*)"

"Holy Mackerel, you two got it on the first try! …I am so proud of you …. Now let us watch some other nations' kids go through the blue light."

Chapter Seven
The Nation of Wixans

Willow's eyes follow the next group. Two girls approach, both freckled redheads with a Scottish dialect as they say their own words in Scottish Gaelic; they strongly resemble twins.

They go through it dressed in the customary Scottish ceremony attire. They, too, have their left hands held high, forming a W.

Mrs. Applegate says. "Ladies, you know, 250 years ago, their attire was a formal ceremony in Scotland. The gowns were crafted from opulent material, like silk or satin, boasting a fitted bodice that gracefully met a voluminous skirt adorned with a gold inlay with the flowing red or green satin skirt."

"Willow, do you see them? Their hair is so beautiful, it flows in the breeze."

"Yes, I like their headpieces; they look so natural, with green foliage and yellow flowers making a crown."

Then Kalei watches this Hawaiian boy approach the tree. She couldn't put her finger on it but felt she knew him—like she saw him on the Big Island at a family gathering.

"Makuahine (*mother*) Is that Freddie Nephew over there?"

"Yes, **Keiki, Alii Nui** (King *or Moi highest of royalty*). King Kamehameha (Kah-Meh-Ha-Meh-Ha) was his ancestor. That is why he wears the Lady Franklin Cap. I don't see his Manhole (feathered helmet)."

"Kalei, that is the Hawaiian Polynesian royalty outfit. I remember seeing one at the Bishop Museum."

"Yep, you're right. **Alii Nui King Kamehameha** (Kah-Meh-Ha-Meh-Ha) people wore similar clothing."

"I am simply amazed that his **'ahu'ula** is so vibrant and intricate. The whole outfit is breathtaking."

"Yes, my **keiki** I agree in real life it is astounding versus the museum where you view it under glass."

Kalei's eyes follow this islander with his dark hair, round glasses, and beautiful olive skin. He enters through the portal, his left hand held high.

Before long, the trio was next. Mrs. Applegate instructed Willow and Kalei, "When you enter, you must raise your left hand above your head, your middle and ring finger crossed together, your index and pinky finger spread apart, and your thumb tucked in like this making a W.

 This will make the Universal Wixan Wellness sign; it makes a W, see like this…. This will let other magic folk know you have arrived with good in our heart not evil intent."

As Wixan's, we always stand for Wellness for the world, never for evil injustice or mal-intent."

"Makuahine, Keanu told me there are FireStorm Sprites that wanna jab out my eyeballs. Is that true?"

"Yes, keiki, FireStorm Sprites will attack us thinking we are evil if you don't hold up the left hand, making a W sign."

"What happens when we don't do that, Sarah?"

DC Daniel

"You don't want to try to. They come after you with a vengeance; they will jab out our eyeballs with their fiery wands....... These Firestorm Sprites seek out all evil in the magical lands. They are very pesky and gruesome fairies, so it's always better to follow the rules than get attacked."

Willow's rambles with many thoughts....*"Evil magic fairies...... Hmm.... Gouges out our eyeballs. What the heck have I gotten myself into?"*

While Willow is off in a trance about the evil fairies....... Lei' Lei' pulls at Willows' arm, and points behind them. "Back there.... about ten people back.... look behind us! Is Trinity from camp?"

"She is totally vibing! Look … She's, like, totally slaying that outfit......."

Mrs. Applegate told the girls, "It appears that she is wearing the traditional Winnemem Wintu Native American from California in her ceremony wares.

"Her outfit it's so colorful!!!.... and now her hair is jet black."

Kalei said.

Willow burst out, saying. "Check this out; it's like perfection! Her kicks totally rock the animal hide look; her hair's styled into these awesome dual pigtails, each with a cool half-wrap detail. And her top? Pure vibes with that blue leather fringe and beads."

"Yeah, I totally agree…. She is incredibly beautiful.

Both Kalei and Willow wave at her; Trinity waves back. It appears that Trinity had an older brother with her; his wares are the same as hers.

"Kalei, do you see his headdress beautified in large and small feathers from birds, from his head and traveled past his back's nape, down his back."

"Yes, he looks strong and dreamy. I see his face is different from Trinity's."

"Oh wow, see that bobcat walking beside her?" "Yeah, buddy, looking straight out of the national geographics."

They turned around to see they were second to next.

"**Makuahine**, Willow does not have her customary wares. Will the tree let her in mom?" Mrs. Applegate takes her wand and casts a discovery spell.

"**Vanquish Qill**"

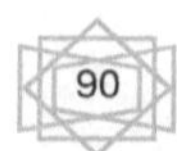

Just then, a flood of Glam pixies flew from the tree, encircling Willow with a whimsical engulfment. They finish creating her; she appears from the Victorian era.

Willow takes a bow like she is greeting the lords and ladies of the town.

Kalei shouts out, "Oh My goodness!!! You look like a maiden princess."

Willow returns to reality, looks down at her hand, and sees the crescent moon change from that to many other insignia's. She can hear the people behind her gasp in shock. Someone from the back screams out.

"She is one of the chosen one's."

Then, the tree speaks up. "Willow, we have been waiting for you for many years; only time will tell if you are chosen one."

"Now, Professor Applegate, please see that Willow goes to Professor Votoggle's at the Vintage Craft and Stone Emporium."

'There, Willow, you will find your answers to her questions."

As the tree finishes speaking, Kalei and Mrs. Applegate use their native Hawaiian tongue to gain passage to Manu'ahi Summit. Willow has an out-of-body experience in which her mouth uses a dialect she has never spoken or known before.

"Os gwelwch yn dda *(Tree of Magic)* anfonwch fi *(send me)* Feniks vuurvogel hoogtepunt *(Phoenix Firebird Summit)."*

"Mom, is that a Welsh Dialect?"

"Yes, dear, I believe Willow is from England or a providence of Wales."

Then both Applegate says. "Aloha" *(Goodbye)* as they hold their hands up, bow to the tree before entering.

Professor Applegate spoke to the girls. "Girls, are you ready?"

Willow and Kalei gleam with smiles, nod, and, in sync, say, "Yes…. oh yes…. I am ready!" the girls are excited to start their enchanting adventure.

Willow's left hand is held high above her head as she enters the tree, speaking Welsh. "**Diolch yn fawr.**" *(thank you very much)* They started to enter the magical opening in the tree. First, Kalei, then Willow followed, walking through the opening. She is greeted on the other side of the sidewalk of this remarkably busy Manu`ahi Summit. Kalei arrives to the left Willow.

Then, within moments, Mrs. Applegate appears with a smile. "See, girls, that wasn't so bad. You can let your worries stay in the realm we just left. Embrace your new beginnings and flourish in your newfound Wixan life."

Appearing before their eyes, they could see all the diverse cultures, all dressed in their native wares. People dressed in Dutch wares, Ming China wares, and more native cultures. Everything here was a blend of cultures from around the world. Even the architecture was done with global artifacts. Each store has its individual charm, adorned with various cultural emblems and symbols. Enormous awnings lining the streets, each color a unique representing the cultural melting pot of Manu`ahi Summit.

As Willow's mouth hangs agape, she hears Mrs. Applegate

saying, "It's beautiful, isn't it? So, girls let me be the first

one to welcome you to Manu'ahi Summit, the trading capital

of all seven Magic Schools."

Chapter Eight
Manu`ahi Summit

Willow looks down the street to the left and right, with storefronts as far as the eye can see. They have everything from Abigail's Amulets to The Quill and Scroll," Mrs. Applegate says.

"Girls' first stop is to get my darling **Keiki** *(child)* her familiar; we must check out Flannagan's Finest Familiars," They arrive, Sarah enters first, the girls trail behind; this store is strange and spooky.

Kalei looks up at a big black crow in the corner. As it stares her down, it gives off an echoing "kaa-kaa…caw …caw…" startling her. Then, it continues to watch the group carefully, paying close attention to Kalei.

"Kalei looks down; "It's a beautiful fluffy fox."

Kalei takes her next step; the sleek red fox gracefully weaves around her feet. Unaware, she stumbles over the clever creature, falling down.

"Ahhhh!"

CRASH!!

"Hey, are you good?" Willow plops the cat and carrier down, then turns to assist Kalei.

While her back is turned, an enormous fruit bat dramatically lands on Aurora's travel carrier. It clings to the cage, flapping its wings like it's throwing a tantrum.

Willow snatches the carrier.

al

"Shoo, you loony bat."

The white bat leaps off the carrier, takes flight, and circles Kalei's head. It makes a daring dive toward Willow, swoops past, returns, and decides to perch on her head. Flapping its wings once again, chaos continues.

"Help, Kalei! Get it off! Shoo it away!"

Willow starts flailing about, thrashing, trying to swat the bat off her head. The mysterious albino bat, with beady red eyes, it flies away, she regains her composure and remarks.

"Well, what a warm welcome! That crazy bat sure knows how to make an entrance."

Kalei chuckles.

Suddenly, the bat swoops back in, drops a tiny scroll into Willow's hand, and flies off again. Willow unrolls it to reveal:

"Welcome to the neighborhood! P.S. Duck next time."

Kalei laughs even harder, "I think the bat just RSVP'd to your next party!"

Chapter Nine
Spellbound Excursions

As they reach the middle of the store, the back area remains dimly lit, with wall candles flickering and casting shadows.

A silhouette of a man emerges and advances toward the group. The girls become aware of the approaching figure, and as he draws nearer, they start to discern his features.

Professor Flanagan comes into view—a short, compact man dressed in ruddy knickerbockers, a ruffled white top featuring a pirate's collar, and a brown leather sleeveless jacket fastened with four buttons down the front. His 18th-century colonial hat appears weathered, much like his worn and tattered clothing, including the knickerbockers. His face and hands bear time marks like he has lived for a century. With his pillowy artist hat, in a raspy yet chipper voice, he speaks.

"Good Mingling Morning Ladies, here to search for your familiar? Here at Flannigan's Finest Familiars, we have a plethora to choose from. Let me introduce myself.

"I am the Great Professor Flannigan, producing the finest familiars. We have everything from bulgy eye bats to sneaky slithering snakes that spit acid. And, of course, every Witches and Wizards favorite, the mundane and usual… dragons, black cats, owls, bats, rats and foxes, and even adorable hedgehogs. If you can think of it, we probably have it. We receive shipments from all over the world, helping you find your familiar."

"So, ladies, how can I help you today?"

"Well, this girl needs to get her familiar," Willow points to her friend, and a pack of Owls starts chattering and Whoo-ting.

"Whoo! Whooo! Whoooo!"

Willow speaks loudly over the chattering owls as she points to a cat.

"Look, Kalei, over there, there is a black cat like Aroura."

"I see; it has the same color of golden eyes; except it's missing the W mark on its forehead."

"I see it, Will; hey, Mom, how do we know what kind of familiar to get?"

"Kalei, I had the same problem when I was your age…. ask Mr. Flannagan… I bet he'll have the solution…."

"Mr. Flannagan, I can't choose; there are so many to choose from."

"Well, Kalei, let's go to the tea leaves and ask."

The professor prepares tea, and the girls wander to the back of the store to investigate and explore.

"Hey, Willow, take a look at that Sign. (Spray this over the Spider's web, and a secret message will appear.)"

The Spider sits on its bright red and white-topped mushroom in the middle of the web, waiting for a question to go to work.

"Can you tell me what my familiar should be?"

"The Spider stretches its eight legs and nods its head. It starts running back and forth in the web, making a web to decode."

It confidently places its hands on its hips, delivering a shake with a hint of attitude as it declares.

"Well, darling, what's the holdup? Snatch that misting bottle; messages don't have time for witches to wilt. Start spraying, girlfriend!"

Kalei takes the bottle and sprays the web. A few seconds later, a large bird appears on the web.

"Spider, what like an owl?"

The Spider shook its head and spiffed and hissed with sighs of disdain.

"Wait a minute…Reality Check! Did that Spider talk to us? And did that thing spiff and spit at you, giving you sass."

"Yip Yip, Willow, I think it did; this realm is wildly magical."

"Hey, I think it is trying to give another message."

The Spider ran back and forth for two minutes like it was on excessive caffeine.

The Spider finally stops and gets on its mushroom perch, centered on its web.

Willow reaches for the bottle. "Here, let me spray it this time."

After she spritzes it, a lengthy road in a forest materializes, pulsating with a surge of vitality at the distant end of the road.

"Ok, Spider, what kind of familiar is that? Spider, like, am I supposed to find a black hole or excess energy? "

"I don't know, Kalei. It has me stumped, too. Let's move on to the four baby water dragons."

Willow points to the table on the left, viewing a sizeable 100-gallon aquarium.

These H2O dragons are doing acrobatic stunts and gracefully gliding in the water with flawless effort.

The Sign hangs above it:

Attention Students and Staff Notice:

!!!DO NOT TOUCH!!!

Rainbow Pocket Pet Dragons Hatchling Pocket Pets

BEWARE!!!

Dragons, even at this young age, can cause large welts upon skin contact. Exercise caution!

• Order of the 12 Elements Ministry of Magic •

DE Daniel

When the two girls finished their staring contest with the creatures, they returned to the table at the front of the store.

Kalei nervously approaches the tea leaves, unsure of what to ask. Mr. Flannagan motions her to come and take a seat.

"Kalei, brace yourself for the cosmic inquiry!"

With closed eyes and a look of utmost seriousness, she belts out.

"What is my familiar?"

She continues to put her mind on hyper-focus. She was mumbling like a mantra…over and over.

"What is my familiar… What is my familiar… What is my familiar."

"Alright, my mystical maven, I reckon the universe is ready to spill the magical beans!"

DE Daniel

He looks deeply into the tea leaves; Kalei anxiously waits for his response. After a few moments, he looks up and smiles.

"Your familiar is a wise-old Hawaiian crow or 'alalā *(Crow)*.

It will guide your journey and help you see things differently when needed, and with its agility and speed it can get messages to far and wide, if needed."

"Here are some keynotes for my young 1st year student."

"Kalei, you're familiar, is significant in Hawaiian culture. It is the Hawaiian crow 'alalā .'"

Kalei feels excitement and curiosity about what this could mean for her future.

He gives three quick bursts of high squeaks and says the name.

"Squ'eek…. Squ'eek…. Squ 'eeeeek ! Rocky… come and meet your new student, Kalei."

Rocky, the crow, swoops down and lands on Kalei's lap. He lifts his claw up to give her a special delivery on ancient parchment paper. It reads:

Dear child of the universe, Today, Kalei, you are embarking on changing your destiny.

When embracing your change, always be positive and know your worth. Endowed, You are with the ancient Bird of Hawaii; your ancestral **'alalā** will be your spirit guide. Your past family member resides in this bird. As your **aumakua**, he will help you with adventures and give you guidance and knowledge from the island people of the past. He represents gods from the water, and his extraordinary powers are.

- Bearer of great tsunamis.

- Parts the waters.

- Creates whiteout rains.

- Brings life of fertility to any baron land.

Sincerely,
RuthAnn Longquist
12 Elements Ministry
Director of Familiars
Secret Island of Ancestral Spirit Guides

Then Professor Flannagan reaches out and gives Kalei a leather-bound book.

"Dear Kalei, child of the Universe, please read this important book on theology, caretaking, spiritual magic, and what qualities you can expect from your familiar."

"Thank you so much, you are a fine man, I will… I promise to read it cover to cover."

"Very well, my dear Kalei, do you and Willow have your wands?"

"No sir, not at this time… do you recommend a place?"

"Certainly, the only place in Manu`ahi Summit…. When you leave here, take a left, go past the big Dragon Colosseum, then just about 10 to 12 magic carpets lengths long. Then you will see The Ministry of 12 Elements Sorcerer's Caveat on your right… just past that, you will find Professor SpellBee's Spellbinding Sticks.

Professor SpellBee will be there to assist…. My only warning is don't let his Troll Beasley have any bubblegum Beatles. Beasley can become a mischievous and malevolent Troll known to swing from the chandeliers, blowing bubbles as big as a seal… Beasley loves to get right next to students and pop the ginormous bubble all over everyone."

"Ha ha ha."

"It always turns into a sticky situation… if you know what I mean. My darling friends, you must be on your way now."

As they were leaving, Mrs. Applegate said,

"Thank you for everything, Professor Flannagan."

Chapter Ten
Unleash the Elves

Mrs. Applegate's belly rumbles, so loud, "Girls, let us find some delicious eats…"

Just then, two kids zoom past the trio.

Willow grabs Mrs. Applegate's arm, shaking it like an excited little kid.

"Are you serious, we get to ride brooms now? OMG… this day just keeps getting better!"

"Well, girls, there are strict rules here on the summit. You cannot fly in the streets, only on campus or if you are in grave danger."

"Evil fairies may chase them for not representing a good Wixan."

"Mom, my stomach is making a scene like it's auditioning for a food drama show!"

As the trio ascends the summit, the air fills with excitement and the promise of lunch.

 DC Daniel

The girls chat animatedly with Professor Applegate about the array of options awaiting them.

"There's the famous Castle de' la' Crem, known for its heavenly fruit crepes and dragon drop stew with glowing dragon essence. Sounds like a feast fit for royalty!" exclaims Kalei.

"Indeed, but let's not overlook the quirky delights on the right," Professor Culinary Explorer points out as they approach the signs for Leilani's Famous Magical Cookies.

Leilani's Sign:

"BAT Cookies (Let's hear past the noise)"

"Freaky Lip-Smacking Goodness"

"Disappearing Cookies"

One of the girl's chuckles, "Disappearing Cookies? Now that's a disappearing act worth witnessing!"

Continuing their ascent, they discover Henrietta's Howling Sundaes and Specialty Candies, each with its own charming Sign.

Henrietta's Howling Sundas & Specialty Candies.

A howling good time to be had by all.

Pretty Pixie Pops
Unwrap the Magic, Taste the Wonder!
Beetle Bubblegum
The Bubble That's Larger than Life!
Trilogy Levitation Taffy
One bite, and you'll be on Cloud 9!

Dragon Breath Candy
The Brave, The Bold, The Supersonic Life!

DE Daniel

Willow grins, "I've never heard a sundae howl before. It should be an interesting experience!"

They decide to stop at Henrietta's. They sit on the live toadstools as the pixie server takes their orders.

"Ribbit… Ribbit…. Ribbit"

Willow orders first. "Please, may I order a lemon-watermelon cooler? I also would like to order two Dragon Breaths and a Trolling Good Time Cupcake."

Then Kalei requests, "May I have a box of Beetle Bubblegum and one Pretty Pixie Pop?"

The fairy server looks at Professor Applegate. "And you ma' dam…What stupendous food may I get for you?"

"I would like to order a Fizz and Pop Sparkling Sundae and a Dragons' Breath.

Also, please add one order of Googely Gooseberry Fries with a side of Bucking Bronco Berry Sauce. Thank you."

She sprinkles fairy dust on the table, swirls it into a mini circulating vortex, and then swiftly heads to the back of the kitchen.

The girls wait; they play in the cloud of fairy dust. They take turns blowing it on one another, making pixie elf ears on each other. Two miniature fairies fly around the table as they play in the dust, blowing fairy dust out of a spirula shell at each other.

Professor Applegate sits watching the girls engage without electronic devices, unplugged from the world. This is special within itself.

Within minutes, the food arrives, and two tiny 5-inch Elves present the Trolling Good Time Cupcake. They march right off the carrying tray.

"Thud"

"Kur…thump"

With the desert in hand, it is presented to Willow; they then make Googely eyes, stick out their tongue, and blow a raspberry at her.

She jumps back, squats down, scoots closer, crosses her eyes, folds her arms, and makes a big old raspberry at them. It covers the girls in wetness. The elves take offense as the two capricious Elves shake like a dog, to dry of a little, then turn to their backside, shake it at her, and give a mischievous laugh.

"He He He Ha ha ha."

The delivery pixie snaps her finger as if to say stop your shenanigans. The two of them jump back onto the tray.

Professor Applegate's Fizz and Pop Sparkling Sundae has a sparkle of 3 small flames on top instead of cherries.

Kalei says to Willow.

"Ready, Willow; on the count of three, we bite into our magical bites together."

"Ok, this will be fun!"

"1…. 2…. 3……"

"Ha ha ha…. Willow, look at you. Your skin is green like Fiona, Shrek's wife…."

"You're not looking so bad yourself, Kalei…. full-blown Pixie status there. I should have chosen that; you don't even have wings, and you can fly?

"Look, Kalei."

"Yep, look at me… I can do somersaults in the air…. Whhheeee"

As Willow purses her lips tight, cheeks full of air, eyes almost popping out of her head."

"Stop, Willow, you are going to make me pee myself."

She laughs, tumbling through the air. Without warning, Kalei comes tumbling down into her seat…. She shakes off the hard landing by shaking like a wet dog, head to tail, as she changes back to her original self.

"Willow, if you are willing to share your 2 dragon breaths with Kalei, we can all experience it together. I think you girls are going to love this."

"Sure… here, Kalei, do you see the fine print?"

"Yes, listen to this. It says one is required to exercise caution and respect for the dragon's power."

"ooohh la laa, that sounds mysterious," Kalei says.

Willow reads on, "Caution: Colors may seem brighter, sounds can be more intense and smells more vibrant.

"Ok, girls, I will go first…."

DC Daniel

Said Professor Applegate with a mischievous smile on her face.

Her pupils dilate as she places it in her mouth, and bits of smoke protrude from her nose, mouth, and ears, just like a real dragon. The girls are overwhelmed with excitement as they pop it into their mouths.

All the girls sit around the table, steaming like dragons and belly-laughing.

"Mrs. Applegate… everything in this room is in super-duper techno-color mode."

"Yeah, Mom, can you hear the fairies in the kitchen talk about food orders…. Sure enough, this is like supersonic hearing…"

The professor nods her head. "I can hear it too, Kalei," Willow says.

The three of them continue to enjoy their treats before A short time later, Professor Applegate announces.

"Well, girls, we must get to a few more places before sunset. Let's get on our way."

The trio packs up and heads to SpellBee's Spellbinding Sticks.

Chapter Eleven
Professor SpellBee's Spellbinding Sticks

The group briskly walks over to SpellBee's place.

"Look, girls, it's a fire dragon hatchling."

DE Daniel

The enchantress trio stops and watches a purple straggly-tooth dragon try to get his fire on.

"Looks like he is trying to learn how to blow fire. He is so cute trying to muster up a flocka flocka flame."

"Yes, keep trying, little one, you will get your fire soon enough."

Kalei giggles as they watch this purple, and lime green dragon blow a few small puffs and one big puff of smoke.

"Don't let it destress you, little man. Be the engine that could… keep trying."

The fire dragon looks discouraged and gives it one last try without success. He puts his hands on his hips and stomps off, feeling defeated.

The group keeps on their trek to find their unique wand. The BFF's make their way into the emporium. Two elves Micka and Bella greet the young Wixan's with mischievous smirks.

These two elves are captivated by Willow. They begin sizing her up and down with a steadfast gaze, paying close attention to her embellished Victorian outfit. The elves circle her, and a voice rings out from the back.

"I will be with you in a few shakes of a dragon's tail. I'm busy back here training the magic monkeys on unicycles.

Be right there and have a look-see around my exquisite emporium."

Willow quietly says to Kalei, "Do you see this? It's unbelievable. Look over there, potions for every elixir, from dragons' breath to Cyclops' dust."

"Yes, I see, Kalei. Hurry come over here, look at this cobra venom…. Oooohhh, I wonder if that can turn you into a snake or knock the scales off a lizard…just kidding, but Willow, whatever it is, it looks deadly with the cross-bone icon on it."

Mrs. Applegate points to the stone ledge with water dragon eggs and fire beetle shells. "This is the place to be when casting supplies are needed. It has everything you can imagine, from air protection supplies to water spells and everything in between."

Professor SpellBee bellows out. "OK, ladies, come to the front of the store. Let's get started."

When Willow approaches, she deciphers that she is a remarkable, well-aged lady.

Her glasses are strange, two big squares for eye frames.

This pair of glasses, over stage her forehead and cheeks. The Professor's smile is calm and inviting. She holds a few extra pounds like Miss Juno. The closer she gets to her, the more she realizes she is taller than 6 feet. Her hair is set in a messy bun at the top of her head, with a lei flower on the left. The untucked hair strands flow with hints of red that shimmer through the thick blonde hair.

The Professor's robe waves in the wind as she approaches; it is a very noticeable shimmery periwinkle. Under her robe, a black ruffled blouse peaks with Victorian lace sleeves cuffed at the wrist.

"Oh! Willow and Kalei, there you are! I've been eagerly awaiting your arrival. I notice your names on the roster of first-year students at WillowBrook on the Island of Solaris. What an exciting journey lies ahead for both of you!

DC Daniel

By the way, I stumbled upon a list of names from the Norse Academy of Craft in Norway, and 1st-year students Jorgen and Haakon were here about an hour ago. As for the second-year students, Björn and Kacper those two scamps are known for their humorous antics. So be warned on those two, whenever they can, they cause laughter and antics"

SpellBee reaches out to grab Willow's hand; the Professor becomes startled. She quickly retracts her hand and spins around in front of them, halting everyone in their tracks.

"What's wrong, Professor SpellBee?" Willow asks.

"Oh, my dearest, sweet child, are you of the same bloodline as Sir Charles Brook of England?"

"No, Madam, not that I know of......why."

"Are you quite certain? You're not a cousin or a relative... You possess the young lad's potent Mana..."

SpellBee grabs her hand again and holds it more intently.

"Ahhh! Yes!! The Mana is powerful, yet I sense the touch of Spector. This confuses me; you look like a beautiful light being, not possible of much Spector. Let me concentrate... Hmmm... quite intriguing.

I sense it now; I can't quite grasp it... It feels familiar, like a good energy, right on the edge of my awareness. Yet, I can't quite pinpoint where it's coming from."

Willow's face is blank, and she looks at Mrs. Applegate. "What does she mean, Mana…Spector? Is that bad?"

"Willow, don't fret child, let's get to your wand…"

She gives a loud whistle, and both Micka and Bella come inside from the court yard. "Yes professor! is it time for fittings?" asks Bella; she is always more energetic than most. Mika with an evil laugh. "Yes, we love to size up the new students… Boou'whaaa ha ha."

Mika points to the roof and draws a silver lasso around him as it spins in a circle to the ground. He disappears with it and reappears behind her. And even louder yells a sinister laughter. "Boou'whaaa ha ha."

Willow is startled a bit; she jumps forward into the Professor. The professor puts her cold hands-on Willow, "Willow child, please be still till they finish.". She looks down at the two helper elves "Now you two get to work, please size her up and give me the Parameters to her wand needs."

The elves pull out their tape measures and start to get to work. They measure from foot to head, elbow to wrist, and one shoulder to the other. They speak to the Professor, finishing every other word.

Mika starts, "Oooooh …ahhhh."

Bella says "Yes, we see… she is a perfect specimen."

Mika says "We believe a wand"

Bella "Of 10 to 14 inches,"

Mika "Will do her justice."

"Thank you, Mika and Bella, for your help." Professor SpellBee smiles at them, looking delighted from their findings.

"Sure, No Problem." Bella and Mika say in harmony, giving each other a high five.

The Professor goes into a spiel about this young Enchantress who went bad after her third year at the China School of Spells many years ago.

"Do you girls know what Spector is?"

"No, professor, what is it?" Kalei says.

Willow with puckered lips and a scowl on her face. "Yes, please tell us what it is. It sounds bad… and I don't want to be part of it."

"Well, it is what dark magic is made from; sometimes, as rare as it is, young witches and wizards follow the dark magic road, leading to travesty and devastation. I met this young lady many years ago.

Her name is Aynat, and she grows old and wicked after she loses the love of her life. She also had a little girl 13 years ago; But the Order keeps it, hush-hush… if you know what I mean.

Then, exactly 14 months later, she delivers a baby boy; I can't imagine what will happen when that boy comes of age—being raised by such a dark and vile lady.

She has been causing ripples in destabilizing the Order of the 12 Elements for years."

"I am confused professor, what does this have to do with me?" asked Willow.

Don't worry Willow, let me tell you more; I swear to you…. because she went to the dark side, that lady and her lad are shell-bent; Spector can take over any soul when the right situation arises."

"Why is that, Professor?" Kalei asks.

The Professor lowers her voice as she whispers. "You see, my children, most babies are instilled with god's grace. The gods create Mana, which embodies the spirit of the young.

DE Daniel

However, sometimes Spector, the dark side of evil…...when the young ones embrace it, it can creep in unnoticed. Taking the soul to the dark side."

Then the Professor loudly shouts. "WHAMO…One day, out of nowhere, there you have it, a full-bound, shell-bent witch or wizard…… please, please, girls, I ask you to always be positive in nature, keep your Mana strong, and never do harm to others."

Both girls simultaneously nod and speak, echoing one another. "Of course, Professor, we promise to always do good and harm none." Both Willow and Kalei put up three fingers in the shape of a W, the uniform Wixan sign of peace and wellness.

"Well, young ladies and educated elder, moving on, enough about that shell-bent witch and her son.

"Now…. enough with the gossip. Willow let's get you a wand. Humm…… let me see here…. California Redwood stick…. (Strong and resilient, 12 inches long. With a little snap of the wrist… you'll have it. It will be a fine specimen for protection and spellbinding."

She places it down and picks up a 13-inch Rosewood Branch... "Very whippy looking, coming to a point, beautifully handcrafted."

She places it next to the other, on a 30-inch-deep circle of a stump, the base of an amazing California Redwood with many rings. The tree looks to be well over a hundred years old.

She picks up one from a pile on her left and says… ah… yes… moderate weighted, subdued grain pattern, hues of red and purple, hardness is an 8… This oak stick will do just fine"

She then places it down next to the other two. "Let me look for a fire stick in the fire runic room. I will be right back. Hold tight, OK?"

SpellBee returns with a 10-inch stick of mahogany. This stick signifies fire. The owner will represent passion, energy, and creativity, with great transformation qualities."

She places the fourth element wand down on the fire element spot on the giant sequoia tree platform.

With the four wands there, one for each element. She gives a command to Willow. "Willow, please wave your hand over them with a flick of the wrist upward. Let's see which one is calling you."

As Willow waves her hand across the four wands, nothing is happening. She waves her hand again, nothing, no spark, no vibration… nothing… just stillness. "Do it again, my child…and flick your wrist like this." SpellBee demonstrates and directs Willow.

She watches as Willow does it again. Same results, nothing.

"Oh, Fiddle Sticks…. not again! Ok' let me try."

SpellBee waves her hand over them with a flick of her wrist.

"Valio!"

They all react instantly, levitating over the stump, ready for a commander. She removes her hand away; they all fall back into their perspective element boxes.

"Humm… this is peculiar and strange…."

She points at Kalei. "Kalei, do you mind going next?"

"No, madam, this will be fun; I am so excited." Kalei steps up to the stump, eager to find her magic stick. She waves her hand across the group with a flick of the wrist.

Kalei's wand flows to her hand with ease, now with her wand in her hand. She noticed the base of the wand had a water symbol on it; it was the Redwood Wand.

"This means you are a Water Sign; you will do great things with water. Have you met your water protector yet?" Inquiries the Professor,

"Yes, Madam, when we were at camp a few weeks ago, he…showed himself to Willow and I; his name is HydroKnox." She pulls out her necklace, the Shell whistle HydroKnox had bequeathed her with.

"Oh My... Oh My…. that is beautiful." As she inspects it with an adoring."Ohh!"

"Make sure you always carry your wand everywhere in the magical world. You never know when you will cross paths with a Night Marcher or one of Telamisis's creatures."

"Yes, of course, Professor, I will. Thank you."

"Now on this trisket of a task, Miss Willow. I have the solution to this wand conundrum." She then says.

"Stay here, I have the perfect one… I will be back in a snap of a dragon's tail." "…. Doodle Lee Dummb… Doodle Lee Bee, a Wixan's life for me…. Snaggle dragon pop, it's the perfect life for me, you'll see." Says Professor SpellBee, then she drifts off to the back of the building.

Kalei looks at Willow after the Professor vanishes. "Did you see what door she entered.?"

"Nope, looks like she faded into the air before she reached any of the doors."

A few minutes later, she reappears with the presence of a willowy branch with a fuzzy large willow bud infused into the tip.

"I have a very special wand attached to the moon's spirit; it is made of the Willow tree."

"This is awesome. The tree name has my name in it." Willow says as she gets full of excitement again.

The Professor places it in the element water spot on the tree trunk.

"OK, girl… what are you waiting for? Go ahead, wave your hand, and flick your wrist."

As Willow raises her hand, all the wands cogitate together, binding into one, and then 3 of the wands fall back into their perspective element spots.

Leaving the water sign and floating. The 14-inch stick lights up and jets to her hand, Willow swirls around once as she grasp it firmly, and a magic trail of sparkles flew from the tip.

Then, a flash of seared flames flow from it. One giant spark hits the top of a cage where a barn owl sits. It knocks the cage free from the roof; just then, Professor aims with her wand and speaks.

"Higher Gavotusus"

DC Daniel

Saving the Owl from dismise, SpellBee levitates the owl in its cage and gently placing it on the counter, unharmed.

"Skiddlee doo, sweetie that was a close one for the Owl."

While this commotion happens, Willow's hand ignites the moon's hieroglyphic symbol, and it starts to flicker the earth, water, wind, and fire, resting back on the moon sign.

"Ahh, I see you have found your wand…."

As Willow looked down, she saw a runic symbol of a larger-than-normal water sign followed by an earth symbol in a carving beneath it. Willow turns the wand over, and a Metatron symbol is engraved on the base.

"You are a water element with a secondary power of the earth element. However, I did notice that you could command the other signs. This must be because you are a moon child of the universe."

With a puzzled look on her face, Willow looked at the Professor. "Professor, I am confused; what does that mean?"

"Well, Willow, in time, you will see. You are a special enchantress; it's rare for a child to have the ability to command more than two magical powers in their first year. Your parents must be proud of you."

Willow becomes emotional, tearing up, wiping the tears from her face, and trying not to cry in front of them, as she tells the Professor.

"I find it hard to believe my parents would be proud of me. You see, I don't have a dad or a mom; my mom had me and abandoned me at the hospital. And the kids at the group homes always gave me grief."

As she grabs her shirt, embracing the necklace in her hand. "The only thing I have is this necklace given to me when I was placed with my guardian, Miss Juno."

"I see, child; I am so sorry you had to go through such turmoil growing up. You will find friends and loving guidance from your new school and professors. So, my child, dry up your crocodile tears and believe everything will be OK."

As she wipes her eyes, her frown simmers with a glimmer of hope of a new chapter unfolding. She grabs her best friend, Kalei, hugs her, and speaks. "I am so glad we are together, And I am so glad we are best friends."

"Mee too, Willow. I am glad you're my bestie, for today, tomorrow, and always."

"Alright, ladies, it is time to get going. We still have one more stop before the Manu'ahi Carriage leaves for WillowBrook."

"Come on girls, gather your stuff, and let's get a move on it. Thank you, Professor SpellBee, for all your help. We are headed to Professor Votoggles in the Vintage Craft and Stone Emporium.

Chapter Twelve
Whispers of the Talisman:
A Destiny Awakened

As the trio steps into the room, Professor Applegate announces their arrival. "Hello, I'm Professor Applegate. We're here to see Professor Votoggle."

DC Daniel

Votoggle smiles and replies, "Well, you've got him right here. How can I help you?"

Mrs. Applegate looks at him, puzzled. "You seem shorter than I remember. Not to be rude, but I recall you being much taller as a kid."

"Ah, yes, Professor," Votoggle chuckles. "You were a half-pint yourself! I used to be taller, but then I ran into one of Hades' goons and used an ant spell to hide. Unfortunately, I never returned to my original height of 5 foot 9 when it wore off. Now, I'm stuck as a mini version of myself. Ha ha ha!"

Professor Votoggle, now just three and a half feet tall, has a bushy white beard that sways as he talks. His pointy hat stands tall above his head, casting a shadow over his face, while his plain black robe gives him a mysterious air. He glides just above the floor, almost as if he's floating. Willow, standing shyly behind Professor Applegate and Kalei, finally musters up the courage to step forward.

DC Daniel

Votoggle suddenly stops talking and stares at her, as if he's seen a ghost. He narrows his eyes and speaks to her.

"Hmm… well, well. Look who we have here. You've been quite the talk of the town. Since your birth, the Order of the 12 Elements gave you a special necklace. Willow, did you bring it with you?"

"This one, Professor?" Willow asks, holding up her necklace.

"Yes, that's the one," Votoggle nods. "Take it off, so I can show you something."

Willow removes the necklace and holds it in her hand. As she does, it begins to pulse with colorful light, swaying back and forth. She stares at it, wide-eyed.

"That's it exactly," Votoggle explains. "This necklace is a protection talisman. Wear it always—it offers balance, harmony, and a connection with the universe. You're going to face some dangers, Willow.

If you encounter a being engulfed in Spector, hold onto your talisman and say, **'Departure No Low Aires.'**

It will vanish and return to where it came from."

Looking bewildered, Willow asks, "I'm not sure I understand. What do you mean?"

"It's called the Norse Protection Spell," he says, resting a hand on her shoulder. "Don't worry; when the time comes, you'll know what to do."

Still feeling a bit overwhelmed, Willow turns to Professor Applegate. "I'm so confused, Professor. Why would I need protection? And why don't you or Kalei have something like this? Does everyone need protection?"

"Take a breath, child," Applegate reassures her. "I know it's a lot to take in, but all will be explained in due time. Stop letting the unknown rattle you. Just remember, I'll be here with you every step of the way."

Chapter Thirteen
The Journey Begins

Reaching the top of the summit is a magnificent volcano named Mauna Loa. Its fiery smoke billows up the sunsetting night sky, and its rumbling can be felt across the countryside of the Big Island. This is a magic portal, one that can transport anyone who enters it.

DE Daniel

The Manu'ahi Summit leads to the 7 Schools of Magic. This eye-catching volcano adjoins a long landing strip where Phoenix Firebirds line up for transport to all the schools of magic, accommodating 6 to 12 people at a time.

Sometimes, on special request, a professor and select Wixan students can travel to the Hypogeum Secret Ancestry Island, where students seek mentorship from their ancestors in times of need and self-discovery.

As they approach the enormous Manau'ahi bird, a feathery creature whose feathers shimmer like gold in the sunlight. A rainbow of intrepid colors covers its body, from bright yellow to deep hues of blue and purple. It sits two kids' side by side, in a straight row of three, with its length of six meters long (19.5 ft) and three and a half meters wide (11ft)

The trio's ears flood with the Birdmaster's voice as she shouts.

The group approaches, and the Birdmaster slides down from the bird's wing. "All Aboard……this Manau`ahi Carriage…. Leaves in 15 minutes."

The bird conductor wears a large top hat and flowing puffy pants striped horizontally in red and black. The blouse is crisp, bright white; it flows out at her hands, with a white ruffle that cuffs and then appears again around her neck. The boots she is wearing resemble jockey boots up to the knee. She is wrapped in a long-sleeved black jacket with a high straight collar with tails.

As they approach the Birdmaster, she speaks out again. "Welcome, new and old wizards and enchantresses. Everyone, please have your tickets ready when boarding your bird."

Kalei squeezes Willow's hand as they walk closer. Willow feels a bit excited about the magical escapade.

They step up to the platform, the sign reads (loading dock here).

The bird master is sharply dressed and attentively standing. "Tickets please!"

"Come on up, this bird is headed To WillowBrook. Have your tickets ready!"

"Tickets please…. loading now."

Willow presents her ticket first.

Click! Click! Click!

Click! Click! Click!

The Birdmaster takes it and punches out an image of the phoenix firebird. After the Birdmaster punches the girls' tickets, Professor Applegate pulls out her left hand and twists her elemental ring.

A holographic image emits the Ministry of 12 Elements symbol; the image speaks to the Birdmaster.

"In direction under the Order of the 12 Elements, Professor Applegate is requested to attend first-year students at WillowBrook. Please Admit One."

In the distance, the girls hear a stout British man yelling from his megaphone in the distance.

"This Manau`ahi Bird is going to WillowBrook. The second bird back is going to the Oriental School of Magic Arts, and the third bird in line is the Norway School of Craft. All birds leaving now, please find your way to the loading ramps."

The three of them board the bird as they settle into their seats. They are surprised when they see Trinity boarding, behind two blonde boys, identical twins.

"Bjørn, I want to sit there; you can sit behind me."

"No, I am older, Kacper, by two minutes."

"Don't care, you big baby… I want to sit there."

The bird master gives 2 quick bursts from her whistle.

"Tweet Tweet."

"Stop the caterwauling, Johanson twins, find your seat… stop bickering. Before I put a spell on your tongues."

Both boys promptly settle in their seats and comply. The Birdmaster makes her way to the head of the bird; with a giant glowing megaphone, she bellows out.

"Welcome, all first-year students and returning Wixan's. Please remain seated while the bird is in motion. Always keep your hands and feet inside the carrier. We don't want any missing fingers or loss of limbs. You are going to be transported to WillowBrook. May your journey be filled with a sense of wonder and enlightenment."

After everyone is loaded safely, the Birdmaster looks over to the loading dock where all their personal belongings remain.

She pulls a golden lasso and ropes a figure 8 in the sky, this glowing lasso, drops down tentacles, then lifts and encases all the personal travelers' belongings, totes, bags, foot locker's, backpacks etc. She enchants the lasso by saying,

"Crasporta transfer stow"

Then magically the lasso turns into a golden net, as it circumferences everything compressing in on itself. squishing everything into a flat rhombus disk. It compresses so tight, that it disappears into a flash of light.

She then raises her wand to the travelers' familiars, she blows a purple sleepy dust at her wand, which flows to and settles on the animals. As they fall into a deep slumber, her stream of magic then encapsulates them, the animals gently float to the rear of the bird. With all the familiars nestled into the rear storage.

She hands the bird some sparkling food in a small bucket.

As it pecks away, it gobbles the magic transcending food. The bird master walks down the rows of travelers and carefully inspects everyone's seats, making sure all are secure and fastened in the travel carriage. This carrier has a beautiful beacon light on the front, helping the bird guide them to their destination.

The bird master jumps off and blows her whistle in a long attention-grabbing sound. "Phwwwwwhht"

She yells out. "Be good, Do good, Be Kind, Harm none."

The bird tightens its grip on the carrier, a wing appears from each side, cascading over the passengers. She motions for the bird to take flight. With a running start on the airstrip, the bird huffs its wings up and down. With a few massive flaps, it is airborne. The Manau`ahi bird takes to the sky, soaring high in the sky. Everyone holds on tight, their hearts pounding with fear and excitement.

Willow looks over the carrier's side as they fly over the rugged mountains and verdant forests.

Suddenly, a super bright light flashes before Willow's eyes, and she feels like she is getting pulled through this crazy energy tunnel. The firebird does all these fancy moves in the energy tunnel, like spinning and diving.

As they all go through the tunnel, Willow sees the colors around her changing. It's like a mix of incredible blues, pinks, and purples all swirling around, making everything look like a super cool kaleidoscope. Even though it's confusing, Willow starts feeling super excited. She just knows this trip is taking her to something big.

Finally, what feels like an eternity, the energy tunnel begins to fade away. The brilliant colors around them start to soften, and they can see a light in the distance. As the group approaches, the light grows brighter and brighter until it completely engulfs them.

When the light finally fades away, Willow finds herself in a new place. She dismounts the bird with the others. Everyone looks around, taking in their new surroundings. She is standing in the middle of a clearing surrounded by towering trees. A gentle breeze rustles the leaves above her, and she can hear the distant sound of a babbling brook. In the further distance, the trio and the others can see the entrance to WillowBrook.

"Hey, Willow, you've got that grin like the Cheshire cat!"

"Yeah, I'm stoked to be here, my brain is like a race car thinking about all the magical stuff that is going to happen."

Kalei chimes in. "This school is legit wild! Check out these intricate symbols and carvings on the walls; they're like Hogwarts on steroids."

Trinity then says, "Totally! But it's not just any old shape; This school is like a hexagon.

There is six sides to the castle, see those buildings 'Water Hall,' 'Earth Hall,' 'Fire Hall,' and 'Wind Hall. And then look over to the left, see the Dining Hall, then to the right is the Shadow Dome."

"I see it Trinity, and this so like a flash from the Japanese past with each one having a **sōrin** erected at the center of the roof top. They say it's for the belief of shapes sacred to Buddhism. Believed to repel evil and fulfill wishes." says Willow.

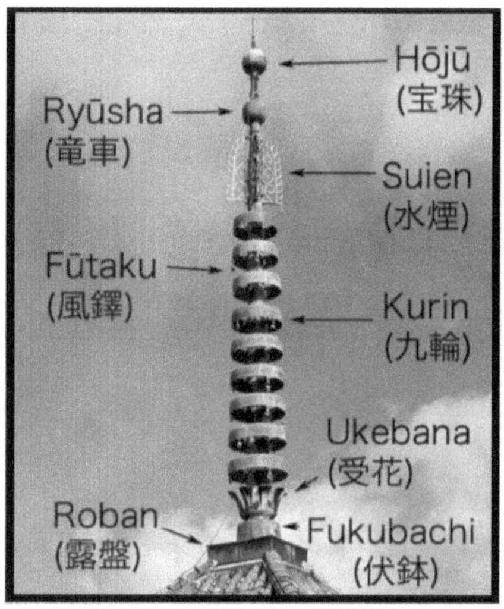

As the girls approach the crossroad, they see directional signs with arrows that appear. "Hey, look Willow, arrows pointing to the Great Hall, a Ballroom, and Dining hall." says Kalei.

"Oh, yes Kalei, looks like we have specialty classes, too! This wizard school is so fire. Maybe we can turn a stone into a bat?" Willow says with a playful giggle.

When they enter the school's courtyard, they are greeted by a bustling teacher, Professor Crowley, making announcements on the giant megaphone. "Alright, young ones, if you need help discovering your dorm, see Professor Nightengale and Professor Onyx standing next to me, and we will help you find your way."

Willow notices this excellent professor, Professor Nightingale, who's half human, half owl.

DE Daniel

Her eyes are super sharp, and you can just feel she knows when a person is lying, she can see right through them."

This human owl has special eyes, with 100 times zoom than a normal person. Adorned with feathery wings that make her look magical when she moves around.

Professor Nightingale's feathers make a gentle swishing or soft rustling sound like they are quietly whispering secrets in the air. Her wings glow with an ethereal glow. She seems to be a living example of the mysteries she teaches, shining with the light of her wisdom. She is a living mystery, full of wisdom under the moonlight.

Kalei is surprised that Professor Onyx is half human and half time, with a shimmering hourglass embedded in his chest. The sands within the hourglass flow with past, present, and future currents, and a subtle hum of chronal energy surrounds him. It's as if he is a living chronicle, carrying the essence of time within his very being, a mysterious fusion of humanity and the eternal march of moments.

Willow feels a sense of exhilaration building within her as she takes her first steps into the world of real wizardry and magic. Two fluttering fairies come bustling in front of them,

"After you get settled in, please make your way to the great dining hall. You will receive a sweet ~treatful welcome meal and a WillowBrook student handbook."

The students are in awe as they enter the castle dining room. They are immediately struck by the space's magical ambiance.

Above their heads, a dazzling array of floating objects fills the air with buzzing bats and careless owls. Nothing less than imagination and wonder fills the air.

The girls are totally amazed by the magical atmosphere around them, which feels like something out of a dream.

Kalei yells out in disbelief. "Ahhhh! Willow, dunk, incoming from your left, watch out!"

"What was that? Something just flew past my head, making some giggling noises."

"I think it was that pack of fluttering fairies or those mischievous pixies." As she points to the air above Kalei's head.

The room is lit by tiny fireflies that float through the air, emitting a soft, otherworldly glow. Also, colorful lanterns and magical orbs can be seen floating above, giving a radiation of glow with ethereal light, casting shimmering shadows on the walls and adding a touch of wonder to the scene.

Chapter Fourteen
The Castle of Tricks and Treats

The young Wixan's are eager to explore their new environment. After dinner, they begin their adventures in the castle. The girls walk through the castle's many corridors.

DC Daniel

As they pass the Neophyte Study Hall, the floor seems to come alive, shifting and moving beneath their feet.

Trinity bravely takes the first step, but the floor is sticky. As she tries to take another step, she slips and falls face-first into the gooey surface.

Trinity screams, looking frightened. "Ahhh, I am stuck slipping in this slime! Help me, Willow!" Willow offers her arm for support, and Trinity stands up, covered in green, slimy goo drippings from her face and hair.

Willow laughs. "Ha ha ha, it looks like you've been sneezed on by a nasty troll."

Trinity shakes herself like a dog after a bath, splattering the slimy goo all over the other two girls.

"Ha ha ha, who's laughing now? You both have been slimed!"

"Trinity, this is not funny. What if someone sees us? We look unbelievably gooey," complains Kalei.

Professor Nightingale appears from around the corner. "Ah, I see you're up to sticky business," she says, casting a spell. **"Remarble goo abish."**

The girls are instantly cleaned, returning to their original selves.

"Next time, girls, don't walk on the moving floors. Beware, there are tricks and traps throughout the castle."

"Thank you, Professor Nightingale, for your quick thinking," says Willow.

"I would hate to be made fun of on my first day here," adds Kalei.

The girls continue exploring the castle. Willow starts to do the potty jig, with a wiggle in her step, she says, "Hey, I have to find the bathroom."

"I see a sign up ahead on the left," says Kalei.

The girls approach the sign and push open the heavy wooden door. The sign reads **"baño-de-chicas"** (Girls' restroom). A blast of cold air hits them, chills run down their spines as they enter. The room is dimly lit, with flickering candlelight casting eerie shadows on the walls. A row of mirrors are ignited by the candle light, as they pass suddenly, the mirrors start talking. "I see you made it to the **baño-de-chicas**," they say in unison.

Willow's eyes widen. "This is so weird. Should we talk back?" she whispers to her friends.

One lady in the mirror rolls her eyes. "Oh, please do! We've been dying for some good gossip."

DE Daniel

Another mirror adds, "Yeah, it's been a while since we've heard something juicy. Last semester was a girl crying a river about her split ends. We almost got flooded out."

Willow exchanges a look with her friend. "Uh, we just came to use the restroom, no gossip here..."

A third mirror chimes in, "Sure, sure. That's what they all say. But we know you've got at least one embarrassing story to share."

"Or a secret crush," another mirror teases. "Come on, spill it. We're like the walls, we won't talk... much."

The girls laugh despite themselves. "Maybe we should just wash our hands and go," Willow says.

The middle mirror above the sink grumbles, "Fine, leave us hanging. But remember, we're always here to reflect."

Willow giggles. "At least they have a sense of humor,"

"I don't know. Maybe we should just do what we came for and get out," Kalei giggles nervously.

Willow heads towards one of the stalls, nervously eyeing the animated pictures on the walls. She opens the door to a stall, but it creaks loudly, revealing a toilet with a shimmering, almost magical glow. A feminine funny face appears, it begins to talk.

"Welcome! Sit down and relax, take a load off. I've been expecting you," says the toilet.

Willow freezes, with a perplexed look on her face, unsure of how to respond. The toilet continues, "Don't worry, I'm the throne of comfort! All your troubles will be flushed away."

Startled by the talking toilet, Willow jumps back out of the stall. Looking at her friends she says, "Did that toilet just talk?"

Trinity laughs. "Yeah, this place is lit! A talking toilet, with a dash of animated mirrors, looking for gossip."

"Willow, just use it already," Kalei tries not to laugh.

Willow hesitantly sits down. The toilet hums a gentle tune, making the situation even more awkward. Meanwhile, Kalei and Trinity explore the rest of the room, noticing more mirrors lining the rear wall. Each mirror reflects not just their own images but scenes from different times and places within the castle.

One mirror catches their attention, showing an old man with a long beard, sunken cheeks, and a bony stature, looking straight at them.

"Ah, new visitors! Welcome to the **baño-de-chicas**. Need any directions?" says the old man in the mirror.

Trinity, looking appalled, with her hands on her hips, asks, "Directions? From a mirror? Come on, is this a joke?"

The old man in the mirror chuckles "No, dear. No joke! I know this castle inside and out, and by the way, you have a little green something on your face."

Trinity quickly checks her face. "There's nothing there, you foolish old man."

"Gotcha!" The old man chuckles again.

The girls burst into laughter, the tension easing as they realize the enchanted mirrors might not be so scary after all. Willow finishes up and flushes, causing the toilet to cheer. "Hooray! You have gifted me! May your troubles swirl away like yesterday's leftovers. Thank you, friend. Thank you for your input! Have a magically flush-tastic day!" the toilet exclaims.

Willow laughs, "Alright, you too. Don't let the poo get to you."

"I love doo-doo droppings, no worries here, I am always full of it" replies the toilet.

She walks out of the stall laughing. "Let's finish up and continue exploring. There's got to be more to this place than a talking bathroom."

They continue down the hall and come across some funhouse mirrors.

"Look at this one guys. I have a shrunken head," says Kalei.

"Look, I am a tall giant," Willow responds, making fun wavy moves.

Trinity yells, I think I just saw something. Quick, come over here! Did you see that lady in this mirror?"

Kalei looks at Trinity in the mirror. "I don't see anything, just your funny face."

Willow pops out from the side of Kalei. "Yeah, it looks like you have huge eyes, a tiny nose, and an enormous mouth. Make a funny face."

Just as Trinity sticks out her tongue, making a hilarious funny face, the lady appears again. She wears all black, has long black hair that hangs mid-waist, and long, bony fingers extending from the sleeves of her cloak, tipped with sharp, claw-like nails. Her broken black teeth show when she speaks.

"Hello, my name is Abigail. Tell me a joke, I love to laugh," she says.

Trinity says, "You look frightful, and anyway, I am not very funny. I am quite nerdy. I know a lot about everything."

"Yeah, she is a Miss Know-It-All," adds Willow.

Abigail repeats, "Tell me a joke. I love to laugh."

"I don't know any jokes right now," replies Trinity.

"Ok then, have you seen the frightened group of girls in the castle?" Abigail asks.

"No, we just got here," Willow replies.

"That's alright. I want to tell you a joke," Abigail says.

"Okay, I am all ears," Trinity says.

"Come closer. I want to get a good look at you," the scary lady in the mirror says.

Trinity leans in a little closer. "I want to see you up close," Abigail says in a creepy, soft voice. "A little closer." Trinity is almost touching her nose to the mirror.

"Okay, so you are so smart. What do you call a wise penny?" Abigail asks.

The other two girls stand behind Trinity, waiting for the punchline.

"I am smart, but I don't know," Trinity responds.

"It's called Pennywise," Abigail says.

Trinity looks at Willow through the mirror. "That's makes no sense, it's not even funny."

"But this is," Abigail responds and disappears in the mirror.

Pennywise the clown leaps out of the mirror, suspended in midair inches from the girls face, and says slowly, "WE ALL FLOAT DOWN HERE!" He gives off a creepy laugh. "Bawhhaa hahaha!"

Trinity falls back into her friends. They all scream in terror, tumbling to the floor.

Abigail reappears and laughs. "Now that was funny. I see a frightened group of girls in this castle, don't you? Ha ha ha."

Willow brushes herself off as she gets up. "That was not funny at all. You tricked us."

Trinity says, "You are an awful mirror with bad jokes."

"Well, Trinity, Miss Know-It-All, you didn't know any jokes. So, I got a good laugh, and you asked for it, next time come to the loo, bearing a joke. Now move on," Abigail says.

The girls' glance at one another, and Kalei says, "Let's get out of here before something more frightful happens."

They skedaddle out of the loo, running as fast as they can. They run down the hall and reach an ornately carved door with a sign that reads "Room of Whimsies." Trinity, still catching her breath, glances at her friends. "Should we go in?"

Willow, a hint of excitement returning to her voice, nods. "Absolutely! This place has been full of surprises; nothing can be as scary as that Pennywise clown. Let's see what this room has in store for us."

Kalei, regaining her composure, pushes open the door. They are greeted by a room filled with floating furniture, levitating teacups, and playful shadows dancing on the walls. The girls step inside, their earlier fright forgotten in the face of this magical wonderland.

As they walk further into the room, a soft giggle echoes around them. "Who's there?" Trinity calls out, trying to pinpoint the source of the laughter.

A small, mischievous fairy, no taller than a teacup, flutters into view. Her wings shimmer with iridescent colors, and her eyes twinkle with mischief.

"Welcome to the Room of Whimsies! I'm Pippa, the guardian of this delightful chaos. Would you care for a spot of tea?"

Willow grins. "Sure, as long as it doesn't come alive and start talking to us too!"

Pippa waves her tiny wand, and a teapot gracefully pours itself into three floating teacups. "These won't talk, but they do enjoy a good spin!"

DC Daniel

She flicks her wand again, and the teacups begin to gently rotate in the air.

The girls laugh, sipping their tea and marveling at the room's enchantment. Suddenly, the shadows on the walls start to take shape, forming into a troupe of shadow puppets performing an impromptu play. The characters – a brave knight, a cunning fox, and a clumsy dragon – act out a humorous tale of a quest gone hilariously wrong.

Kalei, giggling uncontrollably, nudges Willow. "This is amazing! We should have brought popcorn."

Trinity, finally relaxing, looks around the room. "I love this place. It's like living in a fairy tale."

DC Daniel

Chapter Fifteen
The Malevolent Troll

Alarms of deafening sounds and glowing red emergency lights are seen rolling.

"Buzz… buzz…buzz..."

Willow with Aurora, Kalei with Rockey. Purple robes undone, rolling in the wind as they run. With their Wands out, ready to banish any threat. While running through the corridors to a safe place. The two Nuffer'do's, these young teenagers, stand in the hall, dumbfounded.

Willow yells out at the boys. "Get your familiars, head to the great hall, and find Harmoney or Patience, one of the fairy guardians. This is real, this is not a drill…. hurry…."

The boys run back into their room and slam the door in her face. Willow stands there for a moment as other kids whiz by. Kalei nabs Willow by the scruff of her robe as she pulls her down the hall.

"Come on, Willow... We must go... NOW! Forget about the Nuffer'do's; they will be engulfed by their own demise. We have to get to safety."

They make it to the great hall and meet with Harmony, their guardian fairy. The girls sit with their backs facing the castle walls. Students are in front of them, and the angelic 8-foot-tall windows are behind them. The colored ancient panes illuminate purple, yellow, and red hues throughout the great hall.

All students make a circle facing the great hall doors, with wands in hand. Harmony and Patience, the guardian fairies, come fluttering by everyone saying.

"Be quiet and be still."

"There's nothing to be alarmed about."

"Professor Or'dinger and the headmaster, will be here soon."

"Be on alert, be quiet, and be still."

Just then, a rumble can be felt from the floor. The towering windows start to pulsate with vibrations, like something large outside is stomping, making the ground move. The students and Willow exchange worried glances as they hold their wands tightly, ready for anything coming their way.

Suddenly, the great hall doors burst open, and Professor Vanderbuilt, the school's headmaster, rushes in. Professor Or'dinger and two Aurors follow.

Professor Or'dinger commands.

"Everyone, please remain calm!"

"There has been an incident. The protection barrier has been breached. A troll has made its way onto school grounds."

Gasps of fear echo through the room as the students realize the gravity of the situation. Trolls are known for their enormous size and strength and are extremely dangerous.

"We must work together to subdue the troll." Professor Or'dinger continues. "Each of you will be paired with a partner, and together, you will use your wands to cast a spell that will immobilize the troll. Remember, teamwork is key."

The two Nuffer'do Boys run into the room and slam the large doors behind them, yelling.

"The giant is coming… The giant is coming."

The professor quickly reinstructs the two boys to join the fight if the giant is to breach this room. Nun then screams out, "I don't want to die."

Asim clutches and shakes him violently like a rag doll, scolding him. "Stop it. We are not going to die. Get ahold of yourself, you big baby."

The students quickly pair up, and Willow finds herself with Kalei as her partner. They stand back-to-back, dueling in a circle, their wands ready.

The troll's footsteps grow louder and more frantic, and the room shakes with each one. Suddenly, the troll bursts into the room, flinging the ginormous castle doors off the hinges.

It is enormous, with green, slimy skin and sharp, jagged teeth. Its eyes glow with fierce, fiery wickedness, and it swings its club-like arms wildly, smashing the candle torches off the wall and the paintings to bits.

"I smell something tasty…. I smell little humans… I am Hungry…."

With one scoop and little effort, itt scoops Tanner up as Tanner is curled up in the corner, crying. Willow and Kalei shout in unison, and their wands glow bright red.

"Danza Pacato!"

The Spell hits the troll square in the chest, and it stumbles backward, dazed. It begins to dance, dropping Tanner the by its side. Willow and Kalei are still making the creature dance in place.

Isabella comes running up and shouts to the girls, repeat after me! **"Ru`Danza Pacato,"**

They repeat it; this starts to subdue the dancing giant. The other students and professors join in, casting the same Spell. **"Ru`Danza Pacato."**

All Wixan's from left to right shout and point their wands and reenact the same incantation. The troll fights back with all its might, but the combined efforts of the students and faculty are too much for it. As its legs turn into jelly, finally, with a deafening roar, the troll falls to the ground, thrashing on the ground and moaning.

Trinity commands a spell. **"Ivy corperalis."**

The Ivy grows from the far reach of the room's corners. It twirls up, wrapping itself into a large, unbreakable rope. As it whips back and forth, it quickly slides down the wall, entangling the giant's lying arms and legs in Ivy until the troll is completely immobilized.

The room erupts in cheers and applause as the student's high-five each other, grateful for their victory. Willow, Kalei, and Trinity come together for a group hug. The Wixan' Teers are laughing with relief.

As the commotion dies down, Professor Or'dinger steps forward. "Well done, everyone,"

He says, his eyes shining with pride. "You have shown incredible bravery and teamwork in the face of danger.

DE Daniel

Remember this day, for it is a testament to the strength and resilience of our Wixan community."

The students file out of the great hall, chatting excitedly about the adventure they have just had. Willow and Trinity walk with Kalei and their familiars, feeling accomplished with pride.

"Who knew we were capable of something like that?" Kalei says with a grin.

Willow smiles back. "I guess we never know what we're capable of until we're put to the test."

Isabella is walking in front of the trio. She overhears the three of them talking about the day's events. Isabella can't help but stop and spin around with her familiar Ozzy the Owlet on her shoulders, doing almost a three-sixty with its head. As Isabella starts to speak, Ozzy interrupts.

"Who!... Who…. Who!.."

 The trio freezes in the middle of the hall.

Isabella speaks out.

"Hush Ozzy. Those Nuffer'do students better get to studying, my dad once said. Beware of the Nufferdo's kids. Be nice, but don't befriend them for power. They are not as powerful as us. They are said to only have one magic parent; the other was a plain-jane human. Their power will never be as strong as ours."

"My dad also said my Great Grande Zia came from Salem Village in Massachusetts. So, our blood is blue and true." Anyways…. Did you know!"

"Your spell made the Giant dance; you forgot the Ru' in the Spell. You were trying to Subdue him, right?"

"It goes like this…**Ru… Danza Peab'cato**, flick and point."

Kalei speaks up. "Isabella, I have heard gossip about you, now I know it's true. You always pick on others, thinking you're better than them. Why do you have to be a know-it-all, like a snooty patootie. And for your information, Miss Know it all, I am a full-blooded Enchanter too. Both of my parents met at the Polynesian Magic Lore in the 1970s. That was before Poseidon, the sea queen, took the island out with a tsunami she created. Her rath on the island flattened it and then sunk it into the ocean by 50%.

Then, of course, you know WillowBrook was created to take the strain off the Order. To house and teach strong Mana to the young Wixan minds."

With a snarky tone, Willow asks. " Well, Miss know everything, then whom was it built by? The **OEM**? Headmaster Vanderbuilt? Who and Why? Why not just rebuild the Polynesian Lore?"

OEM (The *Order* of the 12 *Elements* of *Ministry*)"

"Well Willow, I guess you and your friends never read the handbook, on the first day? So, it's like this, Sir Charles Brook of England, designed and built our school."

 Willow replies. "Well … uh…, not really. I figured it wasn't that important. I was here, and we were always safe, surrounded by professors. Now that I know theirs a story behind this school, I will get educated on the theology of our school, and more on Sir Charles Brook."

Kalei with an eyebrow raised, looking at Willow, "I will join you, I didn't read it much either, but I do remember one of the important rules. If you're caught going into Forest Hollows, you can be sent home if your soul survives from the DW's."

Willow looks at her perplexed, "What the heck is a DW?"

Kalei says lowering her voice, "We are not supposed to say their names…. so come closer."

Willow leans in as Kalei cups her hand over Willow's ear, looking at Isabella then Trinity and whispers. "DeathWeavers"

Trinity puts her hand on her hip and looks directly at Isabella with a little attitude. "Bella, since you are so smart, what's the deal with that forest? Talking Encyclopedia, why go to the library when you can recite everything, you're like a walking dictionary on wheels. I got a fire nick name for you, we will call you, WE OK."

Well Trinity, why do you have to get so spicy with me? And why would you call me WE OK?"

Well, you have a photographic memory, right?"

"Yes, it's a blessing and a curse."

Well, you can be known as WE OK when people are around you. Everyone will be ok, because of your wealth of knowledge. WE OK, stands for a Walking Encyclopedia Of Knowledge."

"Sheeesh, you guys, that sounds like an insult, you all can stop with the brow beating…. enough already."

Well on a more serious note, what about the Forbidden Forest Bella? Do tell…"

Isabella puts her hand on her hip and says, "If you must know, apparently, we can go everywhere on the island, but NOT there to the forbidden… Forest Hollows."

Then Isabella crosses her hands, feeling attacked. "My name is IS'abella, not Bella. Are you getting cheeky with me, Kalei?"

She removes her hand from her hip and, with a straight face, looks Isabella in the eye. "No, I am sorry for making fun of you. I guess I am not being a good Wixan."

Isabella puts her hand on Trinity's shoulder and says, "Apology received and accepted, but I gotta say WE OK, has a nice ring to it, and it's not a lie, I remember everything from how much to put in elixirs to 3rd year practices."

Kalei redirects the conversation. "I really want to know more about the Forbidden Forest and Sir Charles Brook. Since you're a renown photographic walking encyclopedia…"

Willow says, "Yeah inquiring minds wanna know."

"Well, my friends, I am not here to tell more, I have to get going.

I suggest you go to the Moving Library. It's in the fifth tower on level six or nine, depending on the day. You will be there, as you pass the mimicking knights of armor.

There, ask Professor Great Scotts for insightful reads of WillowBrook's Memoirs and the Forest Hollows and how it colligates to the Lore of Iris at Telamisis. The two of you may get some appreciation and the magic smarts to obtain your real witchery magic."

Willow interjects with. "Isabella, what are we? Wixan's, Witches, Wizards, Enchanters... What are we supposed to address ourselves as?"

"Well, Willow, our graduation certification says Congratulations for Graduating your 1st through 4th year as a Wixan at WillowBrook. Sign from the Order of the 12 Elements. Now as for my family, my **Sorella** *(sister)* calls herself a **Strega** *(witch)*. My brother identifies as a Wixan.

My papa has completed many accolades; he says he is a **procedura guidata** *(wizard)* So, it's really what you feel in your heart.

"Listen, you two. I must go now. My class is starting soon. Per my father's orders, I am learning and getting my certification in jousting. I will see you around."

Kalei, chuckling a little, "Sounds good, WE OK." She looks at Willow then Trinity. "Hey Trinity, Willow and I need to head over to see this Moving Library. Do you want to tag along?"

"No, I can't. I promised Professor Or'dinger I would help him clean the 6000-gallon aquatic tank for the school of one-eyed electrifying eels. Horus and Katana always give him problems. And anyway, he is teaching me to use the dive tanks. Well, Cheerio, you three."

With that, the four of them continue their separate ways, their heads held high, each in their own realm of thoughts about the endeavors ahead.

Chapter Sixteen
Whispers in the Tower

Willow's mind races as she thinks about Tower Five, the Forbidden Forest Hollows, the Moving Library, giants storming castles in search of children, and magical blood. As they walk, she turns to Kalei.

"Kalei, are we in danger here?" Willow asks, concern in her voice.

DE Daniel

Kalei shrugs, looking around. "I don't know, Willow. But it feels like something really strange is going on. We should talk to my mom as soon as we're done at the library. Our Potions and Brews class isn't until 3 p.m., so we've got some time."

Willow nods. "Yeah, good call. Your mom's been an Enchanter here forever. If anyone knows what's up, it's her. Maybe she'll even spill the magic beans."

"Exactly! But first, let's find Professor Great Scotts in the Moving Library," Kalei says, speeding up her pace.

They hurry through the halls toward Tower Five. As they reach the winding stairwell, Willow stops, looking up. "Whoa, check this out. I've heard each tower has 12 levels, but I can barely see past the second. It's just… darkness."

"Yeah, Tower Five is weird like that," Kalei replies, peering into the abyss. "They say you can't see past the second level because of the Transcending Mirrors Room."

"The Moving Library is supposed to be on level six, right?" Willow asks.

Kalei nods. "Yep. But it's always a game with these stairs. Let's go."

They start climbing, but halfway to the second level, Willow gasps as two more staircases appear in front of them. "Wait—where did those come from?" she exclaims.

"Who knows? This place is a maze," Kalei says, cautiously stepping onto the new stairs. "Watch out—some of the risers are missing. And there's that black abyss again."

"Look!" Willow points ahead. "The stairs aren't even going straight up anymore. It's like they're twisting all over the place. What with the Eye of Horus is an ancient Egyptian symbol?"

Kalei squints, nodding. "Yeah, it looks like it follows us as we move.

Holy Batman look! It's like the whole staircase has turned into some kind of rolling staircase."

"Sheww! I thought we would never find out way, Use your energy ball and shine light on the top of the staircase."

Finally, they reach the top of the stairwell, where Willow spots something to their left. "Check it out—the mimicking knights of armor are here," she says.

Kalei looks to their right, noticing a gold plate with the number "16" and an infinity symbol beside it.

"And that's new. Level 16 with an infinity sign? I thought this tower only had 12 levels."

"Let's just stick together, Kalei," Willow whispers. "This place is stranger than I imagined."

Chapter Seventeen
Mysteries of the Knight

Willow nudges Kalei, saying, "Hey Kalei… see those knights over there? I hear they're the mimicking knights. So, I say shenanigans, Kalei!"

"Really, Willow, this is neither the time nor the place," Kalei replies, shaking her head.

"Oh, come on, Lei Lei, it'll be fun! Just follow my lead."

Willow starts doing the Egyptian King Tut dance, singing "Walk Like an Egyptian" by the Bangles.

Kalei can't help but laugh, joining in as they raise their hands beside their heads, swaying them left to right like ancient Egyptian kings.

Suddenly, the knights of armor begin mimicking their moves.

Clatter, clang, bing—the knights clink and clank in unison, perfectly synced to the dance.

"Hey, Willow, let's see if they can do the Macarena!" Kalei suggests.

They jump right into the dance, swinging their hips and moving through the Macarena steps. Together, they chant, "Hey, Macarena, ay!" as they laugh and continue the dance.

The knights creakily step down from their platforms, echoing the rhythm.

Creak! Clank! Rattle! The sound of metal fills the room as they move and sway, awkwardly humming along. One knight even puts its hands on its hips, attempting to sway before making a grating, screeching noise and collapsing into a heap of disorganized armor on the floor.

Giggling, Willow and Kalei skedaddle down the hallway. They arrive at the moving library, its grand doors towering at 22 feet tall (6.7 meters), with each door measuring 8 feet wide (2.4 meters).

It's large enough for a giant to pass through comfortably.Professor Great Scotts can be heard grumbling in the distance as the girls enter the foyer.

"What in God's green earth is all this commotion?" he calls out, approaching the girls.

Kalei's eyes widen as she points, whispering, "Willow, is that the professor coming our way?"

Willow squints, then gasps, "Yeah… but what's he wearing? Is that a Scottish kilt?"

Kalei nods slowly, her face going pale. "Yes, that's him. But… look closer. Do you notice anything strange about him?"

Willow's eyes widen in shock as she covers her mouth. "Oh my gosh, Kalei! He's missing half of his body!"

Kalei's voice trembles, "I know, right? It's like he's floating—almost ghostly, like he's from the afterlife."

Willow takes a cautious step back, eyes fixed on the man. "And his face… with that handlebar mustache and that two-toned beard. He's just… floating over to us."

Kalei shivers. "Yeah, it's like he's some kind of spirit. This is really eerie."

Willow glances nervously at Kalei. "Do you think he's good… or evil?"

Before she can finish, the professor is right in front of them, repeating, "What in God's green earth is all this commotion?"

Willow swallows hard, her voice barely above a whisper. "Our apologies, sir. We were just having a bit of fun."

He raises an eyebrow. "This is no place for jokes. Were you two rat-tapping with the Mimicking Knights of Armor?"

Kalei tries to keep her composure as she explains, "Yes, sir. We heard they mimic whatever people do around them."

The professor's expression remains stern. "Well, clearly you're first-year students. Let's avoid any more rat-tapping with them next time, shall we?"

Changing his tone to a helpful one. "Know that, this is out of the out of the way. Let me introduce myself, young Wixan's, I am Professor Great Scotts. Welcome to the Moving Library, where you'll never find a book in the same place. Do you young ladies know what you're looking for… or do you need time to rummage and read?"

"Well, we were told you had a book of the exploratory reads of The Forbidden Forest Hollows?"

"Yes, of course ladies, knowledge is power. Now go with Libby, the librarian troll. She will take you to your moving corridors and help you find your knowledge."

Chapter Eighteen
Unlocking the Pages of Power

Libby leads the way, wearing a green sun dress covered in beautiful yellow sunflowers; this troll is extremely easy on the eyes. She wears a flowing sunflower skirt, her hair is in big pink puff tails, and freckles lightly cover her face, with a mole at the corner of her left eye in the shape of a heart.

Libby's big glasses, with her noticeably big shimmery blue eyes. Her skin is light, with rosy cheeks, and not green like most trolls on the school grounds.

]Libby takes them through the intricate corridors that lead to row 71, finding and presenting the Forbidden Forest Hollows book.

"Ahhh ha, here you go, Forbidden Forest Hollows; she sits it on the table. Is there anything else I can help you find? If not ladies, then happy reading."

"Thank you, Libby, for helping us. I think that will be all for now," Willow says.

Libby looks back and gives them a wink. "Have a great time." She leaves the corridor. The girls turn back to the book, and there is a Papa owl and his owlet sitting on the book.

"Ladies, knowledge is power; don't let the bewitched babble get the best of you.

who!   who!

          who!   who!"

The girls open the book Written by Headmaster Professor Vanderbuilt.

Chapter one reads.

The Forbidden Forest Hollow is prohibited to all students and staff. This is a summary of what is in the Hollows, we hope this is enough to keep your imagination at bay.

As you step into the forest, a creepy atmosphere thickens the air. The towering trees with twisted roots give off a spooky vibe, like they're reaching out to grab you. This forest has been haunted by witches and dark magic folk for centuries, and their presence lingers in every corner.

You'll notice strange symbols carved into the trees and small altars tucked among the roots. The rumor is that witches and wizards come here to perform their dark magic and ask assistance from evil spirits. At IRIS with Hades' guardians at the underworld on Telamisis.

It's not just the witches and warlocks who make this forest so dangerous—other forces are at work here, too. Strange lights can be seen dancing amongst the trees at night. It should also be noted that if you listen carefully, you can hear the distant cries of the forest spirits.

As you venture deeper into the woods, the trees grow closer together, creating a thick canopy that blocks out much of the sunlight. It's easy to get lost here, with the winding paths twisting and turning in all directions. And if you're not careful, you may stumble upon some of the forest's darker secrets—

—like the hidden groves where the dark ones perform their most potent spells or the ancient burial grounds where the spirits of the dead still linger.

Despite the danger, kids are often lured to this forest. It's a place where the veil between the dark arts and reality worlds grows thin and where anything seems possible.

It should never be entered, that's why it's called the FORBIDDEN Forest Hollows. Be warned for those who are not careful, for they may find themselves caught in the web of the witches' spell or be put under a spell by the Nightshade Beast.

The Forbidden Hollows are known to be a place of great danger, feared by all who know it. It is said to be home to the castaway PMB's that went to dark magic as well as the hell-bent Spector beings, who were once human but are now cursed to roam the woods as ghosts.

This forest is also known for the DeathWeavers; some are demonic evil spirits enslaved to Hades. Hades uses them as protectors in his lair. These DeathWeavers are said to be malevolent and dangerous, haunting the forest and attacking anyone who dares to venture too close to the headquarters on IRIS.

The trees at the forest edge seem to reach out and grab at any unwary traveler who passes by as if warning them to keep out. 

The GrimSpire is one of many dangers in the Forbidden Hollow. Too many Firestorm Sprites And we will leave it with its name, nothing more to be said.

There are also rumors of other malevolent creatures, such as the Ferris' arachnid, who are said to be the cross between a wolf and a giant spider. It is monstrous and immense, standing taller than a man at full height.

They roam the woods seeking revenge. Ferris' arachnids are said to set elaborate traps and lure unsuspecting beings into their lair, where they become entangled in its massive webs, leading to a grim fate.

Then there are the nasty, mean trolls called SnickerQuibbles.

Don't let their name fool you; they are not to be reckoned with; they're cunning and robust, capable of overpowering even the strongest adventurers.

The most inconspicuous threat in the Forest Hollows is the sleeping mushroom plumes. These mushrooms emit a potent sleep-inducing gas, knocking out anyone who breathes it in. Once asleep, the victim is at the mercy of the Ferris' arachnids and other forest creatures. All in all, the forbidden Forest Hollow is a place to be avoided at all costs, for those who venture within its depths may never return.

As they turn the page to chapter two. The words disappear with a quarter-size silvery blob, moving across the parchment paper.

A light beam appears, and a holographic image beams up far above the book. The holographic image of an English dapper-looking man in a castle, he begins to speak.

Hello, I am Sir Charles Brook of England. This is the third chapter in the WillowBrook Memoirs."

The image turns to him at the ribbon-cutting grand opening of WillowBrook. Sir Charles and his two-headed dog disappear's into video footage. He then walks to a podium and takes the microphone.

"Thank you all for coming, and a special thank you goes out to the OEM for your support.

DE Daniel

I, Sir Charles Brook of England, dedicate this school WillowBrook to a higher learning for all students. And it is dually noted it was also for my lost daughter so she may one day come here to study and expand her horizons in good Mana and the universal Wixan beliefs.

Our Mission Statement.

"WillowBrook is here to enlighten and teach students to grow into their best self-awareness, helping them believe in themselves. Inspiring them through strong Mana, to become their best selves and be self-aware of who and what surrounds them.

We remember our sister school, the Polynesian Magic Lore, which was lost to us. Our wizards and enchanters remained steadfast on the island, June 10th, 2007, despite Poseidon's wrath. Though the loss of the magical island saddened us deeply, we've now built this new one in its memory.

The only place we could find to create the school was the island of Solaris. To get a portion of the land, we made a treaty agreement that the dark ones may inhabit ONLY the Forbidden Forest Hollows, and we get the rest of the island. We don't bother them; they agree not to bother us. Once we signed the agreement, we proceeded to build WillowBrook.

Young Wixan's, we provide this information, for all students who may take heed of our warnings: PLEASE…. PLEASE …. for your safety, stay out of Forest Hollows. Most importantly, follow your rule handbook. Please honor our request for your safety.

From this illusion of Sir Brook's speech, it appears to become pixelated, now growing more extensive. A giant, mean-looking purple-horned dragon appears, almost reaching the ceiling, red eyes beaming at them. Breathing fire across the top of the air. Then, a loud voice comes from the book in a deep, growling scream.

Chapter Nineteen
A Warning from the Fire & Shadows

"STAY OUT OF THE FOREST HOLLOWS!!!"

Then, the holographic Dragon vanishes back into the silvery-moving blob on the page.

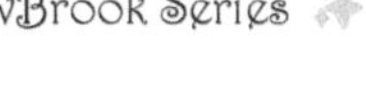

The girls quickly slam the book shut, terrified of the

fire-breathing Dragon, both looking at each other in terror.

Willow breaks the silence.

"Did that really just happen?"

"Yes, it did."

"Well, I have no need to go there."

"I will take heed to the warning. No place for us, right Willow…"

"Yes, Lei lei, I am never going in there; I don't want my soul sucked out by the Deathweavers."

"Me either."

The girls grab their wands and head to the main lobby. As they see books flying over their heads, in leather-bound ties—books with bat wings—Kalei immediately sees a book zoom past them that glistens. It has a Metatron cube embedded in it, glowing with all the rainbow colors. The book cover reads Cosmic Creations.

The duo heads out with their minds on turbocharge, as they head over to Professor Applegate's living quarters.

Kalei's mind races with thoughts, *would the creatures stay in the boundaries of the forest? What creatures lurk in the darkness and the unseen?*

They make their way to her cottage. Professor Applegate stands at her table with a map made of sheep parchment.

Chapter Twenty
Secrets in the Flickering Firelight

The flickering firelight cast long shadows across Professor Applegate's enigmatic cottage. The air was thick with the scent of rose oil and Pīkake flowers, creating a comforting yet mysterious atmosphere.

Before they could reach the door, Applegate waved her hand, and the door creaked open, admitting her visitors.

Kalei entered first, her serious demeanor contrasting with the warmth of the cottage, followed by Willow, whose worried expression betrayed her thoughts.

"What seems to be troubling you, keiki (children)?" Applegate inquired, concern etching her features.

"Well, Makua (parent), it seems we have evil living on the Island," Kalei replied, her voice steady but her eyes betraying unease.

"Yeah, Professor. Are we in any danger from Forest Hollows?" Willow added, glancing nervously at the darkened corners of the room.

"My dear keiki, you have nothing to worry about. Just follow the rules and stay out of trouble. Nothing bad can happen if you keep your distance," she reassured them, a gentle smile gracing her lips.

"Yeah, makuahine. I guess they have that treaty. If we stay to ourselves, then they are supposed to stay in the forest," Kalei replied, trying to ease her own worries.

"Professor, I think we just let our minds run wild with 'what ifs.' I should've known better; we have all of you protecting us, kiddo," Willow said, her voice a little brighter.

"Well, I wouldn't go as far as to say you're completely safe. Hades' goons and the Greek gods have been known to wreak havoc on the Twelve Elements and the schools in the past. So, anything is possible. Always practice your dogma, wear your special protection amulets, and the best advice is to keep your wand ready. It's just not likely to happen here on school grounds. Unless, of course, that shell-bent Aynat decides to throw one of her disruptive temper tantrums again," Applegate warned, her tone turning serious.

"Alright, Makua, we gotta get to our class. We just wanted to check with you to make sure there was nothing more to this Forest Hollows thing. Mahalo, Makua," Kalei said, pulling her into a loving hug.

Willow stepped forward for a hug too. "Mahalo, Professor Applegate. You squashed my worries. I'm sure nothing bad will happen to us," she said, her voice filled with gratitude.

As they approached the hall for their Potions and Brews class, they spotted Trinity waiting for them, and, behold, there were the Norwegian twins.

"Hey, Willow," said Björn, his cheerful demeanor lifting the mood.

"Hey there! Are you ready for Miss Crowley's class?" she asked, her spirits rising.

"Yes! We're going to work with portal trees!" he replies enthusiastically.

Trinity piped in, "No, that's second-year teachings. The professor said we would learn about deadly flowers, Dragon's breath, and levitation this week."

Kalei tugged on Willow's hand. "Come on, Willow, stop gabbing. We'll be late, and no one likes to be put on the spell spot."

With that, the group hurried down the corridor, the weight of their earlier worries lifting as they prepared for the magic that awaited them in class.

Chapter Twenty-One
Cyclops Snaps and Fairy Drama

The 5 of them enter the door and get seated, a few minutes later a group of Nuffer'do kids enter, acting a fool as always. Then, to no surprise, follows the Vanderbuilts' poshy girls with their familiars, the gossip fairies.

Professor Crowley walks around inspecting everyone for proper supplies. "Class, today's assignment will be Deadly Flowers, the Sleeping Trumpet Hearts."

"Now let us begin; add a sif of Dragon's breath to your quaffle'nick beakers. Class, be sure to carefully sprinkle it in, not dump it. Ah, now add, a wee bit of beet pulp and an ounce of sugar ants."

 "Now wave your wands over your quaffle'nick, with a downward flick, and speak."

"Victor Victor Bish Hisk."

DE Daniel

The professor's quaffle'nick beaker begins to grow a plant with the beautiful Sleeping Trumpet Hearts hanging from the branches.

She makes eye contact with Willow as she moves around the room. "Class take a look at Willow's. Now there is a fine specimen of the Sleeping Trumpet Hearts."

The professor glances away from Willow trying to figure out what and where that chomping sound is coming from, she gazes to the left of the room.

"Chop!"

"Chop!"

"Nun and Asim, what are you doing!"

The Nuffer'do twins are trying to figure out how to control a Cyclops Venus fly trap, snapping at the Victoria Vanderbuilts Fairy.

"Chomp! Chomp! Chomp!"

Professor pulls her wand and chants.

"Asultre petrified" Turning the shrewd creature to stone.

"Let that be a lesson, Mr. Nun, BE MORE CAREFUL NEXT TIME! SPRINKLE, DON'T DUMP OR POUR. We don't want more of the dark side illuminating itself in the lab."

Victoria was cuddling her fairy, giving the evil eye to the Nuffer'do twins.

"That is it for class today. Make sure to study this handout on the four major elements. There will be a quiz next week."

All the kids file out of class, but not before the other Vanderbuilt Girl, Olivia, gives her unwanted remarks to Nun and Asim.

"You're nothing. You're a half-breed; better watch it before I tell my dad. He can expel you for trying to eat my sister's Fairy." Says Olivia.

With the evil eye still on them, Victoria shakes her finger at them, "Sheesh! You're a numskull; you good for nothing, Nuffer'do."

"It wasn't my fault, I added what the professor said."

"No, you dumped it in, not carefully sprinkling it like Crowley said… you brainless amoeba."

"It figures you are half magical Nuffer'do's; you will never have the Midas touch."

Willow stands up before Nun, gives Olivia a disgusted look, and points her finger at Olivia.

"Where is your Mana, be nice, Olivia. It's not his fault that he only has one magic parent; he is doing his best."

"Well, that's not good enough. That Nuffro-nothing, almost had Victoria's fairy sent to the fairy motherland."

Victoria shakes her head with her finger out again, pointing at them. "Well, you too, you better watch it.

DC Daniel

I'll be watching both of you screw up one more time, and I'll tell my dad. Then, we will see how fast you fly off this campus. No brooms, in zilch status."

Olivia puts her hands on her hip. "Yeah, that's just what my sister said. Like times two, you ignoramus."

The group watched as the girls left, walking all high and mighty. Their gossip fairies stuck their tongues out towards the crowd, blowing raspberries.

Chapter Twenty~Two
Magic is in the Air

Zip!

Zoom!

Whoosh!

Tinkle tank!

Victoria's cheeky, tattling fairy flies by Trinity's head. It turns around and flutters in front of the trio's faces.

"Psst! Do you hear… Ding Dong the Witch is Dead… the witch is dead… YES she is! The ditzy 3rd year Sarah Sunders is nothing but Wixan dust now."

Trinity grabs Zara the Tink by the wings.

"What do you mean…? Is there another troll on campus? Did it eat poor Sarah?"

"No! Now let me go at once before I tell Vee." Zara says as she squirms and struggles to get free.

Trinity holds her by her wing, brings her closer to her face, and glares directly at her. "Then spill the beans, my troublesome Tink."

"Well, she was in Spell casting 103 and trying the Ignis Morpha spell. She mixes the gooseberry droppings with a few whiskers of a Black Panther…. And wham! Wouldn't you know she forgets the few tadpoles before the two whiskers? Ha ha ha! Now she is dust…vaporized into thin air."

Willow pipes in with a death stare at Zara. "I bet you are spreading rumors again, trying to stir up the school with lies. Trin, you might as well let her go. Karma will find her and teach her a lesson soon enough."

The Tink keeps on with her crazy talk.

"Bwahahahahaha! Dumb, good for nothing, Nuffer'do kids…. Just enough magic to get 'em vaporized…Ha Ha Ha!

Kalei says. "I know she is always trying to either get someone in trouble or tell fables about the Nuffer'do kids… like they don't have enough to worry about."

"Well, Kalei, the apple doesn't fall far from the tree…her owner, you know who! Victoria is an entitled, spoiled Wixan with the manners of a Barracuda, cruel and vicious."

"You know, I really wish I could silence those gossip fairies with a zipper mouth spell. But if I do, Professor Vanderbuilt will surely expel me from the school. He seems to believe those two troublemakers are faultless."

"Yeah, let's just say we do, but don't, I don't want to see my bestie leave." Willow pipes in, giving Zara a death stare

Zara blows raspberries at Willow and flies away.

Chapter Twenty-Three
Tumbling Through Trouble

All the students arrive in the courtyard, and the announcer comes on the air. "Good day! Fellow Wixan's! Today is a special day for all 1st Year Wixan's." Said curator GiGi NovaStar, guest speaker today, the transporter at the Mirror Transcendence Room.

"I am making announcements today. Unfortunately, Miss Echo~Flux your curator got caught in the Tezor Nets yesterday, she has been mildly burned."

The courtyard starts to buzz, the sound of a thousand crickets humming as the students begin chatting about the mishaps.

Gigi says. "Ok, everyone, settle down…Not to worry; our happy-go-lucky Echo-flux will be ok. Soon enough."

"She is recovering nicely in the infirmary. She looks more like a mummy wrapped in a gauge. Nevertheless, Nurse Fred has some SilverLuminX Sav from the Bleeding Hearts plants. The order sent this sav, via the PuddleHopper Express. She will be good as new here in a few shakes of a witch's broom."

The crowd gives a roar.

"3 cheers to Nurse Fred, long live EchoFlux!"

The professor goes on speaking. "Alright! Alright! Everyone calm down, more importantly; get straight on, and be straight with your wits. If the cleaning Norks have signs posted, no broom flying, don't horse around in the tournament courtyard."

"On a brighter note, we have a field trip for all first-year students today. Please have your overnight bag with your notion book, potion bag, and familiar ready by 3 p.m. on the east lawn, just past the pixie quarters."

The first-year Wixan students roar with excitement. They hear crazy stories from other kids about GiGi NovaStar and her field trip antics.

At 3 p.m., the trio is ready, mounted on their broomsticks. They zip through the courtyard, past the fairy quarters. Then, the crunching of trees and branches is heard as one of the Nuffer'do twins flies past Willow's side, upside down, holding on to his broom for dear life. Nun screams as he bumps into the ground and zooms by.

"AHHhhh! Helllppp!"

Bump!

Thump!

Crash!

He tumbles into the east field just ahead of the trio. Asim lands next to him. Kalei and Willow swiftly float over to Nun, making light of the situation.

"Darn broom, they have a mind of their own…. Do you need any help, Nun? That looks like your broom is being a little fruity for a fruity bat spell."

"Yes, it goes bananas, Thank you. What is your name?"

"My name is Kalei." Asim brushes his brother's brushes back off, from the leaves and branches.

Nun looks at Kalei with a severe but puzzled look. "How did you know my name?"

"All the other kids know who the Nuffer'do kids are, and I'm not being mean when I say that. You all can be seen from a distance. Because wherever you folks are, there are bound to be mishaps. And I remember you from the summer when we had the troll breach in the Great Hall." "Ahhh, yes, no one forgets me after what happened with Tanner. By that catastrophic event, I'm sure everyone knows who I am."

"You know Kalei, we all try so hard, but for some reason, it's a 50/50 crap shoot, if our magic is going to work…. LOL."

"Haha, I see; not to worry. With much practice, you will gain more sound Mana and confidence."

"Yeah, thanks for the boost of assurance; I hate it when the kids make fun of us."

"It's all good, my new friend. Be Good ~ Be Kind. Karma always gets her revenge."

"Yes indeed! it does."

Nun (earth sign with no secondary sign) and Asim (Water sign with no secondary powers) are from the Nubian culture of Egypt. Nun is a reddish-orange-skinned teen, and Asim Nun's brother is as dark as Midnight; despite the remarkable difference in pigmentation, they are identical twins. They have notable facial and physical features, and they are similar. The two young men display dark hair and eyes.

These fellas give a gentle smile to Kalei for her kindness.

Gigi NovaStar speaks into a giant megaphone. "All Wixan Students, please get in the retrospective Element line: Earth, Air, Fire, and Water."

"Harmony and Patience will be handing out programs. Please take a booklet and pass the rest down the line. We will be on an overnight adventure to the Transcending Forest on the island's east side."

As the group descends into the forest, the whispering leaves are magical. They are not just green leaves from the trees; magically, the forest possesses a wide array of hypnotic colors not seen anywhere else. They rustle and whisper secrets to each other, carrying messages through the breeze. As they venture deeper, they come across the Song of the Spheres.

Willow hears the melody she heard before; she looks strangely at Kalei and Trinity. GiGi NovaStar directs the class and explains.

"During special celestial alignments, on a full moon, the forest comes alive with a harmonious symphony called the "Song of the Spheres."

It is said that this celestial music can soothe the soul and grant those who hear it moments of profound, uplifting enlightenment."

DC Daniel

Chapter Twenty-Four
Mystic Charms & Wizard Makeovers

They find their campsite, and supplies are retrieved after the camp is set up. Willow, Kalei, and Trinity then begin working on Wizard makeovers.

"Shamlone Pixie Pink" As Willow aims her wand at Trinity. "My eyes feel extremely tight. What happened?"

Kalei and Willow Bust out, "Ha Ha Ha Ha."

In a jokingly Chinese direct tone, Kalei "Ah ha, you look so pretty, like a doll. glinted eyes, rosy cheeks. Yes, yes soo Beautiful."

Trinity takes a bow. "Well, thank you, ladies, you are too kind."

Willow screeches out. "My Turn... My turn... I'm going to do the Country Bumpkin to you, Kalei."

"Take your best shot, Willow (Glamerfy me)."

Willow holds her wand out, points, and aims.

"**Mother serv Van No**," Willow says with a giggle.

"Kalei, grab your partner and dosey doe. You look pretty, with a nice cowgirl hat, hair in pigtail braids, and of course, let's not forget your flannel shirt, jeans and cowgirl boots."

Willow grabs Kalei's shoulder. "Now you cast me." Humm, what can I do? That's funny… Humm.

"A moonwalker…Nah."

"Elvira…the goth witch."

"No, something cute or sweet." requests Willow.

"OK…. Yaris Morfee'is" Willow morphs into a green Ivy Goddess turning her blonde hair to brown curly hair. She has defined high glitter eye makeup, bright cheekbones, and cute pointed elf ears. Live ivy continually moves over her hands and upper torso.

The shimmery green flowing dress sparkles from the moon. Her radiant curly black hair, and iridescent wings flutter as she spins around like a little Cinderella at the ball.

They enjoy the evening and cast spells on objects and themselves.

Willow points across the way. "Hey guys, look over there. The Norwegian boys Björn and Kacper are doing their own thing. Let's go over and watch what Kind of Wizard Shenanigans they are up to."

"Hurry, you two. It looks like they are causing the volcanic stones to become liquid metal, shape-shifting into those crazy things." Trinity runs ahead, yelling.

"The last one gets the stinky broom potion."

"Now, brother, let's get to some real magic; we have an audience."

Kacper looks at the girls and speaks. "Our Mystic Charms will beat your Wizard Makeovers any day.

"My brother, I got the best one for you. It's an 11 out of 10."

"As long as you don't use that Kipper Spell again, I don't want to be a drunken sailor that got a case of the green around the gills. I was sick for 3 days. So be nice this time."

Kacper casts his Spell. "Draco`fly Corneilous."

Trinity laughs with a face of shock. "Hey, look, Willow, Björn, a Mini-Serpent Dragonfly. Straight out of the spell books."

This majestic creature, with a tiny body like a serpent and wings like a dragonfly, comes to life. He gracefully glides through the air, performing aerial acrobat stunts and leaving behind a trail of shimmering dust.

"Well, Kacper, you have nothing on my Mystic Charms. Look at this!"

"**Pano Lumin Wisps.**" A Luminous Panther appears. It is a sleek, cart-like creature covered in bioluminescent markings. It's the size of a toy dog, capable of stealthily prowling through the darkness unnoticed.

"OK… OK… You win, Björn, ding ding ding…. Winner Winner Chicken Dinner."

"Thanks, guys, as he gracefully glides past the group, crop dusting them in the shimmery dust..."

Chapter Twenty-Five
Campfire Magic

After dinner, the Wixan'teers settle in a circle around the crackling Campfire. A few luminescent butterflies flutter across their faces. One lands on the tip of Willow's nose; she goes cross-eyed, trying to look at it. The glowing dust falls on her face as it flutters away, making Willow seem like she has glowing freckles.

"You know, Willow, you are lucky."

"Why Trin?" "Well, I read in the book of Magical Creatures of the Forest. These unique species of butterflies are known as Dreamweaver's. Their vibrant wings carry the ability to influence dreams, granting those they touch with insightful visions and vivid experiences. Who knows what kind of dreams you will have tonight."

"I wish I could dream of my parents and their appearance."

"Do you really wish that, Willow?"

"Most certainly, Trinity, I wish I knew where I came from and why my parents left me. I often wish I never had to experience the trauma that I go through in the group homes."

Kalei speaks up. "It is said that sometimes the hurt makes us stronger."

"Well, you should be tough as nails and strong as an OX." Trinity interjects to change the subject.

"Well, that's a real Debbie Downer thought. I prefer to think about mystical creatures and growing into a strong Wixan… so let's get to our dreams."

The kids spend the rest of the night roasting hotdogs, sausages, smores, and those unique Pixie Pies. The Pixie Pie consists of fluffy red sweet Bavarian cream and fruit tucked in Niffledeck flower petals, which become flakey and crispy when cooked in the pie irons.

Everyone is having fun when Willow is suddenly overcome by a strange feeling. The music that had played on her balcony starts again.

All the students' familiars are getting rowdy. Bats, crows, and owls flying around, cats crying, and frogs croaking… just pure madness. In the darkness appear two golden piercing eyes of light; it is getting closer.

Then, a green-eyed lady appears with beautiful, vibrant red locks of hair that go to her knees. She wears a witch's hat that has a Cedrick symbol dead center of the hat. Professor Gigi greets her. "Hello, Professor Cornelius. How is the Ireland Ministry doing? What brings you out to our school?"

"I come to see if we could speak in private; it's top business of the order."

"Of course, step into my tent."

When they enter the tent, all the kids quiet down to see if they can eavesdrop on the conversation.

The trio creeps closer to the back of the tent to see if they can hear the words being exchanged.

"A Grandmaster from the Order of the 12 Elements tells me to bring you this for safekeeping. You know what will happen if the Aynat or Hades finds it. When you return, take it without haste, Professor Novastar; he'll know what to do with it."

"I understand this could be devastating to the ministry. I will protect it at all costs."

Now I must be going. A branch breaks under Trinity's feet as she leans in closer. Then Willow falls into the tent. Professor Gigi and Cornelius stop talking. They exit the tent as Professor NovaStar tucks the large book-like leather-bound package into her Cloak.

They step out and stare at everyone momentarily, looking around at the kids at the fire, trying to figure out what kid just fell into the tent.

"Cornelius, thank you for stopping by to check in with me, about my owl injury. I assure you all will be taken care of as soon as I return to school."

"Gigi, I'm sure you'll take great care of it, but I must be going now."

Gigi glances around the group of kids, wondering if anyone is acting peculiarly or behaving with guilt.

No one budges, but out of nowhere, Lampfry stands up. "I know who was snooping around the tent."

As Lampfry starts point out the culprit, Johnny takes a rock and bashes it against his toes. "Ouch."

He then retracts his statement, saying. "JK professor, I was just kidding, I didn't see anything."

"Did anyone see or hear anything?" The Professor asks the group. No one speaks up while she is staring at the crowd.

"For all of you who are curious, Professor Cornelius came by to see if my Owl was doing well. News had spread that his wing was injured fighting with an albatross last week."

"Now it's late, everyone turn in for the night."

The group says in sync. "Yes, Professor Gigi."

They gather their trash and familiars and head to their tents for the night.

Chapter Twenty-Six
Blue-Footed, Booby Bird Dust

DC Daniel

The following day, all the students rise; they all gather for morning meditation. The eleven first-year Wixan's gather in a circle.

Camp Leader Gigi NovaStar guides the group through morning meditation. "Hey, everyone! Welcome to morning meditation. It's so important to spend a little time each day to center yourself with the Universe. This could be a quick breather between classes or meditating and stretching when you wake up early.

"Here at WillowBrook, we believe in the consistency of this practice, treating it like a daily routine. It keeps your mind and spirit in sync with nature, its a wonderful feeling! Let's make it a habit to stay connected to the world around us. Remember the 90/10 rule: Life is 10% what happens to you and 90% how you react."

"Ready class, let's take our Burmese pose."

"Next, clear your mind."

"Open your energy channel."

"Find your Gyan Mudra position; remember, thumb to the index finger."

"Now, Close your eyes."

"Release any self-doubt, resentment, anger, anxiety, and or sadness with people around you."

"Breathe in deeply."

"Ready, hold ten; mentally count with me. 10,9,8,7,6,5,4,3, 2 and…."

"One, release your breath slowly."

"Blowing out any Spector or negativity from your inner self."

"Making a SHEEEE or SHAWWW sound when you release."

"Again"

"Breathe in deeply…Hold ten; think with me. 10,9,8,7,6,5,4,3, 2 and… 1, exhale."

"Good job, class. Let's do it again,… Deep …. Deeeepp…breath…. Draw from your diaphragm."

"Hold………1,2,3." "Release slowly…."

"Let's practice the release mantra…."

"Let your soul gravitate to the love, self-acceptance, and receiving positive energy from the universal element leaders."

"Now direct your attention to the humm of the 111 MHz tune coming from the floating Bose Rombisk disk. The class starts in unison and hums together.

"Hummmm"

"Hummmmmm"

Raising their vibrations from their internal lights, releasing all negativity. Willow's nose and mouth start to tingle from her vibration within.

Within a few minutes, Willow feels like she is in a cloud, light as air.

Opening her eyes, she looks down and views herself sitting their meditating, having a outta body experience, viewing herself as she floats above her body. She scans the other areas and sees the other kids floating over their mats, too. Willow is no longer shocked by this; she continues to meditate, knowing (OBE's) (outta body experiences) are expected here.

The end of morning meditation ends with the teachers closing. "Alright, everyone, let's gently bring our focus back to the room. Take a deep breath in and slowly let it out. When you're ready, you can slowly wiggle your fingers and toes, and when you feel comfortable, gently open your eyes.

Take a moment to notice how you feel after our meditation practice."

"Remember, you can always return to this feeling of calm whenever you need it throughout your day. Everyone, great job today!"

Miss Gigi continues to instruct the class. "It is time to get on our adventure. Please gather everything from the campsite; we will not be returning to this site. Please pack everything and be green, leave no footprint behind."

Within minutes, the commotion simmers down, and everyone is ready and packed for today's adventure.

"Class, Let's remain together and refrain from picking up anything along the way. Appearances can be deceiving, so proceed with caution."

"It's a hike but well worth it. We will have a picnic lunch when we arrive."

As they set out on their long hike, on the left of the walking path, a gigantic 6 ft tall Venus's fly trap, large enough to eat a small child, is planted in the ground, snapping at the kids as they walk by.

"Snap,"

"Snap."

A little further down the trail, fruit Bats the size of seagulls zoom by the students' heads. These enormous bats are after an array of purple poppy flowers on the forest floor.

"Swoosh,"

"Whirl."

When they venture deeper into the forest, they approach a bridge guarded by a spiney Murk, lurking beneath it. He pops up on a strump and speaks.

"Cross my bridge, don't have a boat,

Give me some Trisket Zinkers to cross my moat,

Fear not the night, nor the gloom,

For with Trisket Zinkers, your path will bloom.

Through the shadows, you'll safely steer,

So, pay the Murk and have no fear."

Then he winks with a mischievous leer, as you cross my

bridge without a tear."

DC Daniel

The Professor hands this little thorny creature a few Triskets Zinker's and one shiny Rune Stone. It lets everyone cross, ahead in the distance, the path is blooming with light, leading the class to the open prairie for lunch.

After lunch, GiGi addresses the sleeping flowers in the forest. "Those charismatic seedlings are a great collection of your arsenal of tinctures."

"Class, I have a special gift to all of you. She hands out little glass vials sealed with red wax. These vial's glow with a bright bluish light. "My gift to you, the blue-footed, booby bird dust. This dust can give any dark environment an elaborate, luminous array of light. Just open it and stay these magic words '**Avata Nyt**'. A 100 yard light, when you aim the vile in that direction, it lasts for exactly 15 minutes, and it can only be used once, so use it wisely."

As the Professor continues to discuss other important forest information, the trio is getting a little unsettled… looking for some adventure.

Chapter Twenty-Seven
The Tale of Gullinbursti

"Hey, Willow, why don't we venture to the woods? It must be safe; otherwise, Professor GiGi wouldn't tell us about all the cool stuff. We are not in danger or near the Forest Hollows. So, what do you say?"

"I don't think it is right; we should listen to the Professor. Stay with your group, don't touch things… That means don't go into the forest." Trinity says.

DC Daniel

"You know, Trinity, Kalei is right. If we weren't supposed to be exploring, they would not have brought us on this adventure."

"Alright, you two, don't forget I am going to be the first one to say, I told you so, when we get sent to the headmaster's office," Trinity says as she scowls at Willow and Kalei.

"Don't be a worry wart, come on, we are the Wixan'teers…. Remember, "One for all and all for One."

Kalei leads the way, and as Willow and Trinity follow, they venture deeper into the woods.

Trinity proclaims, "I am going to be breaking twigs so we can find our way back."

"Alright, Trinity, that may be a good idea; just hurry up and come on." Says Kalei,

"Willow Exclaims. "Do you hear that?"

"Yes, it sounds like something is whimpering, just beyond that group of bushes." Kalei says.

As they get closer, a giant bore, it's hurt and in pain. This special bore, from Norse Mythology teachings, it has dull bristles on its main, nevermore shining of luminous gold. rather, it is a dull yellow color. The animal is panting and moaning heavily in discomfort.

"Guys, look, the black collar here, it has a blue barrel attached to it." Willow opens and inspects it closer, "I don't see any information about its owner."

As Trinity waves her hands to express urgency. "Come on Willow, open it already, see if there is anything in it."

Willow opens it, with a click and a tug." It's empty guys."

Gullinbursti, gives out a rumble of a moan, from the pain. Willow looks at the other Wixan'teers, with a face of deep concern. "What is wrong with it?"

 DC Daniel

Gullinbursti rolls to its side. Blood slowly rolls down its chest, dripping into a puddle on the ground.

"Look, Trinity, something tried to attack it." says Kalei.

Trinity sits down in the cris cross apple sauce position. She opens her hands and faces them towards the panting unconscious bore, then she closes her eyes and gets into a state of receiving telepathy. "I am trying to telepathically talk to it. It is trying to talk to me; he says his name is Gullinbursti. It's hard to determine what else it is saying. The bore says it lost too much blood. It needs a vile of Elixir of Life Water from the Vitality Brook by the school."

"He says, take the empty vile in the little blue barrel, and get the elixir."

Willow quickly grabs the vial, and hands it to Kalei. "Here attach this vial to your **'alalā's** carrying pouch; he can fly faster than us walking to the water." Kalei sends 'Rocky' her Crow to the Brook.

"Squawk! Squawk!" As the bird takes flight, soaring straight up above the forest canopy.

"Gullinbursti, who did this to you? Why did they want to hurt you? says Trinity loudly.

The creature is gasping when it talks, he explains speaking in quick bursts between catching air.

"Some are after my mana; they know of my ability to light darkness for warriors to make their way in battle. So those evil men are trying to cut my tusks and golden bristles and take my powerful light. For malicious and malice behavior, they want me dead."

"I may look grotesque and even a bit scary, but don't fret; I am here to help the good people. You see, I was created from this legend."

Loki, the trickster god, once lost a contest to the elves Brokkr and Eitri. It all started when Loki, always seeking to cause trouble, cut off the golden hair of Thor's wife, Sif.

To avoid Thor's wrath, Loki promised to get even better hair from the dwarves. Loki went to the skilled elf brothers Brokkr and Eitri and challenged them to create gifts more magnificent than those of other dwarves. Brokkr and Eitri accepted the challenge and crafted three amazing treasures, including Gullinbursti, a golden boar with bristles that glowed in the dark. Mjölnir, Thor's mighty hammer; and Draupnir, a golden ring that created eight new rings every nine nights.

In the end, the gods judged the elves' gifts to be better than Loki's, and Loki lost. As punishment for his trickery, Loki's mouth was sewn shut by Brokkr, a fitting end for a god who often relied on his clever words.

"Ok, but what does this folk tale have meaning to why you are injured?" inquires Willow.

I guess just to know my legacy. I don't think I will make it, from this injury. Now, my life is ending.

Please help me…. I feel very cold, I am losing my sight; everything is going black."

He becomes quiet, and his breathing is slowing. His once lightly discolored glowing armor is fading to gray.

"It's ok, Gullinbursti. Stay with us…. I am sure Rocky has the vitality water; he is returning soon; it won't be long now." says Kalei. In a final breath, he says. As he loses all his color, a twinkle in his eyes remains. "Thank you for trying to help, but it's too late for me."

"No, my friend, hold on. I hear Rockey. He is coming."

Rocky swoops in, his talons extended, as he drops the vile into Kalei's hand.

"Gullinbursti, what do we do now?" Gullinbursti is not answering. He is at the end of his time, too weak to speak.

"I know what to do; I read it in a book.

DE Daniel

If you are a true water sign, take this water, use your water spell, cup it to your hand, swirl your water cyclone, and make a 2ft wave. When you are ready to tumble it on the injured shoulder wound, then say this enchantment.

"AGUA GENT REJUVENATE"

As Kalei does exactly as Trinity instructed, the splash comes over Gullinbursti, vibrating over his fur, soaking into the laceration of his battle. Magically, his wound begins to heal.

A pulsating glow starts, it then becomes strong, radiating bright golden light, almost blinding the trio. Within 5 minutes, Gullinbursti rises to his feet and snorts, making the ground rumble for a moment.

"Hey everyone, thanks a bunch! And Rocky, thanks for showing up just in time to rescue me. I'm super grateful for your flying abilities. You guys didn't let my scary appearance scare you off with my wild boar look and big tusks.

You all came to my aid when I really needed it. I promise I'll have your backs, too. If you ever need me, just call my name Gullin three times. I'll charge in with my horns to tackle any bad guys, and my tusks can take them out super-fast."

"Plus, I'm lightning fast; I am a trans-dimensional creature, moving through space and time in the blink of an eye."

"Thank You, I think that is most admiral of you, Gullinbursti." Says Willow.

"Yes, thank you, Gullinbursti; you never know when a practitioner will need the help of an animal of the forest." Says Trinity.

Chimes in Kalei "I am glad my 'Alala' could help you in your time of need; we will keep you in our prayers, hoping that the Night Marchers don't try to hurt you anymore."

"Well, you better head back to the professor and your class before they notice you are missing." Says Gullin.

"Also, never go into the forest alone; the Night Marchers are always on the prowl. They are the mighty phantom army, the deadly ghosts of ancient Hawaiian warriors … proudly led by the spirit of King Kamehameha, to avenge the people that took over the Hawaiian Islands inhabited by the Indigenous Polynesian people." says Gullin.

"Let's get going before we get caught by GiGi." Trinity insisted.

Chapter Twenty-Eight
Plotter's Figgie's and Gull's

They all head back to the open meadow. Claudell, the tattletale, comes running up as they enter the opening. "Where were you? You know you aren't supposed to leave the group, I am telling the teacher."

"Please don't; I will give you some beetle bubblegum if you keep quiet," says Kalei.

"Ok, show me the candy."

"Here, Claudell, the box of bubblegum, like we promised you; now be quiet," Willow says as she pulls it from Kalei's backpack.

Claudell grabs the package, shoves three pieces in his mouth at once.

Trinity yells out! "You're only supposed to chew one at a time."

"Too late, Trinity, he is air born, now what do we do?" As Claudell tries to spit out the gum, he blows a bubble that keeps getting bigger. Taking him higher and higher up in the sky. It then pops and Claudell starts to fall, rapidly aiming his face to meet the ground.

Kalei asks, looking directly at Trinity and Willow as they watch this unfold. Kalei blurts out, "Spell Casting 101." As she draws her wand, she aims directly at Claudell.

"Benuo Higher Gavotusus" Kalei hones in on him and brings him safely to the ground. By now, the kids are all staring at the action unfolding. They let out a victorious celebratory noise to his wonderful landing. Professor Corbin stepped forward, a proud smile on his face as he looked at Kalei. She raised her hand, grinning, a bit shocked by all the attention.

"I am proud to introduce our next Plotter," he announced. "Kalei, take a bow for your quick thinking and amazing intuition in casting the spell that saved a fellow Wixan." He paused, letting his words sink in. "This wizard and enchantress event is held on the fall equinox, at the end of the first semester."

The room burst into cheers. Classmates hoisted Kalei onto their shoulders, shouting and celebrating.

"Yeah!"

"Woo-hoo!"

Once the commotion settled down, Kalei, Trinity, and Willow gathered in the corner to try to figure out what exactly had happened.

Willow looked at Kalei, his brow furrowed. "What's a Plotter, anyway? And what's this intuition casting thing?"

DC Daniel

Both of them turned to Trinity with expectant looks, like she was some walking encyclopedia.

Trinity put a hand on her hip, smirking. "What… am I supposed to know everything?"

Kalei shook her head, laughing. "Ummm, yeah."

Willow added, "You know everything since we got here, Trinity. So spill!"

Trinity rolled her eyes but finally gave in. "Okay, okay… So, the Intuition Casting Games are part of Wixan tradition here at WillowBrook and other magic schools. At the end of each semester, there's a big competition—the Wizard Mana Contest and the Intuition Casting Arts."

"Okay… go on," Willow said, his eyes wide.

"Yes, please go on," Kalei added, leaning in.

Trinity nodded. "Alright. In the Intuition Casting event, the scorekeeper sends out this purple, glowing ball called a 'figgie'—it's about the size of a tennis ball. The Arena Master places it in the center of the arena. Then, it creates a holographic display, showing one of the grandmasters from the 12 Element Ministry. That grandmaster chooses four players, one from each Element Team: Earth, Wind, Fire, and Water.

"After that," she continued, "the grandmaster picks two more secondary elements, which any player can use if they're skilled enough. Then, a mythical creature gets launched into the sky. The players have to use their intuition to find a way to outwit the creature's spell, either by canceling it or sometimes even sending it back to the dark side."

"Wow, that sounds exciting," Kalei said, her eyes sparkling.

Trinity raised an eyebrow, clearly amused. "Exciting? Sure. Until you get sent to the infirmary because a Durfee's Dragon swats you out of the sky or a Flossy Lucy Burn—a one-eyed creeper—singes your hair. Oh, and there's Huggins, a giant jaw-cupped plant, as wide as six students standing side by side, that spews fire at its enemies." She shrugged. "So, yeah… exciting."

Kalei's expression dropped. "Maybe not the kind of exciting I was thinking of…"

Willow cut in, laughing. "Well, it's a little late to back out now. You're the new Water Element Prodigy!"

Kalei sighed, but then her face softened with a determined smile. "Guess I'd better practice my craft."

Trinity crossed her arms, her voice snarky as she looked at them. "No time like the present, right? Some of us are just… well, more blessed than others, though." She gave a smug little smirk.

DC Daniel

"Daddy says, 'Nothing but the best for my Porggie Puddin' girl.' We blue bloods need to stick together, after all. We're the chosen ones. I hope someday you two get the power I have."

Kalei felt a sting of annoyance but kept her cool, smiling back. "The more we learn, the better we'll be able to use our skills when needed. Besides, maybe I'll make it to grandmaster one day," she said, trying to keep the mood positive.

After that, they grabbed their things for the trek back to the school. As they return, they fly along the coast, gliding over the pristine black-shelled sand beach, side by side like a small pack. Mounted on their brooms, they felt the warm breeze flowing through their hair, their spirits high for the challenges ahead.

The sound of the ocean rolling i. The smell of the sea permeates their senses, the mist of salt that settles on the group's skin.

Trinity alerts the other girls. "Hey guys, can you see the aqua-colored waters? Everything is clear to the bottom as if looking through a see-through window."

"Ohh! I see it; look over there in the distance… spinner dolphins. Spinning out of the water and splashing down with great strength and precision. I just love porpoises." Says Willow.

The Professor speaks to everyone. "Class, you see the shoreline. This black shore here; is caused by crushed Glient shells from the bottom of the ocean. This creates a black beach shoreline as far as the eye can see." The Professor explains as the group of Wixan's were flying across the shoreline.

Coming from a distance, a pack of gulls squawked, headed towards the group.

"Mine…. Mine……Mine"

"Pull in tight, class, a pack of birds at 9 o'clock!" Gigi yells.

"You don't want to mess with the gulls; they will attack you if you show fear," Gigi yells out, racing past the group to the front of the pack.

The kid ahead of Willow yells out, "Heads down, pull in tight… let's make a beeline for the school." Willow was feeling awfully, anxious after the last encounter at camp. The gulls approach the line of students. All the kids tuck in extra close to their broom, streamlined as one.

As the gulls get closer, Willow sees them looking at each student as they pass, like they're looking for someone. They prepare to pass Willow, she holds her breath and closes her eyes. They pass without notice to her. Then Willow leans out of the pack and looks back at the passing two gulls. "*I am*

glad they didn't see me." Just as she finishes her thought, they turn around and heat-sync in on her making direct eye contact. The birds give out this death cry, a long, high-pitched squeal. All the other birds halt in the air. They turn back and head straight for Willow.

Now, the "Mine" Squawk becomes rapid and loud. "Mine" "Mine" "Mine" "Mine" "Mine" "Mine" "Mine" "Mine"

"Kalei, they are coming for me…. Help"

"I got your back," Trinity assures Willow. The girls pull out their wands and ready themselves for battle. The bird made a beeline towards her, with its red beady eyes and hooked beaks designed for tearing and eating someone's eyes out. The first group soars by, taking nano chomps at Willow.

As the trio ducks and weaves past other students to the Professor.

Mateo, one of the Nuffer'do students, spurts out.

"Detener el tiempo"

Willow watches and feels relieved as the bird pack is suspended in time.

"All students, put your brooms in overdrive and head straight to the school!" Professor NovaStar sternly exclaims.

"Well, that seemed to work," Mateo says.

"Yeah, thanks, Mateo."

"No worries, Willow; honestly, I have never seen crazed Seagulls go after anyone like that."

"I have, and it's scarier when that little football bird turns into a prehistoric 6-foot bird." Says Willow, with a discomforted look on her face.

Upon arrival the headmaster was waiting in the courtyard . The headmaster barks order, as the students who are landing into the foreyard, "All students, please report to the Shadow Dome for further instructions and a debriefing." Professor NovaStar walks with a quickness to Vanderbuilt.

Does a slide of the hand, of a small, now glowing, leather-bound package. He quickly slips it into his cloak as they tuck into the castle's side entrance. They both head straight away to Professor Ripley's office.

Chapter Twenty-Nine

Honing In On Their Craft

"Calling all first-year, Wixans, please report to the courtyard. Spell Casting 101 by Professor Crowley. And the expressive Professor Moonfire will be teaching broomstick maneuvers.

Hurry on and get sorted for your class. Spector never waits for broomsticks and potions…

Class begins in 20 minutes…Oh yeah! I almost forgot the big scoop….

Surprise!

Surprise!

Students, we have a special guest from Australia. Come to the Harmony Dome after class for our Shape Shifting Quaffle'lou's guest speaker."

As the Wixan'teers turn the corner to the courtyard, Professor Niffleswips is cooking. They catch a whiff of delicious barbecue smells, like burgers and hotdogs cooking on the grill. Also, a sweet scent is in the air from freshly made elephant ears and churros nearby. Professor Nightengale and the professor from Wizard Math group are running the sweets stand.

"I am so excited to learn new broomstick maneuvers," Willow says as she walks through the courtyard.

"Willow, I am antsy too; I hear Crowley is going to be teaching us FireDrake Theory and the Jubilee Sleeping Troll potion," Trinity says, "Well, you two, that's all fine and dandy, but did you hear that a special guest from the Australia Dundee School of Magic. Professor Wieser will be giving a demonstration."

She pulls a brown scroll from her bag.

"Here, look, I grab one of the floating school scrolls. See, it says…. demonstration on how to turn a quaffle'lou into a shape-shifting animal. I think it's a 3rd-year practice called Animorphus Quafflefication. (**Quafal forum Trans mutus**) That is where my heart lays."

Many kids are gathering in the courtyard. They are all chatting, and the consistent hum grows louder as they wait for the Professor to arrive. Then, Professor Moonfire and Crowley bustle through the crowd as they head to the grand stage.

"Line up, single file, no dawdling. You need to get sorted… Hurry on…. into your learning squad," instructs Professor Moonfire pointing vaguely over the crowd, waving her wand around, a stream of sparkles flies from it adding a mystical ambiance to the scene.

"I sure hope I get into spell casting 101," murmurs Lampfry, "I sure could use the help."

Victoria, in her belittling ways, says.

"Yeah, you need more help than spellcasting 101, you pathetic Nuffer'do. You do just enough to get yourself in trouble. Don't expect to ever be a full-blooded Wixan. You will never do anything amazing or great."

"Sure, I will be a wondrous Wixan; with enough practice, I will become a great and powerful wizard one day. You watch, you snooty patootie."

"Fat chance, Lampfry the loser… nah nah , ha ha."

"Wait and see, Vicious Victoria. You know karma has your name…" Lampfry says confidently.

Trinity is up next as she approaches the Professors.

"Trinity, you will be in Broomstick maneuvers."

Next is Willow, excited and enchanted by the whole experience.

"Willow, you will go to Spell casting 101."

"Kalei, you will be in Spell casting 101."

"Lampfry, you definitely need all the spell-casting 101 classes you can get."

Professor looking back at her, "Victoria, you will be in broom maneuvers. From the looks of it, you cannot stay on your broom without casting magic to balance. Your expertise in this subject reminds me of a Nuffer'do, so practice."

"Sheesh…. Professor. You don't have to be so mean and announce my inadequacies to everyone."

"Well, then, Victoria, you should stop bullying other kids and learn to practice patience, empathy and the zipper mouth spell on yourself. Now moving on." She continues with a smile on her face looking at the boys.

"Up next is Nun, Asim, Björn, and Kacper.

"Nun, you will be part of Broomstick maneuvers."

"Asim, go to the casting 101 line."

"Björn, Broomstick Maneuvers will be right for you."

"And Kacper, please find your way to casting 101."

"Alright, students, there is no time to waste. Please get to your studies. Lunch will be served by the fountain in the middle of the south lawn at 1 p.m. And don't forget, after your teachings today at 6 p.m., we will meet in the Harmony Dome for a special guest speaker from Australia."

DC Daniel

Willow, Kalei, Lampfry, Kacper, and Asim all follow Crowley for Spell Casting 101 class.

Crowley addresses the class.

"Students, today we will be working on the invisibility spell. Understanding this spell may one day save you or your friend's life. Does everyone understand?"

The class replies in uniform.

"Yes, Professor Crowley."

"Okay, class in front of you. You have supplies, including a spell paper. Follow the instructions very carefully. If you have questions, always ask before you mix."

Crowley walks around, paying close attention to the Nuffer'do kids. "Everyone please Follow Directions perfectly, there is no room for error. We do not want to create a vile creature from the dark side or a mischievous flying monkey on motorcycles."

Willow adds a pinch of cloaking air tree root, a sprig of rosemary, and a half teaspoon of dragon's breath to her cauldron. Lampfry is in a daze, trying to figure out where to start.

Kalei assists him. "Lampfry, first put in your pinch of cloaking air tree root, then carefully add your sprig of rosemary and stir."

"Okay, Kalei. Now, what should I do? I don't want to mess this up and have the kids laugh at me again."

"No worries, Lampfry, you have a friend in me. Now, back to the spell; add the dragon's breath next. And repeat after me."

"Okay, Kalei, ready."

Kalei leads the spell, Lamphey echoes her words, repeating it verbatim.

"By the power of the universe and the magic in me."

"By the moon's light and the earth's strength, I call upon the power within to bring forth protection."

"A shield of light around me now, All negativity and harm repel and disperse."

"I am protected, strong, and wise, with love and light as my guide."

"Capote Gerruise"

The protection forms a dome over Lampfry.

DC Daniel

Crowley aims her wand and speaks.

"Cerumen Impaction"

Her beam bounces off Willow's protection dome. She then tries again at Lampfry; he squints, closes his eyes, and hopes for the best. The same thing happens, and it reflects off him. His spell worked; it is flawless. Lampfry's concentration breaks, and he jumps for joy, screaming.

"I am a real Wizard."

Thus, breaking his spell. Crowley aims her wand and speaks the incantation again. **"Cerumen Impaction"**

This time, it turns Lampfry into a muted zippered mouth.

"Lampfry, never let your guard down… it could be your demise."

"Stopple Renew," Crowley says again, holding her wand. This reverses the mute zipper mouth spell, returning Lampfry to normal.

All the kids in the lab, go into a roar laughing.

Crowley addresses the class. "Enough… good time laughs, the next person that laughs at another student, will get the Zipper Mouth Spell."

Lampfry speaks up, "Yes, Professor Crowley, lesson learned. I will stay consistent in my thoughts during my spell dogma."

"Good, now, class. Learn from Lampfry's mistake. Always… stay steadfast in your craft."

Chapter Thirty
FireDrake Theory

Let's all move on to FireDrake theory. For you, Fire Element kids, this spell is super powerful. After that, we will take time to understand the power of the Jubilee Sleeping Troll potion."

"Take your cauldron and mix in 2 cups of Grimm's pepper liquid, 3 bat wings, 2 Spider webs, and a nip of the dust of a phoenix feather. Let simmer for 15 minutes."

"I see everyone is ready; repeat after me….

"Fuoco Ball Organizer"

Now, one at a time, going from left to right, starting with Lampfry, take your wand and aim at the golden Sphere on the stage. Mr. Lampfry, please repeat after me.

"Fuoco Ball Organizer"

DC Daniel

He waves the incent in the air in a circle then aims his wand at the golden sphere, **"Fuoco Ball Organizer."** Suddenly a floating ring of fire burns mid-air in front of him. Kalei made her attempt without any issues. Then, it was time for Willow to complete hers.

"Fuoco Ball Organizer"

With a blue flash, the fire from her wand hits the Sphere. It hits the sphere making it a giant fireball. Then without notice a horrific loud explosion happens and the sphere splits in two.

Willow stands there feeling bewildered. Trying to understand why Sphere exploded the in two pieces.

This is different for a Wixan to do. She has watched over a Lampfry and Kalei cast their spell without issues.

She glances at Crowley as if to say what just happened?

Crowley's eyes meet Willow's eyes and quickly change direction. Never missing a beat, she moves the class onto the next task.

"No worries let us all discuss the Jubilee Sleeping Troll potion. Everyone, clear out your cauldron and make your lab tables tidy. The dorm fairies will be flutter around, delivering supplies on the left of everyone's lab tables. Once Sprout and Hazel deliver all the supplies, we will proceed with the spell directions on performing the Jubilee Sleeping Troll incantation."

"This is IMPORTANT, everyone. Please understand that this spell is only used when you are in danger from a troll that intends to harm you or cause someone else harm, like the one early this year."

We agree here on Solaris Island that we don't disturb the trolls with whom we don't have business with. So, to stay in harmony, NEVER use this incantation unless you are in grave danger."

The class nods their heads to her information, as to say they understand. She goes on further with the instructions.

"Once you have finished your potion mixture, please place it in the glass potion bottles and seal them with a cork and melted wax. When you are ready, say this spell over your bottle."

"Schlaf Blüte" = Sleep bloom in German

"Now, when you encounter the troll, pour a line before you, take 10 steps back, and wait. It will attract the troll and have it tantalized by the scent, putting it into a deep catatonic sleep and letting you pass without harm."

"Okay, class, that is it for now. Please gather your belongings and meet at the Harmony Dome for our guest speaker.

Chapter Thirty-One
Karma Gets Hers

Meanwhile, in the corridor, just past the Elemental conclave on the south lawn, Trinity and Victoria gather with many other students for Broom Maneuvers.

Professor Moonfire directs the class with a stern look on her face. "Class, please pay attention; I forbid anyone to use any form of magic during this class. I have heard that some of you cannot stay on your broom without a bit of magic.

DC Daniel

Professor Crowley chooses you to participate in honing your broomstick riding techniques. So please follow my instructions, and you will learn the craft of broomstick riding."

Victoria makes salty remarks. "I can stay on my broom. Just fine, I am a Vanderbuilt; it is in our bloodline. I don't need this stupid class; I don't know why Crowley put me here."

"Victoria, I heard Crowley tell you, you cannot stay on your broom without magic. So, ha… you're a fibber." Trinity says smirking at her.

"Thats nano crap, Trinity you're a liar. She says I am perfectly fine riding; in fact, she sent me to the class to help the teacher."

"OK Victoria, if that helps you sleep at night. We all heard her, so stop living in your barbie fantasy world. We will see what you're made of soon enough."

"Girls, stop squabbling; you both are here for a reason, so pay attention," Moonfire instructs. "First, mount your brooms, and then once you are study, close your eyes, keeping your feet on the floor, get comfortable, and be one with your broom. Balance is key to staying on your broom."

"See, Trinity, I have no problem staying on my broom," Victoria responds with squinted eyes in a condescending voice.

"Victoria don't be a snobby knobby. You are not even hovering; you are just standing there.

"Shut it, don't be a noob, Trinity."

"Don't get me wrong, I am not crossed. I know I need help, but I am not over there with a Cattitude of attitude like you have superiority."

"Trinity just shut your pie hole, before I zipper mouth you."

"Fat chance, the teachers right there, watching us." She crossed her hands over her stomach. "Just because your dad is our headmaster doesn't give you the right to think you're better than everyone here."

"You two need to stop this mockery before I turn you both into toads and make you practice hopping on brooms instead of riding them!"

"Now class, once you are comfortable with your broom, open your eyes and push off with your toes. You are now hovering above the ground. With a slight effort, lean into your broom and remember your balance.

"Professor, I am doing as you instructed, but something feels wrong." Stammered Trinity.

"It's alright, Trinity, just go with it, be one with your Broom."

"Ahhh, I think I got it…" Trinity says confidently. "Yes, indeed, you have the hang of it, hang on tightly."

"Victoria, what is taking you so long? Please demonstrate your broomstick acuity, as I have instructed the class."

"I have, but my broom is not cooperating with my gestures."

"Give it one more try, dismount your broom, then remount. Once you feel balanced, push off with your toes and lean it to it, like the other kids are doing."

"Ok Professor, like this…" When she gets to step three, she leans into it. The broom gives off a moaning howl, like one from a wild animal.

"WaaaaaaAAAAAaaa... GruuUUuuUuUuUu."

"The broom starts misbehaving. Taking a dark turn with Victoria on it, it is increasingly apparent that the broom is inhibited by a malevolent force. Victoria soars higher than 20 feet above the teacher.

"Victoria, control your broom at once!"

"I caaaaaan't! Professor!" She dips past the professor…
Screaming…. "Iiiiiit's not liiiiiistening to meeeee!"

It starts to shake violently and then suddenly jolts her left to right, up and down, diving towards the lawn.

"Hellllllp meeeee! Please!" Professor Moonfire raises her wand and then yells out. **Bleeck Aroarbus**

The broom makes a hard stop, throwing Victoria off. Then Victoria lets out a squelch as her body tumbles to the ground.

The broom drops to the ground after Professor Moonfire releases her control on the bad-behaving broom. The broom erects itself abruptly and soars toward Victoria; as she rises from the ground, the broom begins to hit her bum and makes a laughing hyena sound.

"Ha-ha-ha-ha-ha! Whoop! Ha-ha-ha-ha-ha!"

OooOooOoo! Professor Moonfire, make it stop…. PLEASE make it stop." As Victoria whines.

Professor Moonfire leisurely arrives at Victoria, and the Professor takes control of it and commands it to self-destruct.

"Morea Resolute." The broom heads for the nearest Monkey Pod tree and self-destructs into the tree trunk. It breaks into many pieces, with scorched broom hairs and tiny slivers of the broom falling from the sky to the ground. The class roars loudly, happy that the Professor handled the Spector-possessed broom issue.

Victoria starts to cry intensely, and the complaining starts. "Now, what am I supposed to do for a broom? I must have a broom; I need it to go around the campus. I should have never been put in this class to begin with. I was doing just fine with a **Bostec** spell I had with my broom. And now I have NO BROOM… WHY … WHY MEEE...."

"Victoria stop whining, you can take the next Manu'ahi bird out."

"I cannot return to Manu'ahi Summit because all the Manu'ahi transportation firebirds are gone till the end of summer."

"Professor, how am I going to get another broom? This is everyone's fault. If it weren't for Professor Crowley sending me here, I would still have my broom."

"Victoria, stop it, just stop this belly aching at once…Nothing is wrong. Go and see Teleporter Professor GiGi NovaStar. She will help you get to the Manu'ahi Summit tomorrow. She will take you to get your new broom between classes at Mystic Broom Stables."

"Where do I find her professor?" Victoria asked.

"Go to the 5th floor past the moving library. There, you will find room for mirror transportation.

There, you will discover Teleporter Gigi NovaStar.

"Now, class, I'd like you all to pack up and head to the Harmony Dome for our special speaker."

"Professor, can you tell us what they will teach?" Inquired Willow.

"You'll just have to wait and see. Now, class, let us get moving. It commences promptly at 6:00 pm. By the way, the courtyard is presently having the BiggleWhomp nets cleaned, and the cleaning Norks require cleared airspace to access the laser beams in the holographic TEZOR on either side of the stadium. So, I'm afraid no brooms will be allowed to fly in that area today or tomorrow."

All the kids from the day classes, plus some 3rd—and 4th-year Wixans—come to the Harmony Dome. Everyone begins to take a seat.

Then walks in an Australian Professor Wieser. He smells of tincture brews, has rosy, red cheeks, and is wearing a Bucket hat. His robe is a distant light red like the plains in Australia.

"Good day, everyone. I am Professor Wieser, your mate from Australia. Today, we will learn about turning the quaffle'lou into a shapeshifting animal."

"Why would we be needin' animals that can shapeshift at all?" Trinity inquires.

The headmaster replies. "Sometimes, you may need to use a quaffle'lou to eavesdrop or protect you when your familiar's not around. You know to keep you safe, mate."

"Oi, mate. You might have to send your shapeshifting animal somewhere to make sure the path's clear or to distract a beastly thing away from you."

"Now take your quaffle'lou, put it on the floor, sprinkle some golden boar hair in it, and cast the spell.

"Animasorbo Transfiguris!" says Willow. Willow looks astounded at the black cougar that appears from her command.

Then Kalei follows suit. Repeats precisely what Willow did. Kalei yells out… "Ewwwwwkkk a snake, what the heck am I supposed to do with this dumb thing? I despise snakes, nasty, vile scaly creatures."

Just then, the rainbow-colored Boa constructor lunges at Kalei; it starts to quickly wrap around her, creating a constricting motion around her neck; as she tries to pull the snake away, it clamps down tighter; Willow takes her wand and casts the snake away.

"Departure No low Aires" The snake vanishes into thin air.

Kalei takes a big gulp of air in à loud breath. "Thank you, Willow. I thought I was headed to the motherland." Kalei feels relieved and hugs Willow for help getting the creature gone.

Lampfry looks at Both of the girls. "I hope this goes well," Willow assures him. "Think positive."

"OK, here goes nothing…. **Animasorbo Transfiguris!"** The girls watch in amazement and behold the most beautiful Owl was standing before them. The bird's bright orange beak and gray and white down feathers fill the bird; the Owl looks around 120 degrees, ruffling its feathers. Its gleaming orangish yellow eyes meet Lampfry's brown eyes.

"Who!"

"Who!"

"Who!"

Lampfry looks around at the other students, feeling unique and enlightened because no other student made an owl as their shapeshifter.

Lampfry yells out. "I got an owl…. Professor. What does this mean?" All the kids glare at him, giving him the stink eye.

"Well, Lampfry, do you have a familiar?"

"No, my Lemur, Mr. Tuggles, died last week; he got loose and ate a magpie mantis.

I don't think he broke it down because later that night, the Magpie Mantis ate its way out of poor Tuggle's belly, killing him. He drops dead with a thump to the floor, leaping no more."

"Well, mate, the only time this happens where the spell forms an owl is when a young lad like yourself needs a new familiar. So, mate, it looks like you own a new owl."

Willow asks him. "What are you going to name it?"

"Maybe I'll call him Orpheus or Zulu," he replies.

"Kalei said. "Whatever you name it, make sure you get a library book titled 'How to Care for Your Owl.' I heard they are trickier to care for than a Lemur."

Willow asks. "What should we do with our creatures, Professor Wieser?"

"Well, class, when you are done using your shapeshifter animal, and it is safe to let it go, cast these words:

"**Reversio Transmutatio.**" This command will return it to its quaffle'lou state until you need it next time."

The kids can be heard casting the reserve spells one after another.

"**Reversio Transmutatio.**"

"**Reversio Transmutatio.**"

"**Reversio Transmutatio.**"

An echoing muttered phrase is heard till the last student finishes. The Professor promptly meets Lampfry with another quaffle'lou, returning the empty shell from when the Owl arrived.

Professor Wieser places his hand in front of Lampfey, waves his wand, and speaks out. "**Avia Docent Come, Ad Manus Meas!**" (This translates to "The Birds Guide Me, to My Hands "Begin book! Let the owl care education appear in my hands!")

This thick book appears enwrapped in vellum. Bestowed on the top of the book, a Tink appears. Gingerberry the Tink reads the book aloud, but she first starts with.

"Lampfry, for your Owl's safety, please listen and, if necessary, reply. That's OK. Listen as I read the instructions to you."

"Thank you, Professor Weiser and GingerBerry. Yes, I want to make sure this new familiar Orpheus lives strong, and for a long time."

He heads off to his dorm as he listens to Tink read the book.

Chapter Thirty-Two
Transcendent Mirrors

Above their heads are floating candles. Tink's wearing tiaras and flying monkeys on motorcycles are also part of the other strange, out-of-this-world things that float above the students at breakfast.

Willow, Kalei, Trinity, and the Vanderbuilt girls sit together this early morning in August.

The trio begins to talk about an upcoming spell theory test. Whereas the Vanderbuilt girls, Olivia and Victoria are talking among themselves across the way. Both their gossip fairies sit attentively, hanging on to every word they say, waiting to hear some kind of gossip to run wild with.

The gossip fairies are trouble starters and roomer creators. If any student wants to know the dirt on the campus about other students and mis happenings on the school grounds, all they have to do is ask Tink or Zara to spill the beans.

"Olivia, did you get permission from father to go to Manu`ahi Summit with me to get my new broom?"

"No, I asked, but he hasn't replied. I feel as if he is ignoring me."

"Olivia, why would he ignore you? He loves us more than life itself."

"Victoria, you know as well as I do that ever since Freya and father started courting, it's been all about her and her boys."

DC Daniel

"Sis, I do see your point. We are like invisible daughters now. Chopped liver. Old news…. Freya is putting on a great show with our father, but she is like the evil stepmom. You see the look she gives us when Dad's not around. Then how sweet she is with her two Oompa Loompa boys."

"Olivia, I agree with you, I can't figure her out, and I don't know if I despise her more or her boys.

"Yep, Olivia, I feel like father doesn't hear us anymore, much less see that we are here and unhappy with Freya and how she treats us when he is not around."

Olivia lets out a huge sigh and voices her disdain, "I hate that lady; I wish she would slither back under the rock where she came from. She is only dating our dad to try to get our dead mother's estate."

"Well, Olivia, if he is too busy with that old hen, you should just come with me; he won't even notice; maybe we can stop by SpellBee's shop and find some Spell brew that we could use to cast her and her two galoots away from our father."

"Alright, Victoria. I will go, but if I get in trouble, I will put snakes in your bed when you sleep."

"No pressure, sis… you go or don't go… it is up to you, but if you are a chicken little, stay in the hen house."

"Now Victoria, don't be a brat… I am going with you; however, I still wonder how we can be transported via a mirror to the Manu`ahi Summit."

Trinity willfully enlightens them. "You know, you two, I heard Transporter GiGi NovaStar has a special mirror that can take you to the future and the past; at least, that's what my dad told me, a long time ago."

Willow stops talking to Kalei and listens intently to what is said about this unique transporter mirror.

"Trinity, is there a mirror that can really take you to the past and the future?"

"Willow, I don't make things up; I always tell the truth, and yes, that mirror is only for students in 3rd year of studies or better."

Willow replies sadly, "Oh, I see. I guess we have to wait until our 3rd year. I would love to go back in time and see who my parents are."

Trinity says. "You know, Willow, sometimes it's better not to know the past. God has a way of protecting us from things that may destroy our balance in life."

Victoria and Olivia get up, plop their fairys upon their shoulder, and head out of the breakfast hall. They go to the Tetris stairs leading up to the moving library.

The girls get to the transcendence mirror room; outside, a sign hangs with this saying.

Through rhyme and spell, to lands unknown,

Step inside, and let magic be sown.

From mirrors of transport, swift, and grand,

To distant realms, we shall expand.

The girls enter to find this room full of mirrors, small ones, big ones, oval ones, and square ones.

"Olivia, do you see this, a Mirror reflecting within itself, 1,2,3,5,7,10,12,15…. It seems like this goes on forever."

"Victoria, do you see this? It looks like a mirror full of static; I bet it's like the mirror that the evil queen uses in snow white. Why don't you say the mirror mirror phrase."

"Okay, here goes nothing…. Mirror, mirror on the wall, who is the fairest of them all?"

The rolling static of the mirror makes a crackling sound.

DE Daniel

The mirror comes to life, and a ghostly genie jets out 3 feet from it. The Genie hands are crossed, glaring at them, he speaks with clarity, authority, and knowledge.

"Oh, Victoria, your soul is ugly, so you could not be the fairest and most magical.

This unique Wixan's soul,

Magic takes flight,

A wondrous essence,

Shining so bright.

Her spirit dances like a mystical breeze,

healing hearts and minds with effortless ease.

In every act of kindness,

A spell is spun, making Willow, the most magical one."

Victoria huffs aloud and says… "You silly Genie…. What do you know?

You're just a dumb mirror; my sister and I are Vanderbuilts, the most powerful Wixans of WillowBrook, and our dad is the headmaster who runs this school."

The Genie tells another rhyme this time looking straight at Victoria.

"In realms of magic, you held great might,

With power bound, potential taking flight,

But ego's grip and words unkind,

Obstructed the path, your mana to be blind.

Let not your pride obscure the view,

True magic comes from what is within you,

Kindness, patience, and humbleness, virtues to hold,

Unlock your Mana, let it unfold."

Olivia with her hands on her hips, and a mean mug on her face she asks Victoria,

"How is this possible? In the storybook, the one asking the mirror is always the most powerful and fairest of the land, right?"

"Well, it's just a dumb mirror. Don't worry about it, Olivia."

Just then, the Genie disappears, and this wicked Cerberus appears in a 4D figure out of the mirror and makes this awful shrieking sound at the girls.

"RAWRR AWW!" as it plunges toward the girls.

This evil creature with three heads engages itself with the girls. Barreling out of the mirror and then, with a flash, sucking itself back into the rolling static, leaving without a trace.

"AHHHH!" screams Victoria.

She falls backward into Olivia, toppling her without warning. Olivia pushes her sister off her. "That about scared the living daylights out of me.

What in the jeepers creepers was that? Victory looking at her sister.

"Did you see the three sets of red eyes?" asks Olivia.

"I don't know. It looks like a Cerberus, Vee. You know that three-headed beast that resembles a dog—the legendary guardian of the Underworld of Hades."

"Yes, I have heard of that; it did resemble that revolting creature."

Gigi NovaStar approaches the girls. "Are you ladies, okay? I heard the screams from across the room."

"Yes, Miss NovaStar, we are okay," Olivia announces.

Then Victoria asks. "Do you know why this mirror had the Hades Guardian Cerberus lunge out of it?

Before Gigi could get the answer out. Olivia bombards her with a flood of questions.

"So, what is this mirror for? Do you really have a time transporter mirror? Are you going to take us to Manu`ahi Summit? Why are there so many mirrors here? I feel like I am in some crazy funky mirror house at the fair."

"Whoa… Girl, please slow down; I can only answer one question at a time." The professor point to the static mirror. "This is a truth mirror; ask it any question, and it will always tell the truth. And yes girls, we have time travel mirrors for third-year students. And this area here is to go to the

Manu`ahi Summit. Now, Crowley told me you need a new broom. Is that correct?"

"Yes Mama, I self-destructed in Broom Maneuvers."

"Ok, now I have no answers about the Cerberus coming out of the truth mirror. This seems bizarre and oddly strange."

Well, I only know of a three-headed Cerberus, this very muscular and powerful dog.

Is generally not depicted as a protector of evil, but rather as a guardian or gatekeeper. In Greek mythology, Cerberus's role is to guard the entrance to the Underworld, which is the realm of the dead, not necessarily a place of evil. His job is to ensure that the souls of the dead do not escape and that the living do not enter without permission.

While the Underworld does contain areas for punishment, such as Tartarus, where the wicked are punished, it also includes the Elysian Fields, a peaceful resting place for heroes and the virtuous. Cerberus doesn't differentiate between good and evil souls—he simply guards the boundary.

Overall, Cerberus serves Hades, the god of the Underworld, and helps maintain the natural order between life and death. He's more of a neutral figure than a protector of evil, focused solely on the duty of keeping the realm of the dead secure.

Now that you've had your mini lecture on Greek mythology, are there any other questions you two might have?"

Well yes, in fact, I do have another question. Who else will be going with us?" asks Victoria.

"Well, Victoria, the foreign exchange students Kacper and Björn, and Lampfry will join us, too. You two are a little early, we leave at 11a.m.today.

We are to leave at 11 a.m. , so check back in an hour. The other kids will be here and I will be qalmostly ready

"Professor, can my sister go with us?" Asked Victoria

"Yes, Victoria, Olivia can travel with us if your father is okay with it. Olivia, you do have permission from Mr. Vanderbuilt, right?"

"Of course she does, Miss NovaStar." Victoria interjected.

Gigi moves her purple hair out of her eyes and glares deeply through her 1950s cat-eye-arched glasses at Olivia, waiting for her response.

"Well, Olivia, do you have permission or not?"

Olivia nods to the Professor as her fingers are crossed behind her back.

"Alright, ladies, I will see you back here, in one hour."

Olivia speaks up. "Pardon me, ma'am. Can we just stay here? That Tetras stairwell is very confusing, it keeps changing, with missing steps and whole levels that disappear. And those paintings, always chatting among themselves... One trip through that was enough for me." Victoria nods, her face clouded with troubled grief as she looks at her sister.

"Yes, you two can stay here, but if you stay on this floor, do not mess around with the mimicking knights. And DO NOT ENTER that room on the left—the one there, you see, with the black door with the red triangle on it, okay?"

Victoria says in a condescending, assuring voice, "Yes, of course. We always follow directions, Miss NovaStar."

"Okay, then you two can mingle, and I will see you after I take care of last-minute details before the trip.

The Professor quickly dashes away, and with a flip of her robe, she disappears into the back of the store.

The girls meander throughout the maze of mirrors. Some minutes pass and the two handsome blonde Norwiegn boys arrive. They are all standing by the the forbidden black door.

Crinkle…. Swooh…. Swoosh ….crinkle

"Hey everyone, do you hear that?"

Björn says to the group.

"Yes, I hear it," Kacper responded.

"I hear it too," Victoria says looking at her sister.

"Yes, it sounds like it's coming from behind that door," Olivia announces.

"we should go in and investigate." Björn says with an intense voice.

"Miss NovaStar our transporter says we are not allowed to enter that door." Olivia the rule follower explains.

"Its ok, she in the back room she wont notice if we make it quick." Kacper proclaims."

"Yeah Olivia lets have a quick look." Said Victoria

As they approach the door handle, there was a giant padlock locking the door.

Stand back guys I wil open it with an unlocking spell." Kacper said.

"avata nyt"

DC Daniel

The Hugh padlock magically opens. Björn grabs the door and begins to open it. All that can be seen by the students isa darkness darker than midnight. They can hear the swoosh … swoosh sound again. But this time, a clawing scratching sound follows the swoosh sounds, with a rush of air that engulfs their body. The group stands in astonishment.

Then two beady red eyes appear, glaring into there souls.

We need light, I cant see anything but those eyes. Victoria says.

As she holds out her hand, she commands the Fire spell.

"firemortus"

As a flame is created in Victoria's hands four more sets of beady red eyes appear in the dark.

The room lightens up as the fire grows in Victoria hand.

Olivia gasps and points. A giant thunder bird standing 3 feet from them. This towing 6.5 foot bird appears to be chained to the floor. As it stands up on its hindlimbs, a leather bound package and a golden egg could be seen in the nest, as the bird rose.

In the rear distance the 2 other birds stood up revealing their golden eggs. The thunder bird that is a few feet away starts to become enraged by their presence. This ghastly bird starts to lunge at the students giving out horrifying screech. In a matter of seconds, it becomes more enraged, and begins to thrash and wallop towards the kids… the crinkling sounds is now overwhelming. The kids dart out of the room, to be met with Lampfry standing there in their path. They tumble all on top of one another, with Lampfry on bottom.

Bojorn closes the heavy steel black door, and Kacper belts out and incantation to lock the padlock.

"Lukko alas"

Miss NovaStar appears from the back almost in distance of appracohing the students. Lampfry is the last one to get up he knopws over one of the mirrors, it crashes into 2 other mirrors, making an horrific sound.

Everyone can hear the Thunder birds in the other room shrieking and making an alarming sound, as if it knew the students were on the other side of the door. Gigi takes her wand and taps it on the door mumbling something, the kids could not make out. However, everything in that mysterious room went silent.

Victoria starts to insult Lampfry.

" Ha ha you're getting 7 years of bad luck, make that 21 years of bad luck. You're such a klutz, go figure always making trouble wherever you go."

Lampfry is quick to respond.

"If you guys would not of pumbled me, I would of never broke the mirrors, getting up. That your bad luck Victoria, not mine."

Miss NovaStar inquires.

"How did you get tackled Lampfry?"

Before Lamprey could answer, Bojorn speaks up.

"We were just playing around teach, weren't we Lampfry." Glaring at him with eyes of you better not tell, otherwise I will get you after class."

Lamprey politely went with the group's clue.

" Yes Miss NovaStar we were just fooling around, I am sorry for breaking the mirrors."

Victoria changes the subject.

"When are we leaving, I have to get my new broom, before class tomorrow."

DE Daniel

Well class if everyone is ok, let get lined up and get ready for transcendence."

They all gather in a circle, holding hands. The transporting teacher Gigi, moves her runic ring from her index finger and places it on her ring finger. Dials it into the Fire bird runic symbol of Manahi Summit.

She says this charm.

"By mystic forces,

I cast my plea,

Grant me passage to realms unseen.

Through the veils of time and space,

Transport our spirits to a sacred place.

With this spell, our journey begins."

They enter the mirror one by one, transportation to the Manahi Summit.

Holding their hands up in the W formation upon arriving at the summit. Making sure the evil Pixies don't attack them, thinking they are intruders.

Victoria gets her new broomstick, Olivia, finds some much-needed potions supplies, Lampfey gets his new robe, since he caught his on fire in Potions and brews 101. The Nordic exchange students get their talismans and amulets for their end of summer project they are working on. After all the students retrieve their supplies they head back to the school. Arriving one by one, coming through the mirror they left through hours before.

Victoria expresses her gratitude.

"Thank you Miss NovaStar."

Thank you Miss GiGi for your time, it was a pleasure. Lampfry says.

The two exchanges students also demonstrate profound appreciation by thanking the teacher in their native tounge.

"Takk Skal Du ha Miss NovaStar" Bjorn expresses.

Then Kacper speaks up.

"Tusen Takk Miss Gigi"

All the students head back to their dorms together making their way down the Transmutairs. These ever changing stiars can be trickey to manipulate. Thr group found themselves at a door that was irrodenscent in color, it have a pulsating ripple effect that went from the left corner to the bottom.

"Why wont the transmutair change." Victoria Stated.

"I don't know?" Kacper uttered.

"what in the Holy Mackerel is this." Asserted Kacper

Just then the door illusively opens, enticing the group too the unknown. Bojorna leader, is the first to step in the room.

The rest of the group follows. As they stand in the darkness the room starts to illuminate with Luminescent Fireflies. These mystical insects radiate a gentle, pulsating light, filling the space with a magical glow as they flutter and dance around.

"What is this place? Do you smell that horrendous staunch?" Lamprey asks the group.

"I have no earthly idea, but look in the distance at the Glowstone Crystals, those shimmery crystals give light to the emerald tablets." voiced Kacper

As the group approaches the tablets.

"I wonder what this writing means, this is an Eclectic

Series of symbols, some looking familiar. While other symbols I have never seen before." Victoria expresses.

As she reached for one of the tablets, to pick it up.

                    DE Daniel

Just then a keeper malevolent troll appears. This 8 ft creature towered over the students, its ghastly appearance with a hunched and twisted posture that gives it a menacing presence. Its skin is pale and sickly, almost translucent, with a hint of an unnerving green undertone. The Troll's body is emaciated, its flesh clinging tightly to the bones, giving it a gaunt and skeletal appearance.

Its face is a contorted blend of horror and sorrow, with sunken cheekbones, and glowing red eyes that radiate its evil intent. Jagged, decaying teeth jut out from its mouth as if forever hungering for something. The Troll's long, bony fingers end in razor-sharp claws, capable of rending flesh with ease.

Covering its body are tattered and moth-eaten rags, the remnants of clothing from a long-forgotten era. The troll emits a putrid odor, a mix of decay and rotten eggs, which lingers in the air wherever it goes.

Its movements are slow and deliberate, like a macabre dance, adding to the sense of unwelcoming dread that infuses the air.

"My name is Gordy… these treasures are MINE….You dare to lay your hands on my treasures?..... You will regret that choice, for I will not hesitate to use my strength to keep what is mine. Turn back now or suffer the consequences!"

"Eeeeek" screams Oliva.

Victoria untethered by the ghastly troll, Stands defiantly, and squares up with the beast.

"I am not frightened of you I am a Vanderbuilt."

Bjorn steps in front of Victoria and the troll.

"Come on Victoria that darn troll doesn't care about your pedigree, don't be stupid to provoke him. He will eat all of us, and not think twice."

Olivia insists. "let's just get out of here."

"I may be a Nufferdo Victoria, But I know we are not supposed to be in here." proclaimed Lampfry.

The kids looked at one another and ran out. but not before Victoria could give the troll the chin flick gesture. She turns to walk away, she is seen flicking her fingers out from under her chin and tipping her head slightly while making a 'ntze' noise with her mouth. This Italian gesture meant Chissenefrega! (Who cares!)

The group feels overwhelmed by what they just saw. Nonetheless, they arrive out of the door and slammed the door ensuring that the troll would be trapped in that mysterious room. They ran from there to wait at the professor's desk at the front of the store.

The group all landed back on the platform ready to depart, but the stairs still were not moving.

Kasper chants the spell out to the Transmutair taking control of its misleading behavior. This sent the group to the bottom of the 5th tower, provoking a sense of relief that they made it to the exit.

They all head back to their dorms. Victoria and Olivia are sitting in the common area, where Willow and Kalei are comingling. The Vanderbuilt twins were unaware of the presence of the other girls in the area. They start to talk about the Transmutair incident.

" Victoria what do you make of the emerald tablets, that the troll was protecting?" asked Oliva.

"I really don't know, but what ever it says , the nasty troll would of rather smashed us, then to let us read it." Responded Victoria

"Victoria, What about the Mirror that can transport you to the past or future. Where would you like to go if you could?"

"I think I would like to go to the future, where I could see who I will marry. What about you Oliva?"

"I would like to back to the past and see us with mom, before the accident. I sure do miss her."

" me too, on most days that end in Y. However, you heard Mrs. NovaStar, not until we are 3rd year students…. However, I can't wait." Said Victoria

Willow sat there in amazement; her mind was flooded with feelings. wonderment about all that they had just talked about. Would she be able to find her family? She had never met her father or her mother the one that left her for dead in the trash. And what were accident Emerald Tablets, what was written on them. Willow feeling uneasy about everything that she heard come from the Vanderbuilt twins.

Remember to bring up the package and golden eggs that the Thunderbirds we're sitting on.

Giving Rebalance teo the package that Crowley received during the outing at the magical forest.

Headmaster Vanderbuilt comes running onto the courtyard… Yelling.

"All Students return to your dorms… immediately.

Chapter Thirty-Three
An Eye for an Eye

The next morning, Willow stands in the archway of an opening to the courtyard. The feeling of intellectual knowledge with the past summer spent in the castle.

DC Daniel

The nostalgic feeling of Solaris Island floods her soul. Willow looks down the hall and sees Kalei coming out of the passageway from Professor Nightengale's room.

As they run towards each other, Trinity and Isabella pop out of Professor Crowley's room, just as Willow and Kalei make it down the hall, and the four girls tumble together.

"We're back? This feels great," says Willow.

"I agree. The small break was fantastic; seeing my brother and father was lovely. But it sure is great to be back," Kalei replies.

The morning announcement comes from a new speaker named MorningStar.

Tap! Tap! Tap!, he taps the mic (umm hum) as he clears his throat… "Can everyone hear me, OK?" asks MorningStar."

The kids at the school roar loudly, whistling and clapping their hands.

"Welcome back, students."

"Let's give a big welcome to the first-year students."

The campus goes into another wild roar and symbolic chant of the WillowBrook Motto.

"We are the Strong, we are the Future, and we unite as ONE. WillowBrook … Hoorah…. WillowBrook… Hoorah…. WillowBrook... Hoorah... WillowBrook... Hoorah!"

Willow, Kalei, Trinity, and Isabella meet in the Precious Gem class taught by Professor Grimsby and Professor Fitzgerald.

As the gems are passed around to all the students, Willow is drawn to the amethyst stone. Her hand starts to glow when she picks it up, and so does the gem. The professor takes notice and comes to Willow's side.

"Willow, it seems like you have a connection to the amethyst."

"Yes, I agree, Professor Fitzgerald. I don't know why this is happening, but it feels like energy flows through my veins when I hold this rock."

"Well, class, take notice; Willow has found her power stone. Now take notice of yourselves, to any rare gem you feel close and connected to, or if your elemental sign on your hand as it glows when you hold the rock. This could be your power stone, like the totem poles at the magic water polo games. Some Wixan's use the totems to power up when they lose some of their power during the game. But you must have your connecting gem when you power up."

"Alright class that is for today, see you next week. Please study the pop quiz on the gem powers."

The girls disburse to the Gathering Hall.

"Hey, Trinity, did you hear about the Labyrinth Maze they built while we are gone?" asks Kalei.

"I heard that if you make it to the middle, there is a beautiful fountain with the Greek goddess statue of Aphrodite," answers Trinity.

"Who is Aphrodite?" inquires Isha.

"She is the goddess of beauty, wisdom, courage, inspiration, civilization, law, and justice," says Kalei.

"Since I am from Indian culture. We have a goddess named Lakshmi, the goddess of wealth, prosperity, and fortune. She can be seen sitting on a lotus flower, which symbolizes purity and abundance. Our culture worships her during the festival of Diwali, as she is believed to bring good luck and blessings. So, does Aphrodite give you special powers?" asks Isha.

Trinity replies, "No, I don't think you get special powers from Aphrodite. I think she was just one of the goddesses from Greek culture.

And as you see, our school takes pride in celebrating all cultures and beliefs, allowing students to understand and comprehend the differences our world offers."

"Let's get to the labyrinth hedge maze after class," suggests Isha.

"I wish I could by I promised to help Professor Crowley after class," replies Kalei.

Then Willow pipes up. "I have practice for the upcoming Magic Water Polo match next week. You and Trinity should check it out."

"I have to go feed my familiar; it's been getting rambunctious in the afternoon. I am free after that, Isha."

"OK, then, Trinity, let's meet me at the hedge entrance after you feed your Sun Bear Sam."

After lunch, Trinity and Isha start at the maze entrance.

"Oh, my, I have never seen so many hedges in one place; this labyrinth is amazing," says Isha.

"I agree, Isha. It's massive in size, once you're in it, the top towers over us like we are shomores. I hope we don't get lost."

As they enter the maze, every turn seems to be a dead end. They retrace their steps to find the next path. As time passes, they find themselves intermingled in the maze.

"I think we have been here before," says Isha.

"I think you are right. Let's leave a trail that we have been here before."

Trinity pulls out a bag of Nipswitches and places one on the ground next to the dead-end wall. This Nipswitch is a colorful array of rainbow colors.

"This should let us know we were here before," says Trinity. They travel on to another dead end.

Trinity places the next Nipswitch on the ground, and before long, she has placed nine of them. They take a left, then a right, then another left to come up on a Nipswitch that has been placed there before.

"I am getting a little nervous because a Nipswitch was in front of a hedge wall before. It is open to walk forward. I wonder if we are allowed to be here in the first place," says Isha with confusion and nervousness.

"I am sure we are allowed to be here because they would have told us no or put up a barricade so we could not enter. Let us go forth and see where this takes us. I bet this is a special hedge that is always changing," says Trinity.

"Alright, Trinity, but I feel uneasy about this place. I don't want to be lost."

They were getting somewhere because they went deeper into the maze without sighting Nipswitches. In the distance, they can hear some creepy sounds of kids laughing.

Trinity is now feeling ambushed by a feeling of loss lessness. She tries to climb the Hedge, and as she gets 2-3 feet off the ground, the Hedge comes to life. A set of eyes illuminates from the bush, and Isabella lets out a blood-curdling scream.

"Ohuchi, why must you be so mean, Trinity?"

Trinity loses her balance and falls to the ground with a thump. She looks up at the Hedge in shock.

"How did you know my name?"

"Young Wixan, I know all the students at WillowBrook. You are no different. Please do not climb on me; I have feelings, too; my branches hurt when you step on them. This maze was grown for you guys to have fun with but not to destroy."

"I'm sorry, Mr. Hedge. I won't climb you again. Please help us find our way out.

"We are lost and a little scared. Are we the only ones in here?" asks Isha.

"No, there are two other boys and a girl in here. But they are not good kids. They are planning to harm my Hedge. I cannot help you find the way out, but I can help you to the fountain. You might be able to conjure up a transporting spell to take you to the room of mirrors back at the castle."

"OK, lead the way, Mr. Hedge." The girls say in a trusting manner.

"OK, I will flutter my hedge top to direct you in the way to go."

The girls start to follow the hedge top and find out they are not far from the fountain. They arrive at the fountain and find a beautiful one with the goddess Aphrodite in the middle.

In the distance, they can hear the group of kids and the evil laugh. They stand frozen, not knowing what to do. For the first time, Trinity is afraid and unsure of herself.

"They're getting closer, Isha; what do we do? Where should we hide?" asks Trinity

Isha pulls out a few Catacorns and the Phantom cloak from her backpack.

Isha casts the spell.

"Umbratus Discretio"

"Come on, Trinity, here, get under it with me. "commands Isha.

They disappear underneath the cloak just in time for the three kids to come around the corner. The kids do not notice the girls hiding. They watch and listen as the troublesome teens disclose their evil intentions.

Karen, Smooch, and Willis conspire about emptying foggle liquid into the fountain.

"Let's do it already before we get caught," says Willis

Smooch pulls out the vile of neon green liquid and hands it

to Karen.

"I don't wanna do it; you're her son; you do it."

"You said you were going to do the honors, you promised

Aynat. Why are you playing chicken now?" says Willis.

"Why don't you do it? Like I said, you are her son. You both

have vengeance towards WillowBrook," says Karen.

"Don't go getting your panties in a bunch, chicken little. Give me the darn vile Karen, and I will gladly destroy the fountain," says Willis.

As he opens the vile, the Hedge speaks up.

"I wouldn't do that if I were you."

"Who said that? Show yourself," says Smooch.

DC Daniel

"There is no one around," says Karen

"Then get to it, Willis; pour the darn stuff already."

Willis pours the Foggle liquid into the fountain. The clear Water starts to sizzle. Just then, a cloud puff floats up.

This dreary black smoke falls into a liquid, mixing with the fountain water. Next, a green, smoky fog floats up from the Water. Without haste, mysteriously, the goddess Aphrodite comes to life.

"Who dares to disrupt the beauty of my fountain," says Aphrodite.

Instantaneously, she reaches down and nabs Karen with the back of her robe. "How dare you destroy all that is beautiful and natural in this fountain."

Aphrodite speaks to Karen angrily, her eyes now beaming red.

The two boy's scramble.

DC Daniel

"We are outta here, Karen; sucks to be you," says Willis

"Help me, you two, where are you going?" shouts Karen.

The girls are shaken seeing the wrath of Aphrodite; fright fills their bodies all the way up to their eyes, and they stay hidden under the cloak.

"We should help her," whispers Trinity.

"Why! They were trying to destroy Aphrodite, and you heard Mr. Hedge warn them."

"Remember we promised….do no harm to others,"

"Yes, I remember, but they are evil kids. They are not from here. Do you remember them saying that Aynat is trying to destroy WillowBrook and everything it stands for? So why should we help this girl?" asks Isha.

"Because we don't wanna get judged by association; let's stay quiet and hidden until it calms down. says Trinity."

Aphrodite tosses Karen into the hedge, "Take this vile creature and do as you wish with her Mr. Hedge."

"Most certainly my goddess, as you wish."

Aphrodite pulls out her own vile of bubbly purple liquid and pours into the fountain restoring her to her natural vitality and beauty.

They stay there, more terrified than ever, hearing Karen screaming and pleading for help.

The boys disappear into the labyrinth hedge maze; they can hear the blood-curdling screams coming from Karen.

"An Eye for an Eye." Grumbles the Hedge as he speaks out with the glowing face from the Hedge before them. The boys beat feet even faster, startled by the appearance of the face in the Hedge. They run faster; the boys turn left, right, and left again. They see an opening in the distance to the outside.

They make a dash for it, and as they arrive closer to the opening, it magically closes, causing it to be a newly formed hedge wall. The face appears again.

The Hedge bellows out in a deep voice.

"Where do you think you two heavens are going? You tried to take the life force of my Hedge; Aphrodite is my protector. So, we will have an eye for an eye."

Both Smooch and Willis turn back to see the Hedge come alive. The hedges of ivy vines grab Smooch and then entangle him, pulling him into the ivy-green wall. The bottom half of his body is entrapped in the green Hedge. Smooch reaches for Willis, flailing to try to get out of the Ivy. Willis tries to pull him out, tugging and pulling with all his might, but he cannot release his friend from the grips of the Hedge.

"Please, man, get me outta here."

"I can't free you; you are stuck in there. I have tried with all my might, dude; you won't budge."

The Hedge calls out from over the wall with a grumbling voice… "An eye for an eye, Willis…. Remember, an eye for an eye."

Then the ivy engulfs the rest of Smooch, as he slowly gets engulfed into the Hedge, he screams, begging for help.

"Willis, where are you going? HELP ME. I thought I was your best bud…. PLEASE, PLEASE, I BEG OF YOU DON'T LEAVE ME HERE, IT'S DARK HERE."

Willis takes off running in the other direction, frightened for his life. As Smooch's screams fade. He tries to get to the next opening and to his next turn in the Hedge; he is pumped, full of adrenaline, and out of breath. Willis stops for a minute to catch his breath.

Panting!

Trying to comprehend what happened, he can't get his racing mind to stand still enough to collect his thoughts. As he stands there, he hears the Hedge speak again.

"An Eye for an Eye."

Willis takes off running again. He smacks face-first into the Hedge. He gets up, shakes the hard landing off, and looks down at the Hedge's end.

"AHHH SMOOCH!"

He sees Smooch's face in the Hedge. As he gets closer and closer, Smooch stops talking. He notices that Smooch is now a stone-embedded face in the Hedge.

"Smooch... Smooch... What happened?"

"What have I done? I am so sorry."

Willis brings out his wand and aims it at Smooch's head.

"Cleverous Be fouis"

Willis repeats...

"Cleverous Be fouis"

"Nothing is happening. What in the Beaver Cleaver is going on? Why is my power and magic not working?"

"I have to get out of here."

He runs off again, leaving Smooch's stone face in the dust. He turns the corner and another corner.

(Wap)

(Thump)

(Kerplunk)

His face plants into Karen's stone face, buried into the bush.

He tries his spell again to turn his stone friend's face back to life.

DE Daniel

"Cleverous Be fouis"

"Cleverous Be fouis"

"Cleverous Be fouis"

Nothing happens; a girl's whinny voice comes from the Hedge; it's Karen.

"What did you do to me? Willis, I thought I was your friend."

Willis yells, with sadness in his voice. "I am so sorry, Karen, I didn't do this to you; the hedge did it."

"No, Willis. You put the foggle into the fountain; this is your fault. The Hedge warned us… and you laughed. Now, I am stuck here forever. Thanks for nothing, you good for nothing, basilisk snake."

"Please, Mr. Hedge, let me out; I will be good, I promise."

The bushy angry green face illuminated in front of Willis.

"I will let you out, but remember you put your evil friends here. Not I."

"An Eye for an Eye, Willis."

The Hedge makes an opening in the labyrinth and lets Willis out. Willis runs out and uses his spell to transport himself back to Iris's headquarters.

"Sortum bledge Abile"

Willis vapors into thin air.

The girls come out of the cloak and head straight away to the headmaster's office. They come in repeating each other's words, talking over one another.

"Mr. Vanderbuilt, we just came from the Labyrinth maze."

"Yes girls, go on."

Trinity with a frightened look on her face, "Well sir, you see, we saw three kids from Iris, they tried to position Aphrodite's water fountain."

Isha wavy her hands and says, "Yeah, and then the hedge ate two of them, but I think that ratty boy Willis got away."

Headmaster Vanderbuilt with a face of shock inquires, "You say Willis was there? Who else was with him?"

Trinity says, "I think a girl named Karen was there."

Isha Says, "And another by the name Smooch."

"Was that it ladies, no one else was there? What did they put in the fountain?"

Trinity with a shacky uncertain voice, "Sir I think it was a foggle position."

Isha asks, "Mr. Vanderbuilt what is Foggle potion?

"Well Isha, it is a liquid that would turn Aphrodite into a creature from the underworld, evil and vile. But more importantly, if too much is added then it can evaporate into the air over night, and settle on the campus with the morning dew, giving everyone on campus amnesia."

Trinity speaks up," Sir I think Aphrodite had her own tincture because she added this bubbly purple vile and it restored her to her natural beauty."

Well, that is good, to hear. Nevertheless, please go find Crowly and Ripley, Applegate and Nightingale, tell them I want to see them tomorrow at 8am."

"Yes sir. right away." Both girls said in sync.

Chapter Thirty-Four
No Room for Error

They find themselves in a purple hall with many windows, as it pulsates a warm glow of green. Fourteen windows in all, seven on each side. In the distance through a bright and long hall, they see a solid black cat with a white W on its forehead and green glowing eyes. It darts off to the left, and they follow without notice passing the elf dorms and classroom for Transcendence. Gigi teaches astral projection to the 4th year Wixans here.

DC Daniel

As they pass the Mimicking Knights; the Knights's heads turn, following the girls. Waiting for some type of shenanigans. The cat continues the path and heads into a mesmerizing inversion tunnel. Like the one on I Drive in Orlando at the WonderWorks Science Center. They follow this cat, and the two girls become dazed as they go through the spinning tunnel. Sparkling colors with twirling lights surround them, engulfing their senses. As they leave the tunnel, they arrive at a ginormous tall mirror.

"What is the cat doing, Liv?"

"IDK, maybe it wants us to follow."

"You silly goose, what like through the mirror? Unlikely, will be splitting atoms anytime soon."

"What the flap jacks! Where did it go, it's like half in and half out the mirror, Victoria?"

The girls come in for a closer look, and the nose and whiskers of the cat poke through the mirror twitching back and forth. The cat comes through the mirror as it paces back and forth, meowing franticly. The girls watch as the cat walks through the mirror again into another dimension, as it disappears into the mirror it cries.

"Meow….Meow…. Meoooow"

Olivia points at the mirror, an electrifying beam comes from her index finger. It hits the mirror, and the mirror explodes into hundreds of tiny pieces, the cat comes flying out. Then an inward vortex starts pulling at the girls and cat.

This spinning, twirly black hole becomes stronger. Sucking inwards everything from the space around the girls. A long cat cry can be heard as the black cat gets swallowed into the vortex.

""meeeoooowww" slowly fading into silence

"There goes the cat. Hold on to me tight Victoria." says Olivia.

As they hold tight onto each other as their hair flies towards the ominous blackness.

A blinding purple flash engulfs them, and they appear back in front of the unbroken mirror in the transporter room.

"What the heck is that, Sis?" "I don't know Victoria. Did you see that electricity flowing from my finger?"

"I did, and saw the mirror explode into tiny pieces. I have never seen that happen before."

"Vee, I wonder where the cat is trying to take us?"

"I don't know, Liv; And I really don't care, we are in one piece...."

"Well, let's keep this between us, sis."

"Okay, Vee."

They venture further into the back of the store.

"Vee, what is that door for? I have never seen that symbol before.?

"Let's peek. The professor never said, we couldn't go to this one."

"Okay, you go first, Vee."

Victoria opens the door to a pitch-black room. She pulls her wand out and speaks.

"Illumine Noob"

They look up and then around, they find a man-made bat cave with hundreds of little red eyes staring back at them. The bats are startled by their presence.

"Click…. Click…. Click…. Click…" Agitated by the light, they begin to click more franticly.

Click, Click, Click, Click…

Click, Click, Click, Click…..

Olivia, out of nowhere, makes a massive rumble from her tummy. Victoria whispers.

"Sounds as if your stomach is eating itself." The bats get scared and start franticly flying through the room.

"AhhhhHHHH," Olivia screams first running out as fast as her feet will take her.

Victoria darts out of the room on Olivia's heels, and then Olivia slams the door behind them.

Victoria notices a rap tapping of something hanging onto her cloak. She begins to spin in a circle, grabbing at her cloak.

"OMG, get it off me." cries Victoria.

"What, where, what is it?"

"It's a dang bat…Liv…. It's on my back, HELP ME.

"Vee…Well, stop turning, HOLD STILL." Olivia grabs the bat and pulls it off her cloak. She throws it back in the room, as Victoria slams the door shut.

The girls stand there collecting their thoughts and composure. From the sounds of the distressed girls, the two handsome blonde Norse boys arrive.

"What's going on, you two," Björn asks.

"Are you okay? What was the yelling about?" inquired Kacper.

They are all standing in front of the room with all the bats. Across the hall, the group's ears are flooded with unfamiliar sounds.

 crinkle….

    swoosh…. swoosh

        ….crinkle

"Hey everyone, do you hear that?" Björn says as he he turns and looks at the group.

"Yes, I hear it," Kacper responds. "I hear it too," Victoria says, looking at her sister.

Olivia announces. "Yes, it sounds like it's coming from behind that door with the triangle." "We should go in and investigate," Björn says with an intense voice.

"Miss NovaStar, our transporter, says we cannot enter that door." Olivia, the rule follower, explains.

"It's okay. She is in the back room and won't notice if we make it quick," Kacper proclaims."

"Yeah, Olivia, let's have a quick look," Victoria insists.

As they approached the door handle, a giant padlock locked the door. Stand back, guys. I will open it with an unlocking spell." Kacper says.

"Avata Nyt"

The huge padlock magically opens. Björn grabs the door and begins to open the heavy door. All that can be seen by the students is a darkness darker than midnight. They can hear the swoosh … swoosh sound again.

But this time, a clawing scratching sound follows the swoosh sounds, with a rush of rotten stench of warm wet air that engulfs their body. The group stands in astonishment.

Then, two red beady eyes appear, glaring into their souls. "We need light; I cannot see anything but those eyes." Victoria says. As she holds out her hand, she commands the Fire spell.

"firemortus" As a flame is created in Victoria's hands, eight more beady red eyes appear in the dark. The room lights up as the fire grows in her hand.

Olivia gasps and points. "Looks guys a giant thunderbird standing there."

Just a few feet away from the group, this towering 6 and a half foot bird is chained to the floor. As it stands on its hindlimbs, a leather-bound book and a golden glowing object can be seen in the nest as the bird rises.

In the rear distance, the 2 other birds stand up, revealing their glowing objects too. A few feet away, the thunderbird starts to become enraged by their presence. This ghastly bird begins to lunge out at the students, giving out horrifying screeching sounds.

"Screeching and Whirring"

In seconds, it becomes more enraged and begins to thrash and wallop toward the kids… the thrashing sounds are now overwhelming.

The group hollers and screams coming out.

"Ahhh!" Olivia hollers. Thud!

"Whoa!" Bejorn yelps. Bam!

"Ouch!" Kacper says. Crash!

"Oof!" Victoria cries out.

"Bang!"

They meet Lampfry standing in their path.

They tumble all on top of one another, with Lampfry on the bottom. Lampfry shrieks out, as he gasps for air. "Get… off me… you're… crushing me."

Björn closes the heavy steel black door, and Kacper belts out another incantation to lock the padlock. **"Lukko Alas,"**

Miss NovaStar appears from the back, almost within reach of the students. Lampfry is the last one to get up. He knocks over one of the mirrors, which crashes into two other mirrors.

SHATTER! CRASH!

Everyone can hear the Thunderbirds in the other room shrieking and making an alarming sound.

SHRIEK!

Gigi takes her wand out.

TAP! TAP! TAP!

She mumbled something; the kids could not make out. The chaotic shrieks of the birds from the room went silent.

Victoria starts to insult Lampfry. "Ha ha, you're getting 7 years of bad luck. NO! Make that 21 years. You're such a klutz; go figure, you always make trouble wherever you go."

Lampfry is quick to respond. "If you guys had not fumbled into me, I would have never broken the mirrors, getting up. Victoria, that's your bad luck, not mine."

Miss NovaStar inquired. "How did you get tackled, Lampfry?"

Before Lampfry can answer, Björn speaks up. "We were just playing around teach, weren't we Lampfry." Glaring at him with eyes of you better not tell otherwise I will get you after class.

Lampfry politely went with the group's cue.

"Yes, Miss NovaStar, we were just fooling around; I am sorry for breaking the mirrors." Professor Gigi waved her wand in a figure eight and spoke.

"Prismatic Revival" instantly the mirrors repair themselves.

Victoria changes the subject. "When are we leaving? I have to get my new broom before class tomorrow."

The professor ignoring Victoria's impatience. "Well, class, if everyone is okay, let's get lined up and ready for the transcendence Mirror."

They all gather in a circle, holding hands. The transporting teacher, Gigi, moves her runic ring from her index finger and places it on her ring finger. Dials it into the Firebird runic symbol of Manu`ahi Summit. She says this charm.

"By mystic forces, I cast my plea,

Grant me passage to realms unseen.

Transport our spirits to a sacred place,

through the veils of time and space.

With this spell, our journey begins."

The petal stool they are standing on rises upward to the opening above, and they are transported to the Manu`ahi Summit.

Upon arriving at the summit, they arrive with their hands up in the W formation, ensuring the evil Pixies don't attack them, thinking they are intruders.

Victoria gets her new broomstick, Olivia finds some much-needed potion supplies, and Lampfey gets his new robe since he caught his on fire in Potions and Brews 101. The Nordic exchange students get their talismans and amulets for the end-of-summer project they are working on.

After a couple of hours all the students retrieve their supplies, they head back to the school, arriving one by one, coming through the mirror they left through minutes before.

Victoria expresses her gratitude. "Thank you, Miss NovaStar."

"Thank you, Professor GiGi, for your time; it was a pleasure," Lampfry says.

The Nordic exchange students also demonstrate profound appreciation by thanking the teacher in their native tongue.

"**Merci** Professor GiGi **pour votre temps, c'est un plaisir.**"

While the kids head to class and begin their regular routine, the headmaster takes over the microphone and summons the girls.

"Willow, Trinity, and Kalei, please report to the headmaster's office." The trio appears in the Headmaster's office. All are wide-eyed and sit with inquisitive looks on their faces.

"My young Wixan's, I have an important challenge for you three. We are experiencing the toxicity of the underworld at Telamisis. Someone or something has poisoned the Life Brook here on the island."

"Ohhh," says Trinity.

"How can we help?" asks Kalei.

"Pardon me, Sir, I don't understand…. How can we help? We are only first-year students." Willow says with a distressed face.

"Well, girls, I choose you three because of your tenacity since you arrived at WillowBrook. I have confidence that you three will bring the magic back to our Life Brook."

"Okay, I am up for the adventure; what about you two? Inquisitively, Trinity asks. Sir, what does this task involve?"

The headmaster explains in detail. "I need you three to go to Capricee's Cottage and ask her for a vile of Vitality to restore the Vitality Brook to its original state."

As Crowley and Vanderbuilt stand before the girls, Crowley pulls out three Talismans. She speaks as protection over the amulets.

"Novos De La Coat."

Then she gives them to Vanderbuilt as he reaches his hand out.

All the crystals on the amulets are glowing.

He hands one out to each girl, giving them a special protection amulet true to their spirit. Willow receives an Amethysts, Kalei receives a Green Emerald, and Trinity receives an Opal.

"May these Amulets give you strength and the protection of the earth, to surround each of you and protect you on your quest, as Hades and his DeathWeavers move about the island."

The girls look at each other with a surprised look as if to say. "*Is this really happening?*"

"You will leave before daybreak tomorrow. May the sunrise give you the light to lead you to Capricee's Cottage without danger and distress? Ex Element Director is a strong Wixan that will know the right Elixir to correct the poison in the waters."

Chapter Thirty-Five
The Brook of Despair

The trio sets out on their adventure. They come upon the forest looking lifeless full of despair.

"Trinity, it looks like the morning sun is fighting against the branches of the trees. It is beautiful but a little spooky, as the half-light pokes through our path."

"Willow, I agree. It feels a little eerie. Like it is conspiring to keep secrets of the forest."

"Do you guys see this? The shadows dancing on our path? I can hear the soft whispers of the trees." says Kalei.

"Well, no matter Kalei, as the Wixan'teers we were picked for this quest."

"I feel like there's something evil, a bad presence, trying to mess up everything that WillowBrook stands for," Trinity says.

The three friends arrive at the Brook and look at each other in shock. Trinity turns to the other two girls.

"Who would bring such evil to our Vitality Brook? It looks disgusting, murky, and ruined. This red-colored water looks like a river of blood."

"Yes, you're right, Trin. I thought the headmaster was overreacting, but he was right; evil has escaped the Hollow." says Kalei.

"Well, let's keep going; we need to find Capricee's cottage like ASAP and figure out how to bring its vitality back," says Trinity.

The girls keep on their walk, they stay on the path, its curvy with crowding trees that hang over the road. Like they are warning weary travelers, we will reach in and grab your soul, if you come any further."

Every step seemed to echo loudly, and the further they went, the narrower the path got, swallowed by creeping vines and trees that looked like creepy fingers reaching out to grab them. The once lively forest now, with an eerie silence, as if the forest itself was holding its breath, waiting for something scary to happen.

Willow points to the path ahead of them. She asks Kalei. "Do you see that ominous mist ahead of us,"

"What does this mean, Trinity? Let's go back to school, my stomach feels a little queasy."

"No, Kalei, the school is counting on us. We must find Capricee."

"I don't know. The fog is rolling in and hiding our path; everything looks different. I am getting an uneasy feeling about this too." Says Trinity.

As the group makes it deeper into the forest, Willow yells out.

"Do you two hear that? I hear whispers of malevolence echoing, they are saying "Go back now; you are not welcome… I will suck the Mana right out of you if you continue.""

Kalei grabs Trinity's shoulder, "Look at your talisman, its glowing."

 Trinity grabs the talisman, looking at the other two with a scowl. "Yes, I hear it too; this feels unsafe. Look at your and Willow's talisman, they are also glowing."

The strange sounds echo from the forest's depths, reverberating through the air. Unearthly cries and chilling whispers claw at the trio's senses, creating an unsettling symphony that permeates the island's core.

DE Daniel

"I think we should go back," says Trinity.

Willow and Kalei look at her with encouraging faces.

"We have to keep going. Our school is counting on us," says Kalei.

"We need to finish what we started. The headmaster wouldn't have sent us on this quest if he didn't think we could do it. He believes in us, and we should believe in ourselves too," says Willow.

As the girls come out of the tree-filled forest, they approach the island's east side, now hearing the waves crash and the smell of sea salt fills the air.

"Kalei, what are those black blobby things? It looks like pockets of mist has turned to darkness and has taken on a malevolent form." ask Willow.

"Trinity says, "The headmaster, warned us about those beasts. Those beings are SoulWalkers; their ghoulish form is floating at the water's edge."

"Should we hide?" asks Willow, "Look at the hollow eyes; their full of despair."

Hey Kalei, let's avoid the beach. We'll go this way instead, back into the forest on the path," Trinity whispered. She seemed to know something like she had eyes everywhere.

Kalei says, "Those SoulWalkers remind us of the danger in these woods. Let's keep watch, everyone."

As Willow, Kalei, and Trinity explored deeper into Solaris Island, they sensed more than just physical threats. There is something dark, something sneaky, trying to mess with the island's magic.

Together, they advance, their souls intertwined with the regal power of water. Guided by their connection to the elements, the Wixan'teers emerge as beacons of hope. Amidst Hades' underworld, ready to confront the malevolence and Spector threats that is to consume their land.

Their hearts beat in unison to unveil the cottage they are searching for.

"Hey, do you guys see that flickering light ahead? Maybe that's Capricee's Cottage?" Trinity pointed ahead eagerly, her voice carrying a mix of excitement and curiosity as they approached the cottage nestled deep in the woods.

As they draw nearer, a boa constrictor slithers down from a tree branch directly in their path, catching them off guard.

"Um, excuse me," Willow stammered, her voice crackling nervously. "Could you, uh, help us? We're looking for Capricee's Cottage."

The snake turned its head to regard them with an amused glint in its eye. "And who might you three be, venturing into my mystical land?" it hissed, its tone surprisingly articulate for a snake.

Trinity couldn't help but voice her astonishment. "Wait, you can talk? But you're a snake!"

"In this enchanted realm, all creatures possess the gift of speech," the snake replied nonchalantly. "I am Taro. What brings you three to Capricee's Cottage?"

Trinity took a breath, explaining their mission earnestly. "We've come to seek answers about how to restore the life force to the bubbling brook. It's been tainted by some evil Spector of the Forest Hollows."

Taro nods knowingly, his scales shimmering faintly in the dappled light filtering through the trees. "Ah, you must beware of Professor Capricee.

Once in good standing of the twelve elements, she was cast out long ago for her dark intentions. She can see the future, past and present and her lies can entwine your minds, leading you astray."

Willow shivered, exchanging a worried glance with Kalei. "So, she's dangerous?"

"Indeed," Taro replies gravely, his tongue flickering thoughtfully. "Procee`zzz with caution, for she may twist`ssst truths`zzz and deceive with illusions`zzz."

The girls exchanged uneasy looks, realizing the gravity of their quest. They were about to enter a realm where reality and deception intertwined—a place where even a talking snake could be both ally and adversary.

"I am baffled. Why would our headmaster send us here to speak with Capricee to find the cure for our sickly Brook if she were banished to the forest?" Willow inquires.

"Do not get it twisted; I understand the peril the school is in with losing its AiraGuard Dome and the life force of the vitality brook, but Capricee should not be trusted."

The girls' necklaces start to glow and heat up. They look at each other strangely, then grab their Talismans.

"Come on you too. Let's get going," says Kalei.

As they approach the door, the rustling in the woods grows louder and more intense, as though the very trees are trying to speak to the group of girls; a soft voice echoes through the leaves. The wind whispers, "Beware…The truth lays in the forest, and the heart of the woods holds the key."

Kalei looks up and yells, "Ahhh!" thrashing her hands about. Willow dunks with a near miss.

Trinity says with ease, "it's just a colony of bats." She looks up at the inlay of the porch. "I think they are all gone. You can relax."

The door to the cottage is detailed with a large reef of pine branches embedded with garlic cloves, firedrake wing clippings, and sage bundles. Willow takes hold of the brass Owl with ruby-red eyes.

"Rat-a-tat-tat"

"Rat-a-tat-tat"

"Rat-a-tat-tat"

This ancient door knocker is an owl, it has its wings spread like they are in flight. Willow taps it three times, and the door opens. The girls exchange glances, feeling frightened and curious. The Talisman glows brighter around their necks, they push open the creaking door of the cottage and step inside.

Chapter Thirty-Six
In the Shadow of Capricee

The interior is dimly lit, with shelves filled with ancient relics, mysterious artifacts, and flickering candles that cast dancing shadows on the walls.

A figure emerges from the shadows, revealing the unmistakable form of an elder woman with gray, flowing hair cascading down her back. Instead of bearing runic symbols or wearing a robe, she is adorned in traditional Vietnamese attire. She wears an **áo dài,** a long, elegant tunic with intricate embroidery that tells stories of ancient legends and cultural heritage. The fabric shimmers in the dim light, reflecting hues of deep indigo and rich crimson. Her black silk pants flow gracefully as she moves, complementing the tunic's sophistication.

Her head is crowned with a **non la**, the iconic conical hat woven from palm leaves, shielding her sharp and intense eyes, lined with age and experience, hold a depth that contradicts the ominous tales from Taro. Her gaze is piercing yet compassionate, revealing a lifetime of stories and unspoken truths.

As she speaks, her voice carries an air of both weariness and wisdom, each word resonating with the weight of years gone by and the knowledge of forgotten times.

"Welcome, young ones," They are stunned for words.

Trinity takes hold of the situation. "Pardon us, madam, we are looking for Capricee. Our headmaster told us we could find her at this cottage."

"Ah, I see... you both made it to WillowBrook after our chat. I'm glad you took heed of my briefing from the Snowball camping trip, the one we had during your visit to Lake la Russo."

As she speaks these words, the air around them begins to shimmer and glow with a soft, ethereal light. Trinity looks at the other two in surprise at the display of the shimmering glow that encircles all of them.

"Come sit with me, I have been expecting you. By the way, it is a great honor to see you have chosen WillowBrook. Wixan`teers your path is full of learning, enlightenment, compassion, and Great MANA."

The cauldron is brewing, and the scent of vanilla and mint fills the air. The girls sit at the thick table, a 6ft circular slab from a Sequoia tree. The slab is etched with symbolic carvings that make an outer ring on the table.

"Would you ladies like some fresh **(gỏi cuốn)** Vietnamese Spring Roll with peanut sauce? Before we start with our deep conversation, let me put on some peppermint tea," says Mrs. Gabrielle Capricee.

As they sit down, the tea kettle rocker can be heard, "tis tis tis,"

"tis tis tis,"

"tis tis tis tis,"

Before long, the water is rolling with a full boil, with a strong hissing sound. Capricee hands everyone their **gỏi cuốn** and tea, ready to tackle the pressing issue.

"Now we are feeding our soul with nutritious and delicious food. So, girls, let us get down to business, what can I help you with?"

"Well, you see, you know WillowBrook has had a treaty with Forest Hollows for quite some time now.

The promises between Sir Charles Brook and Solaris Island, before he broke ground," Kalei announces.

Trinity interjects and takes over the conversation, with a sternness "An evil entity has poisoned the life waters of the Vitality Brook, causing our AiraGuard Dome, the force field has been breached. Our professors have not found a cure to rebuild the Matrix of the protection dome. The dome and the Bubbling Vitality Brook have lost their magical powers due to the loss of their ebb and flow caused by the toxic crimson tide."

Willow hesitates for a moment, then clears her throat. "We were told you might have a cure for the sickly brook."

Capricee nods slowly, her gaze fixed on Willow's glowing Talisman.

"Yes, your brook's ailment is a consequence of the imbalance that plagues not just WillowBrook, but the very elements that govern this realm.

Spector has been trying to take the Mana from the light beings of the island since its creation. The headmaster has sent you three here, to see if I can redeem myself to be a good Enchantress."

You see long ago, I sought to harness the power of those elements for my own gain, and in doing so, I set off a chain of events that led to my exile."

Kalei cannot help but ask. "But why should we trust you now? After everything that has been said about you?"

Capricee sighs, a hint of remorse in her expression. "Because, my dear, I have realized the gravity of my mistakes. I have spent years in solitude, learning the ways of nature and attempting to mend the damage I caused. You should not believe all that is told by the grapevine, and the headmaster believes I hold the key to its restoration."

As Capricee speaks, the necklace around Willow's neck glows more intensely and is pulsating. It responds to the truth in the former professor's words.

The room fills with warm, soothing energy, and the girls feel a sense of connection to the very heart of the woods.

"Time is of the essence," Capricee urges. "The forces that threaten WillowBrook grow stronger with each passing moment. Together, we must embark on a journey to restore the elements, heal the Brook, and save your school."

Willow and Kalei exchange another glance, a silent telepathic conversation passes between them despite their initial doubts and Taro's warning. "Lei Lei, I feel she can be trusted,"

"Yeah Will, I think she is trying to redeem herself too, in the OEM." (Order of the 12 Elements Ministry)

With a sturdy nod, Willow takes her glance from Kalei to Capricee and speaks.

"How can we assist you in ensuring the well-being of our school and community, promoting harmony among students, and growing their Mana?"

Chapter Thirty-Seven
The Whispered Truth of Capri'cee

Mrs. Capricee, do you know why or who is sabotaging the force field and the brook?" Willow asks.

"Well ladies, I can tell you that. There is much talk that Aynat and Willis, they are bringing more terror and wrath to harm all those at WillowBrook. She has been causing havoc at the 12 Elements Ministry for over a decade."

"So, she may have something to do with the Brook turning and the protection barrier collapse. You see, the old saying holds true."

"Heaven has no rage like love to hatred turned, nor hell a fury like a woman scorned."

"Now, you all must understand that Aynat is a good Wixan when I was part of the Order of the 12 elements. However, after Aynat is courted by the great Sir Charles Brook, her father finds out about this relationship; he is against this suitor. Aynat continues to see Charles behind her father's back, which enrages Raphael. He forbids her to see him anymore, thus causing Aynat to elope in the middle of the night on May 15th, 2008."

"She then leaves home and moves in with him to the Abby in England. Within 2 months of marriage, she becomes pregnant with a child. When her father finds out, he raises his wand at her, wanting to end the life of her husband.

She loves Charles so deeply and wants to do anything to stop her father from trying to end her mate. Her magic is too weak, not strong enough to ward off the great wizard's power of her father's wrath. So, she calls the dark forces and makes a deal with Telamisis at Iris."

The exchange is that Telamisis makes a deal to undo the curse on her soul. She would have to produce a first-born male child. She agrees to the terms and promises to give her first male born to the dark force of Iris. Telamisis saves her husband from Raphael's wrath.

Unknowingly, by this action, Aynat sells her own soul to the Underworld of Hades when she makes this deal with Telamisis.

Her husband dissolves the marriage by the time her child is born. He is abused mentally and physically by this woman.

Her attitude becomes scornful and cold-hearted after Spector takes over her once cheerful, happy, and kind soul. Years later, Spector takes over every inch of her mind and soul."

"There are reports that Charlas's abuse is at the pinnacle, days before they file for divorce. The tales are that he is scolded with a hot pot of soup, and it disfigures his left arm and a portion of his neck from the 3rd-degree burns. Others report hitting him with things when he goes against the scorned Aynat and her wishes."

"There is an even more horrible story that after Charles demands that when the baby is born, he wants full father's rights and primary custody, and he tells Aynat that her rage makes her unfit to be a parent. This causes Aynat to go into full-blown rage; she goes off-kilter and gets really spicy in his sleep."

"He wakes again to her cray cray-ness and fights her off; Charles gains control over the spicy situation and flees the house without any more violence from his spouse."

"However, this frightens Charles so much by her aggressively hot behavior that he gets a police escort to get his stuff straight away and leaves Aynat. Not because he doesn't love his unborn child, but because of the wrath of Aynat and her father, it is too dangerous."

"Not to be rude, madam, but what does this story have to do with the crimson-red water at the Brook?" asks Trinity.

"Well, young Wixan, the Vitality Brook holds healing powers. You see Aynat's plans of a diabolical takeover at WillowBrook. So, this sabotage of the healing waters seems like her first big move. Disabling the AiraGuard so Hades SoulWalkers could walk the school and scoop up any unsuspecting souls to build a bigger army of the Underworld… Ladies, WillowBrook is in distress."

"Why has she chosen WillowBrook? We are on an island in the middle of nowhere," asks Kalei.

"You three have read why Sir Charles Brook built the school in the first place, right?"

Trinity responds in her know-it-all way. "Well, of course, who doesn't read the school handbook in the first week."

Willow shuts Trinity showiness down and drives the conversation her way. "Kalei and I went to the moving library and read up on Sir Charles Brook of England; if I am correct, it states that on the first page."

"I believe it goes something like this. (I dedicate this school to WillowBrook. To my lost child, may one day she come here to study and expand her horizons. Learning the ways of true Mana and forming a great bond with the elements and its ministry."

Kalei interjects. "That is right, Willow, and if I remember correctly, the school's Mission Statement.

WillowBrook's guiding light is here to redirect students into their higher being of self-awareness. Inspiring them to become their best self and be self-aware of all around them."

"Oooohh, I now see the relevance. If the dark ones remove the powerful traits of WillowBrook, it will be easier to destroy the school," says Willow.

"Mrs. Capricee, not to change the subject, but I understand you can see past, present, and future of our realm. Have you heard anything about me or my parents?" Willow asks.

"My dear child, I cannot tell you anything other than you are an exceptional child, and many people have been waiting for you to turn of age. You will find all there is to know when it is the right time. Until then, hone in on your powers and learn as much magic as possible. There will come a day when you need to be your strongest to fight the evil powers that are to come to try to destroy WillowBrook."

Willow and the girls' faces turn from happy to puzzled and confused, and they are growing increasingly concerned that Capricee knows more than she is letting on.

However, the trio has no one else to trust, so they are left with their faith in her hands.

"Well, my dear Wixan's, we must be on our way to making a tincture for the Brook. The natural balance and the protection dome need to be restored as soon as possible," Explains Capricee.

"I have another question, Mrs. Capericee. Do you know why I received this Malachite Metatron necklace? What does it mean?" Willow asks.

"Once again, my child, everything will come full circle in due time. I cannot tell much, but never take it off; it's for protection." Capricee enlightens her.

"OK, that's great that we got that out the way. But back to the task at hand. Mrs. Capricee, how do we return power to the Brook?" inquires Trinity.

"Well, girls, let me combine a concoction to help the school." Capricee goes to the cauldron, adds a few things, stirs it, and then adds some Dragon's breath and a few hairs from Gullinbursti, the golden Bore.

'Sizzel…"

After the bubbling sizzle clears, a cloud of green smoke rolls up from the cauldron. She ladles out a putrid-smelling liquid into two vials, closes them with a cork, and melts red wax on top of it to ensure a tight seal. She hands these vials to Kalei.

"Go to the Brook, open one of the bottles, and pour it into the Bubbling Brook. This concoction should work. Repeat this incantation!"

"Aegis solace eternus"

"Only then will the magic work and the spell be broken, returning the vitality to the brook."

"However, if it does not, it will need tears from a fair maiden, true of heart and pure in spirit. Her tears will be collected and mixed with the Brook with the second vile. Use this spell again to reverse the damage done by the dark ones."

"Ok, we are to take this vile to the brook, but I have another question before we go?" Willow said.

"I overheard some students talk about a mirror that can transport you to the past and the future?" Willow replied.

"Well, dear child, you must be certain you want to know the past…. You see, our higher power will often keep us from emotional harm by keeping our past a secret."

"I want to know more about my parents; I don't know anything about my father or my mother, for that matter. I want to know if I have siblings, cousins, grandparents, aunts, or uncles.

I do not even know the nationality to which I am closest related too. The only thing I have to show for my existence is this Malachite Metatron's Cube given to me when Miss Juno adopted me."

"Willow, you can only use the mirror if properly trained. Also, as I remember, they teach about these mirrors in your 3rd year of teaching. So, you must have patience."

"Well, my dear children of WillowBrook, you must be on your way to the Brook. The natural balance and the protection dome need to be restored as soon as possible," Capricee firmly instructs them.

"Come on, let's get on our way, you two," Willow says to Trinity and Kalei. They head out of the cottage, and Taro drops before them.

"Sizzz! Hello again Wixan's. Did you find the information that you were seeking or were they all Lie'zzz and deceit."

"Taro, she was truthful… no lies… just wisdom. We did discover what we were searching for. Capricee has been instrumental in guiding us on initiating the restoration process and restoring balance to the Brook and Air`a Guard dome at WillowBrook." Says Trinity.

"That is good to hear, ladies, but as I said before, beware, she cannot be trusted," Taro warns them.

"We need to get to the Brook. Stop fussing with this snake. You know snakes can't be trusted," says Trinity.

Chapter Thirty-Eight
The Tears of the True Heart

They continue their travels to the Brook; upon arrival, they discover that the crimson water has turned from the blood red flow to a sludgy tar.

DC Daniel

"The Brook is no longer bubbling; rather, the water is stagnant." Kalei exclaims.

"Hurry, Willow. There is no time to waste. Look what has happened. Are we too late to save the Brook?" Trinity asks.

"I am sure Capericee potion will work, but we must hurry." Kalei hands Willow one of the vials, Willow breaks the red wax seal, and removes the cork. The awful stench of the liquid lingers in the air, and she pours it into the Brook without haste. Then speaks the incantation.

"Aegis solace eternus"

"What is happening? I can see the water turning from red to black," Kalei says with a discerned look on her face.

Trinity screams. "Ahhh! Look over there. I see the matrix of the force field of the dome rebuilding."

"Yes, Willow, it is working." Says Trinity.

"Trinity! Willow look! There are still holes in the protection dome."

"Oh my gosh, Trinity, the Brook is now a black tar. What are we going to do?" asks Kalei.

"This cannot be good, guys. We need to report back to Headmaster Vanderbuilt as soon as possible," responds Willow.

As they made their way towards the headmaster's office, they glanced back at the once lively and bubbling Brook, now transformed into a stagnant, viscous tar, devoid of movement. They all return to campus to find Professor Crowley pacing back and forth in the courtyard with a disgruntled look on her face.

"Professor!" Screams Trinity.

"Professor!" Yells Kalei.

All the girls bellow out in sync. "We are in grave danger; where's the headmaster?"

"I last saw him in his office. Did you guys get repair the vitality to the Brook?"

"No time to explain; we must find the headmaster immediately." Says Willow.

As they report back to the headmaster. "Great job, girls… did it work?"

"No sir, it turned the Vitality brook into black muddy sludge." Says Willow.

Things are looking bleak for WillowBrook. Mr. Vanderbuilt has a grim face as if they are facing grave danger.

Trinity speaks up. "It looks like the protection dome is trying to rebuild, but there are gaping holes in it."

"Well, did Capricee say what would work?"

"Well, Mr. Vanderbuilt, she said if the first vile didn't work, we should try the second vile with the tears of a fair maiden, true of heart and pure in spirit. Her tears must be collected and added to the Brook simultaneously with the second vile. She said she was most certain it would work," says Trinity.

"Who is a fair maiden with a pure heart?" asks Willow.

"Willow, it's funny that you ask. I can't think of anyone more fitting than you."

"Professor, I don't understand; I am not a fair maiden; I don't have a true heart, nor is my spirit pure. I have deep-seated issues from my troubled childhood."

"Yes, Willow, your heart is pure. Your past can't change what's in your heart. However, the problem is that you need to give us your tears."

"Headmaster, how do you think we could make this happen?" asks Kalei.

DC Daniel

"Well, Willow, do you have anything that occasionally makes you sad?"

"No, not really. My past is not my final destination. I am the happiest I have ever been. My cup is run'neth over. My life is full of friends, professors who love me, and a school that accepts me. How can I be sad about that?"

"Girls, can you think of anything that would make Willow sad?"

"No, sir. Willow is the most upbeat and happy person I know." Says Kalei.

"Thank you for nothing, Kalei; I thought I was your favorite." Says Trinity.

"You both are my best friends; I didn't mean it like that." Trinity is still feeling sad about Kalei's statement. Her face goes from sad to angry, and without notice, she kicks Willow in the shin as hard as she can.

"Wham!"

"Ouch!"

Willow grabs her knee and starts to cry because of the pain.

"What the heck, Trinity? Why would you hurt your bestie?"

She continues crying, with full flow streaming from her face.

"Quick, Kalei collect her tears." says Vanderbuilt.

Once Kalei collects her tears. Trinity runs up to her and hugs

her. "I am so sooo sorry, I kicked you, Willow, but we needed

your tears. And you said it yourself; you are not saddened by

anything. So, I kicked you so we can save the school from

the dark ones of the Underworld."

"I understand, Trinity, but please never do that again. Look

at the knot on my shin."

"Thank you, Willow, for taking one for the team." Says

Vanderbuilt. "Now girls hurry, take the tears and the vile, and

go to the Brook immediately."

The girls head to the Brook. Once they arrive, Kalei hands Willow the tube of tears, and Trinity hands Capricee's vile to her.

"OK, here goes nothing; cross your finger that this works." She pours the mixture into the Brook. And says the incantation.

"Aegis solace eternus"

"It's working! It's working… look the Brook is changing colors.".

Kalei starts to dance around, yelling "It's clearing up and bubbling once again. I knew we had the power to help."

They all look at one another and give each other a high five. Now that the Vitality Brook is back to normal, they look up at the Aira Guard Dome, which is rebuilding with no holes. As it starts to interlock the matrix, they head back to the school.

Upon arrival, they can hear kids laughing and music playing. They enter the courtyard, and the girls are surrounded by their fellow Wixan's.

Their classmates pick the girls up over their heads, carrying them around the courtyard like they won the best sports game ever. They celebrate WillowBrook's Vitality Brook and the AiraGuard Dome's return to a safe status.

As they're being paraded around, one of the kids shouts, "Three cheers to these girls,

"Hip Hip Hooray!" "Hip Hip Hooray!" "Hip Hip Hooray!"

They all burst into laughter, enjoying the moment of victory and camaraderie.

DC Daniel

Chapter Thirty-Nine
Lampfry's Shellfish Shock

Willow steps into the magnificent Great Hall for the dinner of the Summer Solstice. The enchanting atmosphere embraced her as if the hall itself welcomed her presence.

Kalei stylishly walks up to her and begins to ramble.

"Wow, Will, can you believe it's our first Summer Solstice together?"

Trinity interrupts, breaking the connection and pointing across the hall.

"Have you peeped at the Norwegian twins lately? They're straight-up fresh, and their fashion game is on point!"

"Whoa, did Bejorn just give you the eye, Willow?"

Trinity nudges her friend, a mischievous grin spreading across her face.

"Looks like someone's got a crush on you!"

As Willow looks around, she feels amazed by how beautiful everything was. Laughter and happiness fill the air, mixing with the soft light from the candles that made the room glow warmly. Willow's eyes sparkle with joy as she sees her classmates, their faces light up with big smiles of pure happiness.

Trinity's attention drifts to the tables adorned with mouthwatering dishes.

A smile tugs at the corners of her lips as she admires the succulent roasted chickens, their golden exteriors emitting an irresistible aroma.

Nearby platters of baked fish and heaps of sea scallops called out, tempting all who looked at them. The vivid assortment of vegetables held her gaze, their colorful array forming a breathtaking display of natural splendor.

The yummy smells made her stomach grumble as Kalei reached towards the pastry trays. She couldn't resist peeking at the tower of juicy fruits, practically drooling at the sight.

Kacper said, "Oh boy, those creamy mashed potatoes and warm bread rolls look so good; they are calling my name!" as he helps himself to the floating food tray.

As everyone settles at their designated floating Rombus disks in the Great Hall, Willow, Trinity, Kalei, Lampfrey, Bejorn, and Kacper surrounds in a cozy atmosphere.

The warmth of friendship and positive energy envelops them like a comforting hug, making them feel right at home.

Still basking in the glow of love and companionship, Willow couldn't help but smile at the sight of her friends gathered around her.

Meanwhile, Lampfrey's eyes lit up with anticipation as he reached for one of the floating food trays passing by the tables. Among the tempting offerings, his gaze fixates on a platter of succulent sea scallops, their aroma wafting through the air. The anticipation of tasting those delicious morsels sent a thrill through him, adding to the excitement of the evening's festivities.

"Yum! I can't resist grabbing a couple of these tasty shellfish; they're my absolute favorite," exclaimed Lampfry, his mouth watering with anticipation. Little did he know that the sea scallops he so eagerly devours are a hidden danger invisible to his eyes.

Unaware of the unfortunate chain of events, Lampfry savors the flavor, oblivious to the impending peril.

Within a mere ten minutes, the insidious grip of shellfish allergies tightens around him, unleashing a sudden onslaught of symptoms upon his unsuspecting body.

Waves of nausea crash over Lampfry like a relentless storm, threatening to overwhelm him entirely.

"What's the matter, Lampfry? You look as pale as a ghost," remarked Kalei, concern etched into her features.

"Oh, Kalei, my stomach is in knots," groaned Lampfry, his voice strains with discomfort. "I'm feeling so sick—I've never felt this awful before. It's like Satan himself is taking over my body."

"What do you think is wrong with Lampfry?" Willow asks with concern, looking at the other two girls.

Lampfry's voice echoed through the room in distress. "Ohhhh, if I don't move soon, I'm gonna be sick everywhere, probably all over you three," he groans, his face contorts with discomfort. "Ohhhh... It feels like my stomach getting twisted inside out."

"It hurts so bad," he adds, his voice strained by pain. Beads of sweat form on his forehead, and his skin took on a sickly greenish-blue hue as he doubles over, rocking back and forth, moaning in agony.

Unable to bear it any longer, Lampfry clamps a hand over his mouth and dashes towards the lavatory, leaving a trail of green liquid in his wake. The Professor hurries after him, concern etched on his face.

Minutes later, the children watch in awe as one of the Aeloria Sentinels appears as it rushes into the laboratory. A radiant figure with wings that shimmer in myriad colors like a living kaleidoscope.

She glides gracefully, leaving behind a trail of shimmering light as she went about helping and comforting others in need.

Kalei, her heart fills with empathy for Lampfry, spoke softly. "No matter what he's going through, I'm sure he'll come back with a tale to share—about his encounter with the Aeloria and the peace and healing he found."

Name: Aeloria the Healing Sentinel

DC Daniel

Description: Aeloria is a majestic and ethereal being who manifests compassion and protection. She appears as a luminous figure with iridescent wings that shimmer like a kaleidoscope of colors.

Aeloria envelop students in her wings, creating a protective cocoon that shields them from further harm. This cocoon also emanates a calming energy, easing fear and anxiety.

Once, Professor Ripley emerges from the boys' bathroom with one of the Aeloria Sentinels. The kids see Lampfry being carried by its wings, floating past them. He has a bag over his mouth heaving.

When they walk out of the big hall, everyone watches him spew. His body shakes as he tries to eliminate the bad stuff inside him. Each time he spews, it reminds him painfully of his new allergy to shellfish, which makes him sick like this. He looks ill; his skin is bluish-green, and he is curled up like a baby heaving in the wings of the Sentinel.

After Lampfry leaves for the infirmary, Kacper and Bejorn waste no time in darting towards the serving table, their eyes alight with excitement at the prospect of indulging in the moving Jello bats and Dragon's Breath candy. With their treats in hand, The trio ventures off to the island's north shore, looking for Catacorns for the Phantom Cloak Spell.

Chapter Forty
Catacorns, Cloaks, and Courage

Trinity's demeanor shifts as they tread through the sandy path toward the shore. Her eyes glaze over with a knowing glint as she delves into her reservoir of wisdom.

"Did you know?" Trinity's voice resonates with intrigue as she addresses her companions. "If you take a few ingredients, like 5 drops of scorpion venom, 3 crushed Catacorns, a dash of origami oil, and two black cat whiskers, this combination will create a potent liquid.

When sprayed on the cloak, it releases the veil of Shadows surrounding the Wixan's that use it. This cloaking spell lasts 6 hours."

Trinity knelt among the plethora of Catacorns shells scattered across the beach, her fingers tracing the intricate patterns etched into their surfaces.

Memories of Professor Crowley's lectures flooded her mind, her words echoing like distant waves crashing against the shore.

"I cannot believe there are so many Catacorns on this beach," she murmurs, her voice laced with wonder and disbelief. "This is unheard of. Once, Professor Crowley told me that most people are fortunate to find five of these shells on a mile of beach. And yet, there are at least a hundred within eyesight."

Trinity's attention shifts from the shells to Willow's gaze, seeking assurance from her friend. Willow nods as she emphasizes the gravity of the situation and the rarity they were witnessing.

"I agree, Trinity," Willow whispers, as her voice fills with wonder. "This is something else."

As the trio marveled at the abundance of Catacorn shells, Kalei's voice pierces the moment, directing their attention to the horizon.

"What's that in the distance?" Kalei's voice trembles with worry.

Trinity squints as she follows Kalei's gaze, her breath catching as she spots the looming figure on the horizon.

"Oh, my goodness, you two," Trinity gasps, her voice shaky with fear and excitement. "That's a Zebreth Featherfire. They're rare, hostile, and dangerous flying creatures. And they're headed our way, Trin and Will."

Trinity's heart races as adrenaline surges. This unexpected encounter was about to test not just their knowledge but their bravery and quick thinking. It was a moment that would challenge their friendship and resilience against the unknown.

The Zebreath Featherfire, with its humanoid face adorned with intelligence and curiosity and a chest covered in vibrant bird feathers, was both fascinating and terrifying. Its mighty dragon wings allow it to glide through the sky gracefully, while its zebra-striped body added an eerie elegance. But beneath its captivating exterior lay danger—the Zebreath Featherfire could breathe fire, unleashing flames that could incinerate anything in its path.

"What do you mean, a Zebreath Featherfire?" Willow's voice fills with confusion.

"Look out, Willow!" Trinity's warning came just in time as Willow narrowly avoids a fiery attack.

"Trinity, what do we do? We are in so much danger right now." Willow's voice quivers with uncertainty.

"Yes, Kalei, we're in danger. We need to unify our minds, bodies, and spirits to protect ourselves," Trinity urges.

"Quick, grab my hand."

DC Daniel

"Kalei, use your whistle to call HydroKnox, your water guardian," Willow instructed urgently.

As Kalei pulls out her whistle and blows into it, a series of notes echoes through the air. Instantly, she is connected to HydroKnox through a telepathic connection.

"I hear you; I am on my way. If you remember to use the Aqua Protection Dome Spell."

Within a minute or two, HydroKnox could be seen approaching with great agility and speed on the horizon. The three Wixan's, strong in arms, gathered in a circle, wands in hand, ready for the Zebreath Featherfire's wrath.

The trio spoke in unison.

"Aquuaquellis"

Just then, HydroKnox breaches himself out of the water, ready for head-to-head combat with the Zebreath. The first Zebreath spews out the fury of fire toward HydroKnox. He dove deep into the water, narrowly avoiding being scorched. In retaliation, he forces himself out of the water, using the force of his tail, smacks into one of them out. The creature falls into the water.

"Swipp"

"Splash"

He quickly entangles himself around it, taking the creature to the bottom of the sea, to its demise.

Meanwhile, the trio maintains the **"Aquuaquellis"** protection dome over themselves. The other Zebreath Featherfire tries to burn them to a crisp as it swoops down on them, but the protection barrier holds steadfast.

"Acromesis DeNuglar," Kalei cast her water spell.

As Kalei shouted the Acromesis spell, an immense wave came from the ocean and engulfs the second Zebreath Featherfire. Bringing it to the water, it fails to release itself from the watery abyss. HydroKnox wraps himself around the creature to duplicate his action. The Zebreath thrashes back and forth, trying to free itself from the grips of the long serpent. Without success, HydroKnox's grips were too powerful, and he plummets to the bottom of the sea floor once again, drowning the second creature.

The girls scream for joy as they were now safe from the danger that once threatened them.

HydroKnox came to the ocean's edge, and the girls met him there to thank him for coming to the rescue in their time of need. Kalei gently rubs the top of his blue head, leans in, and gives him a smooch.

"Thank you for coming to our rescue."

"Kalei. I am your protector and will always be here when you need me."

HydroKnox slips back into the water, giving a series of audible sonar clicks and a big splash.

The girls venture back to the campus with their Catacorns

and the supplies they were after, feeling close to HydroKnox.

Feeling empowered, they placed their hands in a circle.

And said in perfect rhythm.

"1"

"2"

"3"

"All for one, and one for all! We are the Wixan'teers Three

times three! Blessed be, everyone around me and including

me."

"Protection around you, be with you, and be with me!"

"Rahhh"

"Rahhh!"

"Rahhh"

Their pinky fingers intertwine, uniting in a dosey~doe, as they all gracefully execute an underarm turn as they depart from their celebration.

DC Daniel

Chapter Forty-One
EchoFlux's Announcement

The girls meet back in the courtyard from their group outing to collect Catacorns. Everyone is in the courtyard and even the ancient oak moves to the center of the yard.

This Oak tree, known as 魔法のオーク (Mahō no Ōku), is ancient, its gnarled branches reaching towards the heavens.

It is said that this tree holds the key to unlocking the magic of the solstice and has been the focal point of the school summer celebrations for generations. The celebration is soon to begin. As dusk descends on the eve of the summer solstice, the Professors and Wixan's gather around the oak tree, their faces illuminated by the warm glow of torchlights.

Appearing out of the crowd, the campus elder **Kenrō 賢老,** the village's wise and revered Japanese matriarch, steps forward. Dressed in her **Kimono (着物),** the traditional Japanese garment known for its intricate patterns and elegant style. It is typically worn for very formal occasions such as cultural events. Her eyes twinkle with a deep knowing, and her voice carries the weight of centuries. She begins to chant in a melodic, ancient language, her words intertwining with the oak tree's essence.

As her voice rises and falls, a hush falls over the crowd, and

a sense of anticipation hangs in the air.

"Solstice fires, spirits bright,

We gather beneath the golden light.

Oak of old, with branches wide,

Grant us your magic; be our guide."

"From sun to moon,

from the sky to earth,

Grant us blessings and rebirth.

As daylight lingers,

spirits play on this sacred solstice day."

"Glowing embers, stars above,

Fill us with your boundless love.

Ancient oak, our hearts entwined,

May your wisdom forever bind."

"In this dance of sun and fire,

We seek your grace, and our hearts aspire.

Renew our souls, make spirits soar,

On this solstice eve, forevermore."

As the final words of the chant are utters, a soft, radiant light envelops the Oak tree 魔法のオーク (Mahō no Ōku).

It spreads like a delicate web, weaving its way through the branches and into the hearts of those who stand witness. A collective gasp ripples through the crowd as the villagers feel the magic of the solstice wash over them, filling them with a sense of wonder and awe.

As the night wears on, the festivities reach a crescendo. Musicians play haunting melodies that echo from another realm, and dancers twirl and sway in graceful harmony.

The bonfire crackles and dances, sending sparks spiraling into the velvety sky. Laughter and joy resonate through the courtyard, carried by the gentle breeze to the farthest corners of WillowBrook.

In the days following the solstice, a transformation begins to take place within the fellow Wixan's. The air crackles with a newfound vitality, and the campus seems to hum with an otherworldly energy. Crops flourish, animals thrive, and the Wixan's themselves feel a renewed sense of purpose and joy.

A week or so goes by as the students buzz about newfound spells they have mastered.

After morning meditation, EchoFlux comes on the intercom.

The announcement comes to the airway….

"Tap… Tap… Tap… Testing 123…"

"Good morning, aspiring Witches and Wizards."

"As the sun stretches its fingers over the horizon, we gather in the east Meadow of wisdom and magic. Today, in morning meditation, embrace the warmth, feel the Earth beneath your feet, and let the essence, like fireflies in the night, ignite your heart with much wisdom and understanding for those around you."

Dit… Dit …Dit… type on typewriter sound. Paper rolls out of the machine, making the sound hot off the press.

"Don't forget students… Sign-up ends at 3 p.m. tomorrow!"

"Calling all Wixan Students…. I REPEAT… Calling all students. It's time for the Quarterly WillowBrook Spellcasting Competition. Please sign up in the Echo Hall today or tomorrow before 3 p.m. The competition is in a few weeks.

DC Daniel

The trio hurry as they head to Echo Hall. They line up with more than 25 other students. When they get up to the table, Crowley pulls her glasses down and glares at Willow.

"Hummm… This will be very interesting, Willow. Won't it?"

"Ummm, I guess." As she says with an uncertain demeanor.

Chapter Forty-Two
Spellcasting Competition

"It is that time of year again at WillowBrook School of Magic. It is time for the Quarterly Spellcasting Competition! Students have been practicing their charms, jinxes, and transfiguration spells for weeks in anticipation of the big event.

The competition takes place outside the school's courtyard in the **Gallo Dome**, decorated with floating candles and enchanted banners for the occasion. The stands are packed with teachers and students eager to watch the spellcasting battles. The Spellcasting Competition is not only thrilling entertainment but also a way for students to showcase their magical abilities.

The drum rolls… "Bum-bum-bum-bum"

"Willow B Juno and Isabella R Profaci`, rise up to take their place on the platforms, stand at attention for the **margin maker** to make his Wixan pairs."

Announcement:

"You all know the name of the game of the Quarterly Spellcasting Competition. On the left, we have Isabella with powers of 1st Fire, and 2nd Force and on the right we have Willow with powers of 1st Moon and the 2nd Earth."

Students, are you ready to compete? The rules are simple. Students compete in pairs. One student attacks with a spell while the other defends with their own spell."

These spells have been carefully selected to be harmless yet dramatic, focusing on the student's specialty. Brightly colored sparks fly as young Wixan duel, casting spells like **Lumiblastis, Rictusempra,** and **flipendo.** The air crackles with magical energy.

Willow is up against Isabella. Both girls mount their brooms and bow, touching the tips of the brooms floating in the air.

Isabella points her wand, and forms a ball of energy, and clearly announces.

"Flipendo Momentum"

Isabella takes control of the object with forward momentum and force. The object is then infused with kinetic energy and thrusts forward rapidly towards Willow.

Willow is taken off guard and maneuvers her broom out of the ball's path to dodge it. A quick tuck and roll with a change in direction, she misses it entirely.

Isabella retakes aim.

"Umbra Morpha"

As a giant zipping ball of energy comes plummeting towards her. Willow thinks fast and deflects this energy ball.

"Aetherial Nexus"

With this, Willow sends out her own radiating ball of energy. As it hits Isabella's, they magically make a large explosion, ending with a super Nova Flash collapsing in on itself.

After many exciting rounds, the two finalists are Willow B. Juno and Björn K. Johansen. They get in place for the face-off, do a broomstick bow, and then take their positions. On the count of three, their wands slice through the air, colliding beams of light dazzling the spectators. The winner decides who can withstand the sustained magical barrage and avoid getting knocked off their broom.

Willow takes aim and belts out.

"Thorin's Thunderclap!"

As the booming thunderclap is followed by a lightning bolt that targets Björn, he aims at the lightning bolt and casts the spell.

"Astrum Reflectum!"

Björn dodges the lightning by using the spell. He swiftly turns and maneuvers through the competition circle, moving as fast as the eye, so the spectators can barely keep tabs on him. He appears behind Willow, takes aim with his wand, and yells.

"Aero Umbrus!"

Clouds start to bum-rush Willow. Within seconds, she is engulfed in a twilight cloud that shrouds her in semi-darkness, disrupting her focus and perception. Not able to see anything but purple mist, she takes aim at where she thinks Björn is. Sparkling fire flows from her wand.

"Vapor Vanishium!"

As soon as the mist and cloud vanish, she finds Björn and begins to derive her next move. Björn, acting like a demigod, proudly shows off his fancy Broomstick maneuvers.

Willow is taken aback by his pompous action. Her heart beats rampantly, her hands sweaty and clammy.

She thinks for a moment, then sends her next spell, hoping to win the contest. In the heat of the moment, Willow decides to cast.

"Wobblebum Bumblefly!"

As the incantation is chanted, Björn's posture suddenly shifts, and his body contorts comically. His limbs elongate and wobble as if made of rubber while his face takes on an exaggerated expression of surprise.

With an equally amusing squawk, Björn transforms into a part owl, part frog, and part bouncing ball. His wings flap wildly, his legs spring him up and down, and his body ricochets in a wobbly dance midair.

Unable to maintain his balance, Björn tumbles off his broomstick with an "oomph" and lands on the ground in a cushiony bounce, leaping across the field with his frog legs, trying to get out of sight from Willow.

Just as Björn's magical mishap is about to become a spectacle, his trusty broomstick springs into action. The broom zips down from the sky, catching Björn in mid-leap, and they share a comical airborne hug as the broom whisks him back to safety.

The spectators erupt into laughter. Even though he knows he has been defeated, Björn cannot help but chuckle as he is reunited with his enchanted broomstick. Feeling the hardwood and safety, he knows there will be other Spellcasting competitions.

Crowley aims her stick at Björn and uses the reversal incantation to bring Björn back to his actual state.

"Reverse Whimsical!"

Björn performs a few whimsical contortions on his broom and returns to human form. Crowley has both competitors together in the middle of the arena. The professor raises Willow's hand to proclaim the winner.

"This Spell Casting Competition winner is Willow B. Juno."

Both Wixan's use good sportsmanship; they shake hands and praise each other on a good game. Crowley gives the Sparkling Spellcaster Trophy to Willow. This glowing crystal wand mounted on a marble base. The entire school cheers excitedly for the winner as they cheer, clap, and stomp in the bleachers to congratulate Willow on her Spellcasting win.

Willow feels overwhelmed, and a tear falls from her left eye. She reflects on once being an inward introvert just a year ago at the group home.

Embracing her achievements at WillowBrook, she has feelings of enlightenment and belonging rush over her. Willow looks at Professor Crowley and speaks.

"Professor, I need to express my feelings…. You know, I would have never thought for one second that my life would transpire to such amazing experiences.

I feel tall and proud to be part of WillowBrook. This belonging and contentment are larger than I could ever have imagined. I am becoming a Phoenix firebird, raising from my ashes."

Willow. I understand being in a group home was tough. Some of our childhood memories are not all rainbows and butterflies. As we grow, we need to embrace our adversity, learn from sadness, misery, and despair. Find the negative energy and grow from the sometimes unfair and awful experiences."

"Professor, I know that some of the other kids here, had it much worse than I did, and if they can flourish and grow with WillowBrook, so can I."

Chapter Forty-Three
The Great Cleaning Spell

The next day, the kids bustle through the corridors of the castle. It's the last day at WillowBrook, all the Neophyte students are going home for the short break before 1st semester starts 08/28/2020.

Nun, Mateo and Asim the click of Nuffer`do's, stood in the middle of the Harmoney Dome, wand in hand, eyes narrowed in concentration. "Just a simple cleaning spell," they mutter. "How hard can it be?"

Taking direct aim, with a big swooshing wave, they point their wands at the broom.

"Bezem Schoonmaken!" *Dutch (broom cleaner)*

The broom shudders and springs to life, but instead of sweeping the floor, it stands upright and began to waddle around aimlessly.

Suddenly, ripples of sparkly magic come flowing out from the broom, washing over the entire common room.

Asim watches in horror as chairs, tables, sofas, and even the old grandfather clock began to quiver and shake. One by one, they spring to life, their wooden faces creaking into expressions of delight.

"Ooh, finally! We can talk!" exclaimed an overstuffed armchair, wiggling its plush arms.

"I've been dying to stretch my legs," a coffee table said, extending its legs with a groan. "CRREEEAAAKKK! GRROOOAAANN"

Nun gulped. "Uh, this isn't right..."

"Oh, look! It's another Nufferdo," a chair with a torn cushion called out. "Remember when they spilled that potion and turned their hair blue for a week?"

A small side table giggled. "And then tried to hide it under that ridiculous hat!"

Nuffer`do blushed furiously. "Okay, okay, spell's over! Disseminate!"

But the furniture wasn't listening. The gossip continues.

"Did you hear about the time Mateo tripped over their own shoelaces during the dueling practice?" a footstool said, bouncing up and down with excitement.

"And **Ashley's** crush on Professor Ripley! She wrote his name in hearts all over her notebook," the grandfather clock chimed in, its pendulum swinging with glee.

Nun frantically flipped through their spellbook, looking for a counterspell. The furniture, now fully animated and quite chatty, began sharing more and more secrets.

"Remember when Trintiy tried to make a love potion and ended up giving everyone hiccups for a day?" a tall bookshelf chuckles, its books rattling.

"Oh, and let's not forget the time they—"

"Silencio Mobilia!" Nun finally shouted, pointing the wand at the furniture.

The room fell silent. The chairs and tables froze mid-gossip, their wooden faces showing surprise. Mateo sighed in relief and slumped into the now silent armchair.

"Well, that could have gone worse," they muttered, though they knew they'd have some explaining to do when the other students found out their secrets had been spilled.

As Asim started to clean up the mess, the broom came back to life, in its animated nature, waddled over and gave a little salute before finally starting to sweep the floor.

"At least that part worked," Nun said with a rueful grin.

Willow, Kalei, and Trintiy Stood in the room during the commotion of the expressive furniture fiasco.

Trintiy looking surprised, "Nun were you and your friends up to no good again?"

Willow gasped, "What happened here? I have never seen such shock on the faces of furniture."

Trinity, eyes wide, took in the scene. "Did you guys cast a spell, or did the common room have a wild party that we just witnessed?"

Nun scratches his head, still clutching the spellbook. "Well, we were just trying to clean up a bit... and things got a little out of hand."

Kalei smirked, "A little out of hand? The grandfather clock was just dishing out Ashley's deepest secrets."

Ashley, who had just walked in behind the girls, turns beet red. "What?! My crush on Professor Ripley?! Who told—"

Mateo, slumped in the armchair, groaned, "Yep, and the footstool mentioned my shoelace fiasco too. Apparently, the furniture has been keeping tabs on all of us all summer."

Asim, who was now gathering up the fallen cushions, looked up. "At least the broom's finally sweeping. That's one success, right?"

The broom, still animated, waddled over and gave a little salute to the group before diligently continuing to clean the floor.

Nun tried to suppress a giggle. "Hey, at least something went right. Though we might need to keep an eye on our new chatty companions."

Willow chuckled, "Well, at least it wasn't another potion explosion turning your hair blue again."

Kalei grinned, "Next time, maybe we should just stick to good old-fashioned cleaning methods."

Trintiy laughed, "Agreed. But you know, this might of just been the most entertaining cleaning session ever."

Just then, the animated broom approaches Nun and hands them a note. Nun unfolded it and read aloud, "Dear Nuffer`do, please refrain from using spells on the furniture. Sincerely, The Enchanted Objects' Union."

DE Daniel

Everyone burst into laughter, and the common room fills with the sound of their giggles, mixed with the soft sweeping of the broom. For now, the secrets were safe, but the memory of the day the furniture came to life would be a tale told in the halls of Nuffer`do for years to come.

Chapter Forty-Four
Wizards, Wands, and Witty Pranks

"You know you guys, I can't believe the summer has ended, it feels like we just got here, I can't wait to see my brother and father," says Kalei.

"I know, I feel you, it feels like just yesterday we arrived, and now we are going home, I am excited to see Miss Juno," says Willow with a happy look on her face.

"Well, I am excited too, Jasper the PuddleHopper dropped off a ChatterStone from my dad. He said we have a new and improved, dueling chamber at home. He said I'll become the best spell caster after practicing with these elemental beings. He also said that over the summer, he finished building a jousting room on the third floor of our house.

I am so excited to go home and try all this cool stuff!" says Trinity with a showy attitude.

DC Daniel

Isabella laughs. "Sounds like you've got an exciting time ahead of you, Trinity! I'll just be happy to sleep in my own bed again."

Kalei nods. "Yeah, and I'm looking forward to seeing my dad and brother. I can't wait to show them all the spells we learned."

Willow smiles, pulling her cloak tighter around her shoulders. "As long as I don't turn myself into a chicken again, I'd say we would be off to a good start."

They all stand by the platform; Professor Nightingale fly's over, flutters her wings for a soft landing, arriving in front of the group of kids. She is calling out on a megaphone. Manu`ahi summit loading here. The girls feel a rush of air, making their hair flutter against their faces.

The large, colorful Manu`ahi bird landed gently in front of them, its feathers shimmering in the late afternoon sun.

The bird extends its large wing, for easier access to the cabin on top. One by one, the students climbed aboard, finding seats and waiting for the Birdmaster to magically stow their belongings.

As the bird took off, the school grounds of WillowBrook slowly disappeared beneath them. The students leaned over the carriage, waving to their friends who were staying behind waiting for the next Manu`ahi bird.

"We'll keep in touch, right?" Trinity said, holding up her cell phone.

"Definitely," Isabella replied. "Group chat, every day. We have to keep each other updated on all the magical mischief we get into."

"And don't forget," Willow added, "We will all be back here soon. This isn't goodbye, just see you later."

DC Daniel

The Manu`ahi bird soared higher into the sky, carrying the students towards the wise banyan tree. They watched the clouds drift by, reminiscing about their summer adventures and eagerly discussing their plans for the break.

Kalei sighed contentedly. "It's been an amazing summer. I can't wait to see what the school year brings."

The others nodded in agreement, their faces filled with anticipation and excitement for the future. They knew that, despite the distance and time apart, their bond would only grow stronger. WillowBrook School of Magic had brought them together, and it would be the place where their magical journeys truly began.

Willow grabs Kalei's hand, "here we go again into that crazy inversion tunnel."

Kalei squints her eyes, "Yep, hold on Will, it's face warp time."

The tunnel looms ahead, a swirling vortex of colors and light. It pulses with energy, the entrance it's the doorway to another dimension.

Inside the tunnel, the air is filled with swirling colors that change and move in mesmerizing patterns. The sounds are a mix of rushing wind and strange, wobbly noises. The volume goes from loud to soft and back again, making the kids feel dizzy and off-balance.

As the bird continued its journey, they chat and laugh, making audible sounds that also sounded like they were face the rear side of a fan. Making wobbly sounds of their own.

The group lands somewhere in space and time on the back side of the tree, the group dismounts the bird with belonging and familiars walking beside them, the get on this people moving escalator, it is heading towards a tree that looks like it was color inverted, drawing of the ancient Banyan Tree.

This Tree image was created by flowing lightning. The tree is glowing with energy, and small, bright balls of light move from the top to the bottom of the tree, and back up the outer outline of the tree, making it pulse and flow.

Willow approaches she gets zipped through the opening, arriving in the meadow where this adventure began. Willow is restored to her authentic Victorian-style wares. Kalei then arrives with her crow, soon after Professor Applegate follows with all the personal items floating behind her on the AirCharm Cart. The professor and Kalei, arrive back in their Hawaiian custom wares. The three of them begin their travels to meet Mr. Applegate and Keanu past the forest.

Remembering the adventures of their summer at WillowBrook, filled with unknown challenges, new friendships, and the magic that tied them all together.

Days after arriving home, they quickly realize that the three of them have become inseparable. They often find themselves sleeping over at each other's houses, alternating between Kalei, Willow and Trinity's.

However, Willow and Kalei's favorite place to stay is at Trintiy's, she has a six-bedroom mansion, over twelve thousand square foot home, equipped with a home theater and indoor Olympic size pool. And her fathers' recent upgrades, including a spell casting barn, a joisting arena, and a dueling chamber.

The girls were having a blast—until Kalei's brother, Keanu, and his best friend, Chase, decided to unleash their latest prank. The boys had set up a hilarious surprise in the living room while the girls were in the kitchen, chatting and snacking.

Keanu leaned over to Chase, grinning mischievously. "Are you ready for this? We're about to turn this cozy house into a horror show!"

Chase chuckled, "Totally! I can't wait to see the look on their faces when they find out what we've done."

As the girls finished their drinks and made their way back into the living room, Keanu and Chase quickly pressed a button on their remote control, activating a realistic-looking fake snake that slithered across the floor.

Willow, who was first through the door, let out a blood-curdling scream. "What is that?!"

Kalei squinted at the floor, then burst out laughing. "Is that a rubber snake? You two are ridiculous!"

Trinity, ever the dramatic one, jumped up on the couch. "I'm not coming down until it's gone!"

DC Daniel

Chase, trying to stifle his laughter, exclaimed, "Don't worry, Trinity! It's more scared of you than you are of it!"

Willow, still panicking, yelled, "Yeah right! It's definitely plotting my demise!"

Keanu couldn't contain his laughter and grabbed the remote again. "Alright, time for phase two!" He pressed the button again, and the snake began to wiggle around erratically.

Kalei rolled her eyes but was still giggling. "Seriously, you guys need to get a life. How old are we, five?"

Chase chimed in, "Five with a PhD in pranking!"

As the girls slowly regained their composure, Keanu and Chase decided to turn up the heat. Keanu pulled out a confetti cannon he had hidden behind the couch. "Get ready for a surprise!"

Before the girls could react, he set it off, and a burst of colorful confetti showers down around them.

DC Daniel

Kalei squealed in delight. "Okay, that's actually awesome!"

Willow laughs and start to dance in the confetti, shouting, "Best prank ever! Let's do this every weekend!"

Trinity finally jumped down from the couch, her fear gone. "Fine, but next time, I'm in on it!"

Keanu and Chase high-fived, proud of their successful prank. "Next time, we'll plan an even bigger surprise!" Keanu said with a grin.

"Just promise it won't involve any more rubber snakes," Trinity added with a mock glare, still trying to get the confetti out of her hair. Willow laughing despite herself, "Okay, okay, you got us. Now help us get out of this."

Kalei still giggling, "Yeah, this was pretty clever."

Trinity smiling, "Just wait until we get you back!

Keanu and Chase help the girls peel the Ishan wrap away, all of them laughing and chatting about the prank.

Keanu grins, "Don't get your big girls' panties in a wad, it's all in good fun."

Chase smirk, "Yeah, but I think we're safe from revenge for a while, right?"

Willow playfully, "Oh, we'll see about that."

Kalei with a mischievous look, "You'd better sleep with one eye open tonight. Revenge will be sweet."

Willow is laughing, "Yeah, you never know when we might strike back."

The break continues with the next few weeks filled with banter and camaraderie.

A few days before they leave for Manu`ahi summit. Getting their foot lockers packed and their stuff ready for another exciting trip to the ancient Banyan tree for transport to the Manu`ahi Summit.

DC Daniel

Chapter Forty-Five
Into the Magic:
Returning to WillowBrook

The night before the trip to fly to the Island, everyone gathers at Mr. and Mrs. Applegates home for a bonfire and cookout.

Everyone is there, Miss Juno, Willow, Trinity and her parents, Mr. and Mrs. Applegate, Kalei, Keauna and his best friend Chase.

They all have a great time; Trinity stays the night at Kalei's with Willow.

Kalei sets Wizzy the Wizard alarm to wake at 6 am. They all fall fast asleep, in anticipation to the exciting day tomorrow.

Wizzy the Alarm Wizard, rings loudly " RING RING RING! Rise and shine, my sleepy witches!

The sun is up, and so should you be! It's a magical morning, and Manu`ahi Summit and WillowBrook await you three dazzling Wixan's!"

Kalei looks groggy "Ugh, Wizzy, do you have to be so loud every morning?"

Wizzy the Alarm Wizard, with his hands on his hips, "Of course, Kalei! How else would I ensure you make it to WillowBrook on time? The early witch catches the spell, after all!"

Willow stretches and yawns, "He's got a point. We can't be late for our first day back. Thanks, Wizzy."

DE Daniel

Trinity yawns and rubs her face to wake up, "You're pretty cool, Wizzy. I don't have an alarm clock like you. Mine's just an old croaking frog gifted by my grandfather. But you put the magic in a witch's wake-up! I love it. Kalei, don't be such a broom bummer!"

Wizzy the Alarm Wizard is full of glee, a smile can be seen under his mustache that is rapidly moving as he talks. "Cheerful? Why, Trinity, a positive attitude is the best way to start a magical day! Besides, we've got quite the adventure ahead. Manu`ahi summit isn't going to climb itself!"

Kalei says "I suppose you're right. Alright, girls, let's get ready. We have the Magic Banyan Tree to get passage to, the Manu`ahi Bird to conquer, and spells to learn."

Willow gleams a look at the other girls, "I'm excited. I love traveling on the transport bird, it is so freaking amazing. Plus, I heard that Professor Ripley has some amazing new potions to teach us."

Trinity says, "And don't forget about the other classes we will have… we are no longer in training. This is our first official year. I can't wait to see the professor, and the rest of our friends!"

Wizzy the Alarm Wizard replies, "That's the spirit! Remember, magic is in the air, and every step you take brings you closer to your dreams. Now, let's get moving! Time waits for no witch!"

Kalei snarky says, "Alright, alright Wizzy, lead the way with that tenacious energy of yours."

Wizzy smiles and points to the door, "Onward, to Manu`ahi Summit and beyond! The path is paved with wonders, and WillowBrook School of Magic awaits its brightest witches!"

Willow smiles, "Thanks, Wizzy. We're lucky to have you waking us up every morning."

Trinity looking more upbeat, "Yeah, you may be loud, but you make it hard not to smile. Let's do this!"

The girls, now fully awake and bubbling with excitement, drag their footlockers to the car, with their belongings and set off towards Manu`ahi summit, their spirits high and ready for the magical day ahead.

After, arriving back at the school and getting settled in, they all head off to bed. Willow and Kalei, keep each other up with a syndrome of chatty Kathy. Eventually, they fall into slumber.

Willow wakes, yawning and stretching to greet the morning. She opens her dormitory door to many early morning faces surfacing through the corridors. The smell of fresh baked goods from the cafeteria infuses the air through the castle.

The Morning Announcer EchoFlux comes on the airwaves.

"GGooodd Mmooorriiinngg fellow Wixans, welcome back everyone! You all know the routine, gather your stuff, and head to the east lawn. Meditation sunrise"

Everyone heads to the morning meditation meeting on the east lawn. On this crisp morning, the lawn is covered with morning dew that glistens in the rays of the peeking sun.

The traditional morning prayer and wake-up meditation are always the first step to a grateful and focused day. Everyone gathers and sits around in a circle in the lotus position. United socially, as a clique of Wixan teens embodying strong Mana.

As Willow looks around, she gazes at these bright-eyed young teens glowing with pride and WB's motto. As the three gong songs, all the kids simultaneously, speak in unison.

DE Daniel

The traditional morning prayer and wake-up meditation are always the first steps to a grateful and focused day. Everyone gathers in a circle, sitting in the lotus position. They unite as a close group of Wixan teens, filled with strong Mana.

As Willow looks around, she sees bright-eyed friends glowing with pride, all inspired by WB's motto. When the three gongs ring out, the first bong echoes through the air, the second bong vibrates in their chests, and the third bong rolls away like distant thunder. Then, all the kids speak together in unison, their voices rising in harmony.

1. Do Good,

2. Be Kind to everyone

3. Practice Peace and Unity in the World.

Willow can't help but notice all the changes in friendly faces. Her classmates she met over the summer have changing facial features, which is unbelievable, within a month

After some are bigger and taller. All this change from childlike features to more young man and woman definitions.

Kalei notices new, fresh faces from a few transfer students joining the school. After morning meditation, the students meet up in the shadow dome.

Headmaster Vanderbuilt takes the podium to give his welcoming address and introduce the new students.

"I can't believe we are back already. We were those scared, inquisitive kids at the start of the summer. Now we have a place and Element to call our own," Kalei says.

"Yeah, Kalei, we get to pick our foreign exchange school for our second-year studies this year." Norway, China, India, Egypt, Sweden, Greenland, and Australia, so many to choose from. This will be so exciting to learn their culture and customs."

"Will, it is going to be an amazing adventure."

"I hope we meet more cool professors and learn some cool spells. I feel it's going to be exciting, I feel it deep in my belly; it's exciting, like a butterfly's dancing in it."

The headmaster starts the introduction of all the new Wixans.

The five transfer first-year Wixans are introduced with their familiars, one by one.

"Please give a big welcome to Zwelithini from Zimbabwe; his name is Zwelithini, and he is named after the King of the Zulu nation from 1968 to his death in 2021: His familiar is Sam the Sugar Glider. His 1st element sign is Water, with a secondary sign of the Moon."

He takes a bow, his mysterious gray eyes glowing slightly, peering out to the crowd.

"Next, we welcome Isha, she is a transfer student from Fahad, India. Her name, **Isha**, means Goddess or protector. Her familiar is her Sun Bear Sam. Her 1st sign is Fire, and the 2nd is power."

A group of 3-4th year girls stand up and shout.

"Go Isha! Show them what you're made of! You've got this!"

 The headmaster proceeds to announce the next teen, "The third foreign exchange student from Egypt is **Akil Mohamed**, meaning determination and power, and his familiar is a leopard named Leon. The elements are 1st Wind and 2nd Thunder."

Please welcome our fourth Wixan Transfer, Björn Johanson, meaning bear or strength and power. He is from Norway and spent the summer with us, getting to know the routine and ways of WillowBrook. His familiar is a reindeer named Skadi goddess of winter in Norse Myths. His 1st elemental power is the Moon, and his 2nd is time.

DC Daniel

Now, give a big WillowBrook welcome to Kacper Johanson who is Björn's brother, meaning treasurer or keeper of the treasure. He is coming to us from the Nordic School of Craft, Kacper is from Norway, too. His familiar is a ferret named Fugo for protection against evil forces or bad luck. His 1st Element is ice, and the 2nd is shadow.

The crowd gives a loud embracing roar, Chanting over and over.

"We Are WillowBrook!

    WillowBrook Loud!

    WillowBrook Proud!"

The headmaster gives three tap on the microphone, getting everyone's attention.

Tap!

    Tap!

      Tap!

He proceeds, "Welcome back, all Wixans. We must also welcome back our summer students. These fellow Wixans have come here to grow and learn the ways of WillowBrook. When I call your name, please make your way to the stage.

Kalei, Trinity, Willow, Nun, Lampfry, Mateo, Asim, **Zhara,** Reba, Jorgen, and Ha'kon. All the kids gather on stage, forming a long line. Standing in single file are the foreign exchange students alongside the returning newbies.

The headmaster instructs, "Everyone take a bow, remember these first moments to the rest of the year here at WB.

All the kids take a bow in front of the rest of the school. Willow feels the warm embrace of the brisk fall winds flowing through her hair as it canoodles her face. The group disbands off the stage. They all meander through the halls for the day.

DE Daniel

CHAPTER TEASER
The Vanderbuilt's Go Missing

The crisp trade winds blow across the islands. The breeze whips the curtains throughout the dorms, and the window curtains flow in the beautiful breeze. All the students are tucked away in their dorms. Kalei and Willow are in one room. Across the way are Trinity and Isabella, and further down the hall are Victoria and Olivia.

Both Victoria and Olivia are sound asleep. A red beam of light appears in the middle of their room, but there is no sound to awaken the young ladies. The light looks 8 feet tall and about 6 -8 inches wide. A set of hands are reaching from the other side, pulling open at the slit of a beam of light. As it pushes open, a tall boy with an olive complexion, with dark hair and black eyes enters out of the portal. Then the portal closes till a flash of light.

Across the room, another large silent beam of red light appears. This, too, produces another boy with a black cloak and jet-black hair.

Out comes Willis from Iris, the land of Spector souls. Both boys look at each other with a perplexing look.

"What are you doing here, Mortis?" Willis asks.

"I am sent by Lord Loki. You are very young, maybe a second-year student at most. So, what are you doing here?"

DE Daniel

"I am sent here by Aynat to kidnap Olivia and bring her to Lord Loki."

"I see, I guess they want all the Vanderbuilts. I am here to retrieve and port over Victoria and the headmaster," Mortis whispers.

Willis pulls out his Astral Leap Sphere and sets up his prism mirror. While Willis is preparing, Mortis is doing the same. Willis drops an empty glass vile on the floor, making a crashing sound.

This awakens Victoria; she grabs her wand and aims at Mortis.

"Departure No low Aires"

Mortis deflects the spell, which hits her familiar fairy Zara, and poof, just like that, it disappears into thin air.

"Departure No low Aires," Victoria commands, aiming at the other boy, Willis, using his Prism mirror.

He catches the flow of the casting and deflects it to the lava lamp on the table. Poof, making the lamp disappear, too.

Now, Willis and Mortis's minds meld as Victoria looks around, dumbfounded, trying to think of her next move while shaking and yelling at her magic stick.

Willis mentally tells Mortis. "Let's capture her in our mirrors, I will enact my AstralLeap Sphere."

Mortis follows Willis's request and aims for his mirror to align with Willis's.

Willis rolls his AstralLeap Sphere out to Victoria's left.

Victoria looks over at it and demands. "What the heck is that?"

A green light appears as it opens.

"**Astra Lumina**," Willis says.

Victoria disappears with a sweeping vortex into the green light…..

DC Daniel

Professors and Casts

1   **Charles Brook** Sir of England

2   **GiGi NovaStar** Camp Leader directed the group in morning meditation

3   **Maxiums Vanderbuilt** Headmaster of WillowBrook

4   **Mrs. Grace Kittles** Transmission from ChatterStone

5   **Professor Cornelius** Ireland Ministry, a green-eyed lady, who appeared with beautiful vibrant red locks of hair that went to her knees. She wears a witch's hat that has a Cedrick symbol dead center of the hat and an Irish sign

6   **Professor Crowley**   Spell Casting 101

7   **Professor Fitzgerald** Precious Gem Class teacher

8   **Professor Flannagan** Potions and Brews class and Familiar finder at the Manu ahi Summit at Flannagan Finest Familiars.

9   **Professor Gabrielle** Ex Element Director Capricee's Cottage Forest Keeper Vietnamese custom and attire.

10   **Professor GreatScotts** Caretaker at Moving Library.

11   **Professor Grimsby**   Teaches Precious Gem class.

12   **Professor Moonfire** Broom Stick Maneuvers.

13   **Professor Nightengale** Wizard Math Group, math club teacher. Professor Nightingale, who's like half human, half owl. It's a feathery wing creature.

Wixan's & Familiar's

Akil Mohamed Cairo, Egypt
Element Power The 1st Wind, 2nd Thunder
Familiar is a leopard named Leon.

Asim Nubian culture of Egypt.
Elemental Power 1st Water sign with no secondary

Aynat Stalemann Willis Mother

Björn Johanson Hermansverk, Norway
Elemental Power 1st Moon, 2nd time
Familiar is a reindeer named Skadi (goddess of winter in Norse Myths)

Isabella R Profaci Cefalù Italy.
Elemental Power 1st Fire, 2nd Power
Familiar Sun Bear Sam

Jorgen and Ha'kon Henderson   "High Coast"
(Höga Kusten) in the Ångermanland province of Sweeden
1st year students
Elemental Power UNKNOWN

Kacper Johanson from Gotland, Sweden
Björn is his twin brother
Elemental Power 1st ice, 2nd Shadow
Familiar is a ferret named Fugo for protection against evil.

     DE Daniel

Kalei Applegate North Kohala, O'ahu
Elemental Power 1st Water 2nd TBD
Familiar Blackbird ('Alalā) 'Rocky

Karen, Smooch, and Willis kids from the underworld in the chapter an eye for an eye, with Mr. Hedge and Aphrodite Fountain

Keanu Applegate Oahu, North Kohala (Now lives in Florida with Kalei's father)

Lampfry (No specialized element) Full Nuffer`do
Elemental Power None
Familiar Lemur Mr. Tuggles 2nd Owl Ozzy

Mateo from Basque Country, Spain (Half Nuffer`do)
Elemental Power 1st Time, No known 2nd Element
Name meaning (Gift from God)

Melinda the enchanter

Nina is a master of potions, a tri-wizard tournament

Nun From the Nubian Culture of Egypt
Elemental Power No known Elemental sign

PuddleHopper Delivery service with an echo-receiving locator in the magic community. A squirrel-like creature with strong hind legs jumping like a Jack rabbit.

<u>Sarah Sunders</u> Wixan student vaporized in a lab from a spell gone wrong.

<u>Steven Applegate</u> from Pu'ukohola Waimea, Hi Keanu and Kalei's Father

<u>Trinity Sisk</u> Winnemem Wintu Native American from California
Mid-length black hair
Familiar bobcat named Tiny

<u>Willis Stalemann</u> Willow's your sept brother

<u>Willow B. Juno</u> from Florida, US
Familiar Black Cat, named Aurora
Elemental Power 1st Moon 2nd

<u>Zwelithini</u> Zimbiwa, South Africa
Familiar is a Sugar Glider named Sam.
Elemental Power 1st Water 2nd Moon

Your Personal Enchantments:

WB ~~ Enchantments:

All Spells are Copywritten by the author DC Daniel and the WillowBrook Series.

Acromesis DeNuglar: immense wave comes from the ocean.

Aegis Solace Eternus: to return Brook back to normal.

Aeris Lepus: The cart can hover.

Aero Umbrus: To make mist and cloud spell form.

Aetherial Nexus: Radiating ball of energy.

Agua Gent Rejuvenate: Water spell, cup it to your hand, swirl

your water cyclone and make a 2ft wave, to repair wounds.

Animasorbo Transfiguris: command for a black cougar.

Animorphus Quafflefication: Turn a quaffle'lou into

a shape-shifting animal.

Astrum Reflectum: Dodges the lightning.

Asultre Petrified: Green light appears

as it opens from a Sphere.

Avata Nyt: luminous array of light

Avia Docent Tome, Ad Manus Meas:

The Birds Guide Me, to My Hands "Begin book!

Benuo Higher Gavotusus: To safely bring something or someone to the ground

Bocca Con Cerniera: Zipper mouth.

Bleeck Aroarbus: Broom makes a hard stop

Brocolean: Both hands to get Fireball.

from hands towards something or someone.

Danza Pacato: (danza Peah`cato) Spell to make someone

or something dance uncontrollably.

Departure No Low Aires: Vanishes into thin air.

Detener el tiempo: Make suspend in time.

Draco`fly Corneilous: Create a mini-Serpent Dragonfly out of Björn.

Firemortus: To create fire from the palm of the hand.

Flama Fussa: To create a Fire Genie from

ball of fire in hand.

Flipendo Momentum: To take control of the object

with forward momentum and force.

     DC Daniel

Frembringe Zweven: Norwegian/Dutch meaning bring forth and levitate.

Fuoco Ball Organizer: Command floating ring of fire burns mid-air

to send flame and scorch the floating golden sphere.

Glidara Levandus: Command to move Aira Cart

in the Meadow to the Bayan Tree.

Higher Gavotusus: To bring someone or something

safely to the ground.

Ignis Morpha: A Spell to make you float, made wrong can vaporized

person doing the incantation.

Ivy Corperalis: To bind something with live ivy, completely immobilize item.

Morea Resolute: This spell is to take control and self-destruct in something. .

Novos De La Coat: protection over the amulets.

Prismatic Revival: To repair something broken

Reverse Whimsica: The reversal incantation.

Reversio Transmutatio: This command will return the

shapeshifting quaffle'lou, back to its original state until you need it next time.

Rudanza Pacato: Turn something legs turn into jelly.

Schlaf Blüte: (Sleep Bloom in German) Casting spell for Sleeping Troll Tinture.

Shamlone Pixie Pink: Incantation for turning someone

into a Glitz doll, during Wizard makeovers.

Sortum Bledge Abile: To transport one's-self back

to Iris's headquarters, vapors into thin air.

Stopple Renew: This reverses the mute zipper mouth spell.

Thorin's Thunderclap: To command a lightning bolt that

gives off booming thunderclaps.

Umbra Morpha: To Cast a giant zipping ball of energy.

Umbratus Discretio: To make a group incognito with magic cloak.

Vanquish Qill: The ORIGIN discovery spell

Glam pixies flew from the tree, to take on the task.

Vapor Vanishium: To vanish or remove mist and clouds.

Victor Victor Bish Hisk: Incantation to make

Sleeping Trumpet Hearts.

Vocare Scopam: To command one's broom.

Wobblebum Humblefly: To command someone to change into a rubber puddle

transforms into a part owl, part frog, and part bouncing ball.

Yaris Morfee'is: This spell morphs into Green Ivy Goddess (Glamerfy Me)

DC Daniel

DE Daniel

Lanaguge Reference:

<u>Hawaiian Language</u>

1. Pūliki or ʻauan = Hū ʻia \hoo\ \ee-ah\ \POO\ \LEE\ \KEE\ Hug

2. Aloha = which means love, compassion, or a friendly greeting like hello or goodbye.

3. Oʻhana = \ʻOH\ \HAH-nah\ Family

4. Makua kilei = \mah-KOO-ah\ \kee-LAY\

    Step father

5. Makuahine = \mah-KOO\ \ah\ \HEE-neh\

    Makuahine specifically refers to a mother in Hawaiian culture. It reflects the importance of maternal figures in families and communities.

    Mother

DC Daniel

6. Makua kāne = \mah-KOO-ah\ \KAH-neh\ Father

7. Keiki = \KAY-ee\ \kee\ Child.

8. 'Anakē = \'AH\ \nah\ \KAY\ Aunti.

10. Aloha wau iā 'oe : I love you.

11. Pa'akai "pā: \pah\ \ah-KAI\ is an important term in Hawaiian culture, as salt has historically been vital for food preservation and flavoring. It is also used in ceremonies and rituals. Meaning salt Barrier in Hawaiian.

12. Nani ke kani: \NAH-nee\ \keh\ \KAH-nee\ expresses appreciation for a sound that is pleasant or beautiful, which could refer to the sound of music, nature (like waves crashing or birds singing), or any harmonious noiseIt sounds beautiful.

DC Daniel

13.   Ke nani kai: \keh\ \NAH-nee\ \KAH-ee\

Ke nani kai is a poetic expression that captures the beauty of the ocean or sea, emphasizing its visual and emotional impact. The beauty of the sea.

14.   He 'ala 'ono: \heh\ \'AH-lah\ \'OH-no\ expresses the idea of a delightful or pleasant smell, often associated with flowers, food, or other aromatic things.

15.   Aloha wau ia oe: \ah-LOH-hah\ \vah-oo\ \ee-ah\ \oh-eh\ is a beautiful expression of love and affection, often used in a heartfelt way.

16.   Mahalo Nui Loa: \mah-HAH-loh\ \NOO-ee\ \LOH-ah\ Mahalo Nui Loa" is a way to express deep gratitude and appreciation in Hawaiian, often used in a heartfelt manner.

17.   Tūtū Kāne: \TOO-too\ \KAH-neh\ Grandfather.

18.   Tūtū Wahine : \TOO-too\ \wah-HEE-neh\ Grandmother.

19.   Kupua puka puka: \koo-POO-ah\ \POO-kah\ Kupua puka puka" can suggest that these mystical beings have connections to portals, symbolizing their ability to move between worlds or realms. It evokes the idea of the kupua navigating through mystical doorways, a common theme in Hawaiian mythology. Magic portal

20.   Kilokilo nā kupua: Kilokilo: \KEE-loh-KEE-loh\ The kupua (demigods) observe" or "The kupua (demigods) practice divination Witches are sorcerers.

21.   Kupua: Pronunciation: \koo-POO-ah\

Refers to supernatural beings, demigods, or shapeshifters in Hawaiian mythology. These beings often have special powers and can exist in multiple forms, such as animals or natural phenomena.

22.   Menahuna: \meh-neh-HOO-neh\

Mythological race of dwarf people, live in the deep forests and hidden valleys of the Hawaiian Islands. 1820 census from the island of Kauai listed 65 people as Menehune.

23.   Mauna-kea-resort: Resort on the Big Island.

24.   Kupuna kane: pronounced \Koo-poo-nah kahneh\ = A term that refers to an elderly man or male elder in the community. In Hawaiian culture,

DE Daniel

kupuna (elders) are highly respected for their wisdom, experience, and knowledge

25. Spam Musubi: spam \moo\ \soo-BEE\ This is cooked rice, a slice of grilled Spam (a canned meat product made from pork), and seasoned with a special sauce, all wrapped in a sheet of nori seaweed.

26. Kumu = \koo\ \moo\ Teacher.

27. Keanu = \keh-AH-noo. Boys name for cool breeze.

28. e ʻoluʻolu, lāʻau kupua = Please magical tree.

29. olona = A type of fiber made from the bark of the wauke tree.

30. a lei niho palaoa = Necklace made from the teeth of whales or other marine animals.

31. Mahiole = a feathered helmet, worn for high fluent Kamehameha socicity.

35. 'ahu'ula = The Lady Franklin Cape.

36. ‘i‘iwi = native birds

37. mamo = native birds

38. ‘A‘ole pilikia = This means "no problem" or "you're welcome" but can also be used to dismiss a minor annoyance in a friendly way.

39. ‘A‘ole ho‘omana‘o = This translates to "no worries" and can be a casual way to brush off a small annoyance.

40. i"ho'ohuihui = Pretentious

41. kū'ēlelohe = bad attitude, not good behavior, conflict,

42. Mahalo = Hello

DC Daniel

43.   'alalā = Hawaiian crow

44.   Aumakua = Spirit guide

45.   Manu`ahi Carriage = Transport bird

46.   Mauna Loa summit = Place.

47.   kupunawahine   (koo-poo-nah-wah-hee-neh)= Grandmother.

48.   hoa hānau Kaukini = Cousins Male cousin of the parents' generation, makua kāne, makua kāne hanauna. Female cousin of the parents' generation, makuahine, makuahine hanauna.

49.   Ala Manu FireBird Alley. The place Wixans go to get supplies.

50.   'Auana Hula: To wander, drift, go from place to place.

Welsh Language

(dialect England or a providence of Wales)

1.   Os gwelwch yn dda = Tree of Magic anfonwch fi I Phoenix Fire bird Summit.

2.   Diolch yn fawr = Thank you very much.

3.   Feniks vuurvogel hoogtepunt = Phoenix Firebird Summit.

Sanskrit Language

1.   Jnana or Gyan Mudra of Knowledge = It is a symbolic hand gesture used in yoga.

Vietnamese Language

1.   gỏi cuốn (Guy c'oon) = Vietnamese Spring Roll

Italian Language

1.   ntze' noise with the mouth. This Italian gesture means Chissenefrega! (Who cares!).

n: A nasal sound, like in "no."[n-tzeh] "eh" sound at the end.

Spanish Language

1.   baño-de-chicas. (Girls Bathroom)

2.   Que soy Buena

Italian Language

1.   Sorella = Sister

2.   Fratello = Brother

3.   Madre = Mother

4.   Papa` = Father

5.   Zia = Aunt

6.   Strega = Witch

7.   Procedura Guidata=Wizard or

procedure guidate

French Language

1.   c'est la vie! = (such is life)

Japanese Language

1.   Kenrō (賢老) = Wise Elder

2.   Kimono (着物) = The kimono is a traditional Japanese garment known for its intricate patterns and elegant style. It is typically worn for very formal occasions such as weddings, tea ceremonies, and other important cultural events. There are different types of kimono for different seasons and occasions.

3.   Mahō no Ōku 魔法のオーク = Magic Oak tree

4.   Kenrō 賢老 = the village's elder wise and revered

Dutch Language

1.   dank je = thank you if you're speaking informally

2.   dank u = speaking formally

German Language

1. **Schlaf Blüte** = Sleep bloom

2. **Erleuchten Licht** = illuminate light

Hindi Language

1. astral body in Hindi. देखें

2. astral body का हिन्दी मतलब

3. astral body का मीनिंग

4. astral body का हिन्दी

5. astral body का हिन्दी अनुवाद।

Norwiegn Language

1. Formell spisestue = Formal dining room

2. Selvabsorbert = Self absorbed

3. Pretensiøs = Pretentious

4. Liten rampunge = Little brat

5. Liten drittunge = Little brat

6. å bli kronet som dronning = to be crowned queen

7. Godt jobbet = "well worked" or "well done." This is another common way to praise someone for a job well done.

8. Frembringe zweven = Norwegian/ Dutch meaning bring forth and levitate

9. Tusen takk - This means "a thousand thanks" and is a more emphatic way of saying thank you.

10. Takk skal du ha - This is a slightly more formal way of saying "thank you" and translates to "thanks shall you have."

11. Takk for hjelpen - This means "thanks for the help" and is used when thanking someone for their assistance.

12. Hamask's – A Norse word that means bear' also meaning state of frenzy in battle.

13. kløende sky - Itchy cloud Spell

❀ Dedication Page  ❀

~ This book is dedicated to all the kids in the world that struggle, every day, with fitting in, self-acceptance, self-esteem, self-worth and finding their unique path in life.

~ You are not alone in your journey, and this dedication is a tribute to your strength, resilience, and the incredible potential within each one of you.

~ May this book serve as a source of inspiration and comfort as you navigate the challenges of growing up and discovering your true selves.

~ Remember, your uniqueness is your superpower, and the world is a better place with your one-of-a-kind contributions.

~ Keep believing in yourself, keep striving for your dreams, and never forget that you are loved, valued, and capable of achieving greatness, no matter the adversity and hardships you have faced in life.

~ When finding your way, find your voice. You are the heroes of your own stories, facing challenges with courage and resilience.

~ Remember, you are never alone, and your uniqueness is your greatest strength. May this book be a beacon of hope, reminding you that you are valued, cherished, and capable of achieving incredible things.

Rhythms

Solstice fires, spirits bright,

We gather beneath the golden light.

Oak of old, with branches wide,

Grant us your magic, be our guide.

From sun to moon,

from sky to earth,

Grant us blessings and rebirth.

As daylight lingers,

spirits play, On this sacred solstice day.

Glowing embers, stars above,

fill us with your boundless love.

Ancient oak, our hearts entwined,

May your wisdom forever bind.

In this dance of sun and fire,

We seek your grace, our hearts aspire.

Renew our souls, make spirits soar,

On this solstice eve, forevermore.

DE Daniel

 Note from Author 

Finding Your Inner Light
&
Following Kindness

Dear Reader,

In this world, where life often feels like a whirlwind of responsibilities, challenges, and expectations, it's easy to lose sight of the most important journey of all: the journey to find your inner light. This light, unique to you, is the spark that holds your dreams, your compassion, and your boundless potential. It's the essence of who you are—your truest, most radiant self. And it's always there, even on days when the world feels overwhelming or unkind.

Finding your inner light doesn't require magic or perfection. It starts with small steps and simple acts. It begins when you listen to your heart, follow your passions, and make choices rooted in kindness—both for yourself and for others. This journey isn't about being perfect; it's about being real. It's about learning to love who you are while growing into the person you're meant to become.

How to Find Your Inner Light

Listen to Yourself: *Take moments to pause and reflect. What makes you feel alive? What brings you joy? These are clues to where your light shines brightest.*

Embrace Your Strengths and Flaws: *Your light isn't just in your talents; it's in your imperfections too. They make you human, relatable, and whole.*

Pursue What Matters to You: *Whether it's writing, music, helping others, or something entirely your own, following your passions fuels your light.*

Practice Gratitude: *Noticing the beauty in small moments can brighten even the darkest days. Gratitude helps you see the good that's already around you.*

Be Kind to Yourself: *Forgive yourself for mistakes. Treat yourself as you would a best friend—with patience, understanding, and encouragement.*

DC Daniel

The Power of Kindness

Once you've connected with your inner light, you'll find it naturally spreads to others through acts of kindness. Kindness is a superpower that can change the world one person at a time. It's in the small gestures—a smile to a stranger, a helping hand, or words of encouragement. When you choose kindness, you create ripples that inspire others to do the same. Your light grows brighter, and so does the world around you.

<u>Here's the secret:</u> kindness isn't just for others; it's for you too. When you give kindness, it feeds your soul, strengthens your light, and reminds you of the goodness in the world.

A Challenge for You

As you turn the page to begin this journey, I have a challenge for you: every day, find one way to honor your inner light and one way to show kindness. These moments can be as simple as journaling your thoughts, thanking someone who inspires you, or helping a friend in need. Small steps lead to big changes.

Remember, you are more powerful than you realize. The world needs your light and your kindness, and your story is just beginning. Embrace it. Shine brightly. Lead with love, hope and inspiration,

DC Daniel

"Become the light being you are supposed to be." ~DC Daniel

"Let your smile change the world,

but don't let the world change your smile.

Just keep swimming." ~ DC Daniel

"Keep your Mana shining bright, and never stop believing

in the power of your dreams." ~DC Daniel

My current situation is not my final destination. DC Daniel

<u>REMEMBER THESE QUOTES FOR LIFE</u>

Life is 10 % what happens to us and 90 % how we react to

it." ~ Charles R. Swindoll

"Success is not final, failure is not fatal: It is the courage to

continue that counts." ~ Winston Churchill

"Believe you can and you're halfway there." ~ Theodore

Roosevelt

"The greatest glory in living lies not in never falling, but in rising every time we fall." ~ Nelson Mandela

"You are never too small to make a difference." ~ Greta Thunberg

"You are braver than you believe, stronger than you seem, and smarter than you think." ~ A.A. Milne (from Winnie the Pooh)

The pessimist complains about the wind. The optimist expects it to change. The leader adjusts the sails and picks up the pace. ~DC Daniels

"Your current situation is not your final destination." ~DC Daniels

Let your smile change the world, but don't let the world change your smile. Just, keep swimming. -DC Daniels

"Keep your Mana shining bright, and never stop believing in the power of your dreams and vibrations." -DC Daniels

DC Daniel

Desiderata

Here is Desiderata, the beloved poem.

Desiderata is a prose poem written by American author Max Ehrmann in 1927. The title comes from the Latin phrase desiderata, which means "things desired"

Desiderata

Go placidly amid the noise and haste,
and remember what peace there may be in silence.
As far as possible, without surrender,
be on good terms with all persons.
Speak your truth quietly and clearly;
and listen to others,
even to the dull and the ignorant;
they too have their story.

Avoid loud and aggressive persons,
they are vexatious to the spirit.
If you compare yourself with others,
you may become vain or bitter,
for always there will be greater and lesser persons than
yourself.

Enjoy your achievements as well as your plans.
Keep interested in your own career, however humble;
it is a real possession in the changing fortunes of time.

DC Daniel

Exercise caution in your business affairs,
for the world is full of trickery.

But let this not blind you to what virtue there is;
many persons strive for high ideals,
and everywhere life is full of heroism.

Be yourself.

Especially, do not feign affection.
Neither be cynical about love;
for in the face of all aridity and disenchantment
it is as perennial as the grass.

Take kindly the counsel of the years,
gracefully surrendering the things of youth.

Nurture strength of spirit to shield you in sudden
misfortune.

But do not distress yourself with dark imaginings.
Many fears are born of fatigue and loneliness.

Beyond a wholesome discipline,
be gentle with yourself.

<u>You are a child of the universe</u>
no less than the trees and the stars;
you have a right to be here.

And whether or not it is clear to you,
no doubt the universe is unfolding as it should.

     DE Daniel

Therefore, be at peace with God,
whatever you conceive Him to be,
and whatever your labors and aspirations,
in the noisy confusion of life keep peace with your soul.

With all its sham, drudgery, and broken dreams,
it is still a beautiful world.
Be cheerful.
Strive to be happy.

DE Daniel

♪ ♫ ♪ About the Author ♫ ♪ ♫

I Choose Joy.

Love ~ Reach ~ Impact

DC Daniel is an author whose life story is marked by profound experiences that have shaped their writing journey, from navigating some of the complexities of child abuse and being an unwanted child to enduring a challenging upbringing. This ignited a passion within them to create a book series. This WillowBrook Series empowers, elevates, and encourages young readers facing adversity and struggles in the path to adulthood. With a deep understanding of the struggles young people encounter,

DC. Daniel has crafted the art of storytelling, captivating children's attention in their novels that seamlessly blend imaginative storytelling with themes of resilience and triumph over hardship.

Their ability to create a magical world with young Wixans and Nuffer`do's. The WillowBrook Series is a testament to their ability to create and transport readers into enchanting worlds.

Desiderata

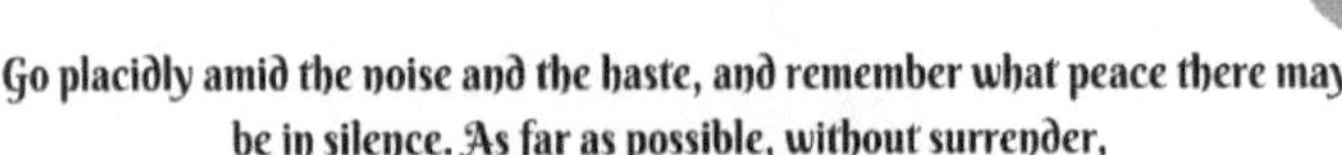

Go placidly amid the noise and the haste, and remember what peace there may
be in silence. As far as possible, without surrender,
be on good terms with all persons.
Speak your truth quietly and clearly; and listen to others, even to the dull
and the ignorant; they too have their story.
Avoid loud and aggressive persons; they are vexatious to the spirit. If you
compare yourself with others, you may become vain or bitter, for always
there will be greater and lesser persons than yourself.
Enjoy your achievements as well as your plans. Keep interested in your own
career, however humble; it is a real possession in the changing fortunes of time.
Exercise caution in your business affairs, for the world is full of trickery.
But let this not blind you to what virtue there is; many persons strive for
high ideals, and everywhere life is full of heroism.
Be yourself. Especially do not feign affection. Neither be cynical about love; for
in the face of all aridity and disenchantment, it is as perennial as the grass.
Take kindly the counsel of the years, gracefully surrendering the things of youth.
Nurture strength of spirit to shield you in sudden misfortune. But do not distress
yourself with dark imaginings. Many fears are born of fatigue and loneliness.
Beyond a wholesome discipline, be gentle with yourself. You are a child of
the universe no less than the trees and the stars; you have a right to be here.
And whether or not it is clear to you, no doubt the universe is unfolding as it
should. Therefore be at peace with God, whatever you conceive Him to be.
And whatever your labors and aspirations, in the noisy confusion of life,
keep peace in your soul. With all its sham, drudgery and broken dreams, it is
still a beautiful world. Be cheerful. Strive to be happy.

by Max Ehrmann ©1927

As this book and story comes to an end, think about the journey the characters took to develop their inner strength, resilience, and self-belief. Now, reflect on your own life. What challenges have you faced that required you to grow stronger?

____

____

____

____

____

____

____

____

____

____

____

SELF EMPOWERMENT PROMPTS:

How do you build confidence in yourself when things feel difficult?

____

____

____

____

____

____

____

____

____

____

____

____

Trusting Yourself:

Self-belief is trusting your ability to handle challenges. Write about a moment when you trusted yourself to make a tough decision. How did that experience change the way you see your own abilities?

____

____

____

____

____

____

____

____

____

____

____

____

Embracing Change:

Change can be uncomfortable, but it's often necessary for growth. Write about a change you've experienced and how it helped you become a better version of yourself.

Resilience in Action:

Resilience means bouncing back when things go wrong. Think of a situation where you had to bounce back from failure or disappointment. What helped you recover, and how can you use that experience to stay strong in the future?

____

____

____

____

____

____

____

____

____

____

____

____

Becoming Your Own Hero:

In the book, each character had to embrace their unique strengths to become a hero. What are the qualities or abilities that make you unique? How can you use those traits to overcome challenges and help others?

DE Daniel

Overcoming Challenges:

In the story, the characters faced challenges that tested their resilience. Write about a time when you felt like giving up but didn't. What helped you keep going? How did that experience shape the person you are today?

DE Daniel

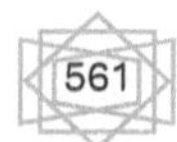

Becoming Your Best Self:

Imagine the best version of yourself. What qualities or skills does that version of you have? What steps can you take to start becoming that person today?

____

____

____

____

____

____

____

____

____

____

Setting Goals:

Think about a goal you want to achieve. What steps can you take to work toward that goal, and what personal qualities will help you along the way?

____

____

____

____

____

____

____

____

____

____

____

Inspiration and Role Models:

Who is someone you look up to and admire for their inner strength or resilience? What qualities do they have that inspire you, and how can you develop those same qualities in yourself?

DC Daniel

Strengthening Your "Mana":

In the magical realm, Mana represents the inner power needed to overcome evil. If you had your own mana, what would strengthen it? What habits, actions, or thoughts could you practice to keep it strong in the face of difficulties?

DC Daniel